CANDLELIGHT
Supreme

"YOU'LL MARRY ME," LEIF STATED SIMPLY.

"You can't be serious!" Tracy cried.

"I am."

"Leif—a marriage like that would be a disaster! Legal, but meaning nothing. In name only and all that!"

"In name only?"

"It couldn't be anything else."

"It would have to be something else."

"I will not go to bed with you again!"

"You never had any problems before."

She glared at him. "I've had problems every time I've seen you!"

"Tracy, if you marry me, you sleep with me. I can't imagine it being that terrible a hardship. If you're my wife, you'll be just that." He added, with a hard glint in his eyes: "In the bedroom as well as outside of it."

CANDLELIGHT SUPREMES

LIAR'S MOON

Heather Graham

A CANDLELIGHT SUPREME

Published by
Dell Publishing Co., Inc.
1 Dag Hammarskjold Plaza
New York, New York 10017

Dell ® TM 681510, Dell Publishing Co., Inc.

Candlelight Supreme is a trademark
of Dell Publishing Co., Inc.

Candlelight Ecstasy Romance®, 1,203,540, is a registered trademark of Dell Publishing Co., Inc., New York, New York.

ISBN: 0-440-14854-5

Printed in the United States of America

February 1987

10 9 8 7 6 5 4 3 2 1

WFH

For my cousin Helen Astrella, with love

To Our Readers:

We are pleased and excited by your overwhelmingly positive response to our Candlelight Supremes. Unlike all the other series, the Supremes are filled with more passion, adventure, and intrigue, and are obviously the stories you like best.

In months to come we will continue to publish books by many of your favorite authors as well as the very finest work from new authors of romantic fiction. As always, we are striving to present unique, absorbing love stories —the very best love has to offer.

Breathtaking and unforgettable, Supremes follow in the great romantic tradition you've come to expect *only* from Candlelight Romances.

Your suggestions and comments are always welcome. Please let us hear from you.

Sincerely,

The Editors
Candlelight Romances
1 Dag Hammarskjold Plaza
New York, New York 10017

PROLOGUE

She came to him in the darkness, in the coolness of the night, and through the years it would be in the darkness, beneath the glowing cast of the moon, that he would recall her.

Of all the things that came and went in life—battles and peace, pain and triumph—of all these things, only she came back to haunt him. She came to him in his dreams, in vivid recall, so that he would wake, drenched with sweat, thinking that he could reach out and touch her again—smell the sweet aroma of her perfume, feel the curve of her breast, the whisper of her caress.

He remembered that very first night.

She was standing in the doorway, framed by the glow of the moon—a liar's moon, they had laughingly called it. Shadowed and soft, a moon that hid sins and sheltered guilt and glowed with softest beauty.

She paused there in that doorway and slowly, slowly bent to cast her heels away. So clearly he remembered the grace of her feline stretch, the supple shape of her legs, the soft thud of her shoes as they fell.

She came into the room slowly and elegantly, her walk easy, luxurious, unhurried. So confident, so sensual. She came that way to the center of the room, where that liar's moon could fall upon her from the bay window that opened to the garden and the night breeze. She reached for the string of her gown at her nape, releasing it, shaking back the lustrous waves of her hair as she did so.

The gown fell to become a pool at her feet. Beneath it, she was naked. No slip, no teddy, no lace, no stockings. Just bare and elegant beneath the moon glow—a glow falling upon the fullness of her breasts, the firmness, the slender curves of her body. Skin like satin, taut and sleek, so breathtaking. Everything—everything about her so perfect. The slope of her shoulders, the line of her back, the flare of her hip.

Her eyes were indigo—sparkling, reflecting, catching the moonbeams, so deep and dark, so touched by brilliance. He knew, because he came to her, scarcely able to breathe. Touched her shoulders and felt her shivering, trembling. Who was she? He had wondered then, but he hadn't really cared. He hadn't known . . .

She had danced with him, laughed with him. And when he had fled the party, she had come to him, telling him silently that she was through with it, too, that she longed to go with him.

He had forgotten Celia—forgotten the problems that had plagued him. And in the moments to come he forgot all else. Schedules and deadlines and tunes and commitments. Survival, fame and fortune.

He remembered that first kiss; folding her into his arms, letting his fingers play over her skin, curl into her tresses, caress her shape, and wonder again at its fullness and perfection. Her taste, her scent! These, too, he could remember. The feel of her small hands against him, touching him . . .

That kiss, that kiss . . .

She was so bold, it inflamed him; yet all the while she

10

trembled. Bolder still, and he was stunned—and taken. Yes, oh, yes, touch me—the fever of his whisper, the depth of his fascination. Her touch, her tongue, her kiss, so refined, so abandoned . . .

Liar's moon.

She'd never made love before.

He'd tried to leave her, but she'd whispered out his name. Soft, plaintive, broken, and he was back. A groan echoed all his emotions, for she was a web of complexities —innocence and deepest knowledge, sensual beauty and quaking uncertainty.

Whispers throughout the night.

Lies and whispers, for none of her words were true. Not the need, not the reason—not even her name.

Still, it was what he remembered. That night. Each kiss, each caress. The feel of her hair against his chest, the soft pressure of her body, the cadence of her heart, of her breath, of her movement against him. There was more in the days to come—more of the fascination, more of the love. He taught her about love, and never knew that there could be such pleasure in teaching. And in teaching he learned. Laughed and teased, whispered and groaned. And fell . . . fell, deeper and deeper, until the loving was a natural thing. Each kiss, each caress, the sway of her hips, the eternal blue beauty of her guileless eyes . . .

Asleep then, he twisted and turned, the sweat beading upon his forehead, his breath coming too fast.

He woke, bolting up in his bed, crossing to the balcony.

Of all things to remember in life! Not the horrors of war, not the pain of loss. Not the magic of success.

Just her.

The streaking month of beauty, kissed by the liar's

moon. The nightmare that always woke him. Jesse standing there screaming—Leif amazed. Stunned. And looking at her in disbelief.

Tracy—is it true?

Her tears; her anger. Her screams against those who had so crudely burst in upon them . . .

That was all he could remember because the blow had come to his head then and he'd fallen unconscious to the floor.

Oh, God! It was so many years ago.

He didn't know why the dream had haunted him so exceptionally vividly this night.

Or maybe he did. He'd been thinking about her. Wondering where she was. No, it had been more than that. If she didn't surface soon, he was going to have to hire a detective to find her. He didn't know if she was in danger or not—he only knew that in remembrance of Jesse, by God, he would see that no harm would come to her. Jesse —her father. And Leif's best friend.

That much he owed Jesse. Oh, God . . . Jesse.

Leif stared up at the night sky. The moon was out. A half-moon, shadowed, cryptic. It seemed like a moon of foreboding that night.

A chill swept through him. He felt a sudden urgency. He had to find her. He had to know that she was near him, that he could watch her. Jamie, Jesse's son, her half brother, was with him, beneath his wing. He wanted her here, too, but no one had seen her, no one seemed to know what continent she was on, much less what city.

Silly, he tried to tell himself. Nothing would happen to her; nothing would happen to Jamie.

He would have said the same thing about Jesse, and Jesse was dead. God, how he missed Jesse. More than Celia.

He stared up at the moon again. A silver crescent there in the sky, shadowed, elusive.

A liar's moon.

Tracy . . .

He'd fallen in love with her then. And nothing had really changed that. Not the betrayal, not the pain. Not Jesse, not her mother, Audrey, or even his own wife, Celia. And he *had* loved his wife. A different love, a different caring.

He would have found Tracy, if they'd given him half a chance.

A man couldn't stay in love with a mirage for seven years. And he hadn't, of course. He'd married Celia, and it had been a good marriage, but Celia, sweet and gentle and lovely, was gone now, and for the life of him, his mirage held the greater recall.

A man couldn't stay in love for seven years . . .

And he hadn't. He just wanted to see her again. For Jesse's sake.

And only maybe for his own.

Leif gave himself a severe shake and stared at the moon again. Foolish. He had debts to pay, nothing more. He'd loved Jesse, and Jesse deserved justice. There was a way . . . but Jamie and Tracy had to be protected and—

Where the hell was Tracy?

CHAPTER ONE

The curtains on the next balcony were open to the night, fluttering gently in the breeze. Tracy hesitated briefly—the two balconies were not a foot apart, but still, the ground was over forty stories below.

She shrugged, wryly admitting that anyone seeing a woman in a nightgown crawling from balcony to balcony this high in the air would have to assume that she was mad.

But she had to see Jamie, and she had to see him alone. He had bodyguards these days, and a host of personnel, and she didn't want to go through any of them—not now. Not this first time.

She thought about running back into her room and dressing in something more substantial, but by then he might have locked himself into one of the suite's bedrooms and she would never reach him. She should have stayed dressed, of course, but when midnight had come and gone, and then one A.M. and two A.M., she had about given up hope that he was returning to the suite at all.

It was really no big deal. Maybe eight inches.

She bunched her gown together, gripped the concrete railing across from her, and smoothly made the little leap. And well timed, too—he was still humming in the hallway, surveying his new domain. She grinned watching him. You little egotist! she thought affectionately. He was just twenty. A little ego wasn't such a bad thing—when she thought of the things she had done in her youth, her brother was way ahead of her.

She leaned back, though, watching him. It had been years since she had seen him. He might not even remember her. But she was convinced that he would welcome her—and help her. They were both Jesse's children, and she was certain that blood would win out.

There was a small, smug smile upon Jamie's face as he closed the door to his luxurious suite and ambled into the salon, looking about himself, as if he were in awe.

Suddenly, he grinned deeply and leapt into one of the beautifully upholstered Victorian chairs—and planted his booted feet upon the gleaming oak coffee table. At his side lay an ice bucket containing an expensive vintage bottle of champagne. Jamie poured himself a crystal glass of the stuff, surveyed the bubbles, laughed delightedly, and downed the glass. Then he poured some more.

Watching him, Tracy hid a wry and secret smile. Oh, yes, he was smug! But why not—the world was his. Far below his penthouse windows, fans were still screaming on the street. All this—for him!

He started to sip his second glass of champagne, then paused, catching sight of himself in the mirror across from the chair.

He looked a lot like their father, Tracy thought, and wondered if he wasn't thinking the same thing.

Jamie Kuger was thinking exactly that as he surveyed his assets. Blue eyes, blond hair, slim—artistic—face. Long, lanky build, a certain, melancholy and mysterious appeal. James, my boy, he silently told himself, you are just like the old man. Just like the old man. Oh, yeah . . .

But at that thought, he closed his eyes and swallowed back a host of tears. That was why he was here, wasn't it? Because he was so much like his father!

Chills riddled him. He'd been feeling on top of the world when he'd come in, and suddenly it was all different. He didn't feel like a twenty-year-old millionaire. He felt like a little boy—alone, lost, confused, utterly miserable. The loss was still such a horrible shock.

Jesse Kuger was dead, and had been dead for almost a year. But he had been a magic man. A magical music man. Together with Leif, Tiger, and Sam, Jesse had been part of the Limelights—a group to rival the Beatles, the Stones—any and every rock group that had ever come along. They were musicians who created songs and lyrics that were already considered classic—changing, flowing, growing constantly. And Jesse had been known and loved, admired and gossiped about the world over. He had been a personality belonging to everyone, to the world.

To Jamie, though, good and bad, he had been so much more. He had been his father. A comet, a burning, blinding star—but above all, his father. Loved and adored for his genius—and his faults. I'm going to start crying, Jamie warned himself. And I've already cried and cried, and it's useless to do it again . . .

He started, hearing a rustling from the balcony. He frowned, wondering who could have gotten past the hotel's security system and his own bodyguards to crawl around his balcony.

He stood with youthful and agile grace, then trod silently across the plush carpeting to the drapes that just whispered in movement from the soft breeze that came in from the park.

He parted the drapes slightly.

17

Night was upon the city. A haze of neon shed magical light upon the elegant balustrade, clearly outlining the slender form of the sylph of a girl who seemed to be awaiting him.

She was leaned against the wall, casually staring out into the night. Her hair was a rich mahogany, burnished and radiant, softly curling around her shoulders. Her eyes were blue, dark as India ink in the night, staring curiously into his. She wore the most entrancing outfit—some soft, slinky, silky thing that clung to her in the breeze. She was small but she was mature. Definitely mature. Slim and tiny but with curves, too, defined by the bedroom outfit—and stunning.

Jamie smiled slowly. "Hi," he told her. He assumed that one of the guys in the band had sent her, as a present, or a gag. They'd been teasing him about his youth.

"Jamie. You're back, at last," she said with a note of annoyance.

"Ah, yes," he returned, smiling and stepping out on the balcony. " 'At long last love!' "

She gave him a most peculiar look, then strode past him impatiently. Watching her, Jamie frowned again. This was certainly not the attitude he would have expected. He was adored—idolized!—by millions of screaming girls. He was supposed to have a smile that could kill—or captivate for life at any rate. And "bedroom eyes." Hadn't one of the magazines described him that way?

And a rich voice, of course. Just last week that senator's daughter had told him that his voice alone could send her into spasms of ecstasy.

So what went? Someone had hired him a stunning and voluptuous little doxy—and she seemed to be clock-watching! He was irritated for a second, then shrugged,

18

his natural humor coming to the fore. Ah, well. He'd be more charming—and she'd forget all about the time.

He followed her back into the room, watching her. She sat on the sofa rather primly, bare feet flat on the ground, hands folded on her knees. A sizzle swept through him again as he appreciated her assets. She was an "older" woman, he decided. At least twenty-five, maybe twenty-eight. Her face was a beautiful heart shape, with full red lips, small, slightly tipped nose, and rich mahogany brows that arched over her deep blue eyes. Sophisticated, yes—it was a sophisticated face, as elegant as the soft, silky material that floated around her. He could already imagine her lips damp and parted from his expert kiss, breasts heaving with the rush of her breath as she responded to his touch. Those eyes, soft and liquid . . .

Only they weren't soft and liquid at all. They were studying him quite sternly.

Keep your cool, keep your cool, Jamie! He warned himself. And he did. Half grinning, he moved around the couch, keeping his eyes on her—bedroom eyes, of course. He'd take his time; she could make the moves.

"Champagne?" He asked her, coming around to the bucket.

She shrugged, then smiled at last. "Sure, why not?"

He managed to pour the champagne without taking his eyes from hers. Cary Grant couldn't have done it a whit better, Jamie decided, congratulating himself.

He brought the glass of champagne around to her, handed it to her, procured one for himself, and sat beside her—giving her distance, of course.

But he rested his arm against the rise of the sofa, just beyond her back. Then he gave her his absolute best smile, inclining his head close to hers—and touching her,

19

touching her at last. Just letting his fingertips dangle upon her bare flesh at her shoulder.

She seemed to freeze for a minute. Her lips tightened and her eyes narrowed.

She shook his hand impatiently away.

"Oh, for God's sake, Jamie! Are you trying to pick me up?"

"I beg your pardon!" To his horror, he flushed with embarrassment. "Hey—wait a minute, what is this? You were out there on the balcony. All dressed up for an intimate encounter!"

"I am not dressed up for an intimate anything!" she replied with irate indignity. "My, Lord, I'd about given up on reaching you tonight. I was ready to go to bed."

"Your bed or my bed?"

"Oh, no, I don't believe this!" she exclaimed.

Jamie shook his head in confusion. "You don't believe this!" He swallowed down his champagne and shuddered, staring at her reproachfully. "I find a negligee-clad woman on my balcony and when I invite her in, she goes bananas! Who the hell are you and what are you doing on my balcony if you're not trying to pick me up?"

She returned his gaze in amazement, then broke into laughter.

Jamie was suddenly on his feet. "What are you laughing at! Honest! Hey! You're barely dressed, and in my room, and—"

"And it never—never!—in a thousand years occurred to me that you might try to pick me up!" she interrupted him, smiling ruefully.

God, was she lovely! he thought. But what on earth . . .

"Jamie—give it up. That lovely, lanky charm means nothing to me. I'm your sister."

He gasped in startled surprise and staggered back. He reached for the champagne bottle and didn't even think about getting a glass—he just chugged down a good swallow, which made him cough. She jumped up and started patting his back. Teary-eyed, he kept looking at her, in awe.

"Tracy?"

"Yes."

"You're Tracy?"

"Yes, I'm Tracy!"

"Oh, my God!"

"No," she grinned, "Just your sister!"

"Oh!" He sank into the sofa. She sat beside him, curling her feet beneath her. Jamie stared at her, totally intrigued, totally fascinated; she studied him in the same fashion, as if they could absorb all the lost years by learning the little visual nuances of one another.

"And I was trying to pick you up!" Jamie breathed.

She laughed a little breathlessly. "Yes. Shame on you!"

Jamie grinned in embarrassment, then he sobered. "Tracy . . . why didn't you call? Why didn't you write? Why did you have to sneak over the balcony like a thief? Or a hooker, which is what I thought you were." He paused for just a second. "Why didn't you come to the funeral?"

She sighed softly, staring idly down at her hands. "I didn't come to the funeral because it was a public circus." She looked up at him suddenly, and in her huge blue eyes Jamie saw a sorrow to match his own. He wasn't surprised. They could say what they wanted about Jesse Kuger, and, sure, some of it would be true. He'd caused a lot of grief in his day, but there'd been magic about him, too. Something unique. Tracy had loved him, just as Jamie had himself. And Tracy had gotten a really raw deal from both of her parents.

"You loved him, huh, Tracy?"

"Yes," she said softly.

"I would have resented them both."

"Oh, I did. But then I got older. I've never changed my opinion about the way they handled things. I just understand a little better that decent people can do rotten things. But that's beside the point. Jamie—someone murdered him."

He stared at her a little blankly, wondering at the tension in her tone, wondering if the trauma that had filled both their lives had taken a toll upon her. "Tracy," he said softly, feeling the more mature of the two of them for the moment. "Tracy, of course he was murdered. He was mugged, robbed and stabbed in Central Park. The police shot the guy who killed him."

She shook her head impatiently. "Jamie, I know that. But someone paid that man to kill Dad."

He inhaled sharply. "What are you talking about?"

She stood, and restlessly wandered back to the drapes that rustled so gently in the night air. "Jamie, I checked into the guy who stabbed him. His name was Martin Smith. He had a record—nothing major, which is, of course, what the police discovered. But I went further. Over the last year, Martin Smith had been carefully depositing large sums of cash in a savings account."

"How do you know?" Jamie gasped.

"I hired a private investigator a couple of months ago." She bit her lower lip and continued introspectively, "You see, I was in such shock at first, so hurt that I accepted the obvious as the truth. That a mugger had simply killed him. But then it occurred to me that we would never know the full truth—because our father's murderer had been killed before he could say anything to anyone. If there had been a conspiracy, he certainly wouldn't be around to admit it. I'm not sure what triggered my suspicions, but I was suspicious, and on that hunch I had Martin Smith's affairs investigated and found out about the money."

Jamie swallowed. "Maybe, maybe he, uh—"

"He—uh—what? Jamie?" she inquired tightly. "Smith was a loser, a petty thief. And a junkie. Jamie, I'm telling you, someone paid that man to kill Dad."

So this was his sister, Jamie thought, chilled and swallowing again. He didn't want to hear the words she was saying. He just stared at her. Small and slim, so elegant and so pretty—and so passionate now, hurt, as he was, and more. Outraged, stricken, and determined. He didn't doubt her. He just didn't want to face it. It had been bad enough to think that their father had died, wounded and alone, the victim of random crime.

It was much more horrifying to believe that someone had coldly and meticulously plotted that crime.

"Jamie?" She spoke softly now, standing tall for her diminutive size, her chin raised. "We have to find out what really happened."

He didn't feel that he could talk. "Who—who—"

"I don't know. The other guys; Leif, Tiger, or Sam. My mother, your mother, or his last wife."

"Our mothers—"

"Mine is innocent, of course. To me. So is yours—to you. Oh, Jamie, I don't know. But that's why I had to see you! We have to know!"

"I didn't have to know," he said glumly. "I never suspected anything until you came."

"Jamie—"

"Okay, okay." He lifted his hands. "So where do we

23

start? What do we do? And you left out your grandfather and your stepfather. Neither of them was fond of Dad. And you still didn't explain why you crawled over the balcony like Spiderwoman. Or Mata Hari."

She laughed. "I'm sorry, baby brother. The last time I saw you, you were wearing Pampers. I didn't want to meet you with anyone else around. I must say you've grown—but you're still my brother."

"But I'm not, Tracy," a harsh male voice suddenly interrupted.

They both froze; Jamie with surprise, Tracy with—something else.

Jamie was just startled. He hadn't heard Leif Johnston come into the suite. But then, Leif was like that. He could walk without the sound of a tread, and stand silently, watching any situation, until he decided to talk. Strange, too, because he was a tall man. And once you noted his presence, that presence dominated the room.

Jamie started to smile at Leif, then he noticed Tracy, dead still by the window, pale, still staring at Leif, still—frozen.

He thought to introduce them. He didn't know if they had ever met or not. He and Leif had never discussed Tracy, and, of course, all he knew about Tracy was what his father had told him.

"Tracy, Leif—" he began, but then he shut up, because they were both staring at each other, and evidently they did know one another, and evidently they didn't like a single thing they knew about each other. The hostility and tension was so thick in the room that he felt like he was cast in the middle of a brewing storm.

But then Leif moved on into the room, casually sitting on the back of the couch, idly lighting a cigarette that he pulled from the pocket of his denim western shirt—and still staring at Tracy.

"So, Tracy makes an appearance—at last," he mused dryly. "And a nice appearance at that. Where'd you buy that frothy piece of near nudity? Paris? Rome?"

Jamie could hear the sizzle as his sister sharply inhaled. Her eyes might have been twin points of flashing blue diamonds.

"None of your business, Mr. Johnston."

Leif shrugged. "I think that it is. Where have you been that you couldn't make the funeral? Ah, yes! Prying into the past life of the assassin! We're after a murderer, now, eh? Brilliant, Tracy. And you've got a nice list of suspects. Where do I fit in on that list, Tracy?"

"Right on top," she replied coolly, having recovered her dignity.

Leif laughed but the sound was harsh. "Me? Right on top? I don't think so, Tracy. Why in God's name would I have wanted one of my best friends dead?"

"Best friend? Most bitter enemy, I would say."

"That was what you wanted, Tracy, wasn't it? But it didn't work. It just didn't work."

"What in hell is going on here?" Jamie suddenly exploded.

Tracy closed her eyes, briefly, painfully, and shook her head. "Nothing, Jamie. I—uh—I'll see you later, Jamie. When you're alone."

"Tracy, don't go! You just got here! Tracy, we've just—"

"Jamie—it's very, very late. I just wanted to reach you without any of the media around. We'll get together in the morning, huh?"

"Uh—yeah, okay. If you have to go."

"I do. 'Night, Jamie. I'm right next door."

25

"And who else is right next door, Tracy?" Leif asked her coolly. "Your mother, your stepfather? Your grandfather—*el dictador?* Maybe you should grab her, Jamie. If they're around, they'll whisk her away."

Tracy stared at him for a moment, smiling coolly, the sizzle of her eyes belying her soft voice and smile.

"If the two of you will excuse me, please . . ."

She turned toward the drapes. Leif was instantly on his feet, clutching her elbow. His smoke-gray eyes were dark and stormy, boring down into her magnificent blue ones. To Jamie, they looked like a movie poster standing there, he so tall and dark, she so small and feminine against him, the sparks flying between them.

"What—" Tracy began, teeth grit, tense as she tried to free herself from his touch.

"You needn't crawl out the balcony, Tracy. Use the door," Leif drawled to her softly.

"Thank you!" She wrenched her arm from his touch.

She seemed to glide, to float, from the room. All dignity, all elegance. Jamie marveled again that she was so stunning; after all, it was quite nice to meet a sibling and discover that she was beautiful and lovely, delicate—and somehow tough as nails, too. Proud and determined.

He was still so stunned by all the events of the night that he didn't even say anything as she left. He just watched her.

But then he noted Leif again. Denim-clad arms crossed over his chest, watching Tracy, too. Smoke eyes dark as thunder. Troubled, brooding, pensive.

Jamie was crazy about Leif. When his own dad hadn't been around, Leif had been there. Through thick and thin—but then Leif had always been the most responsible of the group. The most level-headed, the most determined, and the most dangerous when he had made up his mind about something. Of course, Leif had endured the most hard knocks, too. The only American, he'd been shipped off to Nam during the days of the draft. Then he'd fallen in love with and married Celia, and Celia had died. Then he'd been the first one called when Jesse Kuger had died in the park.

Tracy had put Leif in with her group of suspects! But that had to be because she didn't really know him.

But obviously, they did know one another. Awkwardly, Jamie cleared his throat. "Leif, you and, uh, Tracy have met before, huh?"

"What?" Leif arched one of his jet brows, drawn from an inner reverie by the question.

Jamie cleared his throat again. "You and Tracy have already met, huh? You know one another?"

Leif paused for a second, then chuckled dryly. "Oh, yeah, we know one another all right."

Jamie sank back down to the plush sofa. "I just met my half sister. After all these years. She slips over my balcony, then disappears. My God. I've got so many questions for her."

"You'll have the time to ask them all," Leif said with a little sigh. "She isn't going to disappear again."

"How do you know?"

Leif hesitated again, briefly. "Because I think she's right, Jamie. I think that the man who stabbed your father was a hired assassin. And in this I don't blame her one bit. We've got to find out who it was behind the murder."

"Oh, God," Jamie whispered. "First Tracy—and then you! What makes you so sure that it was some kind of a conspiracy?"

Leif answered softly. "It took me a long, long time, Jamie, just to accept the fact that your dad was really

27

gone. That his life could have been snuffed out like a candle flame—so damned carelessly! Since the killer was already dead, I couldn't shake the man, I couldn't scream at him—I couldn't even hate him. I couldn't stop thinking about what a stupid, senseless tragedy it was. Then I suddenly started wondering if it was really senseless at all. And I hired a private detective to check into it."

Leif planted a hand on Jamie's shoulder. "We'll talk about it in the morning, okay? I'm going to get some sleep."

Leif disappeared into the left bedroom of the suite. Jamie watched him, then glanced at his watch. Three A.M., and he had practice and a concert the next night. He stood, stretched, and went on into the right bedroom.

He was glad that Leif was with him. Leif wasn't acting as his manager or anything—nor was he performing with Jamie. He was just along because it was Jamie's first American tour—and because he was Jamie's friend. Lending support and experience—and probably keeping a wary eye on the happenings to make sure that Jamie didn't fall into any of the traps that could wind around the very young who suddenly became the very rich and very famous.

Jamie lay down and tried to sleep. No good.

Two hours later, he was still wide awake. Obviously. He'd just met his mysterious sister, and he'd learned that his father's murder had been a conspiracy. It seemed that Leif had suspected the same thing for some time and had kept his own counsel. Well, that was like Leif, too. He kept his own counsel a lot. How the hell did you sleep when you had all this running around in your mind?

He frowned against the darkness of his room. Someone was moving around the elegant salon of the suite.

Jamie leapt out of his bed and rushed to the door,

28

cracking it slightly. Maybe it was Tracy again, coming secretively to try to finish her conversation with him. Obviously, she hadn't known that Leif was traveling with him. She'd thought to find him alone.

But when he stared out into the darkened salon, he didn't see Tracy. Again there was movement in the room. It was Leif. Tall and towering in the night, he was a dark lean shadow. Agile, soundless.

He went to the drapes, pulled them back, and disappeared onto the balcony.

A second later, Jamie heard a soft thud, and he knew that Leif had hopped from their balcony to Tracy's.

They were both crazy, he thought first. Insane. Hopping from balcony to balcony when their suites were on the fortieth floor!

Then he began to chew his lower lip in concern. Leif had just gone after Tracy. Leif and Tracy didn't seem to be any too crazy about one another. Tracy had even put Leif on her murder suspect list . . .

Oh, God! What if it was true? What if Leif thought that Tracy had some kind of proof, and what if Leif was hopping over the balcony to go and kill his sister in the night.

"Oh, God!" Jamie groaned aloud.

He couldn't believe that. He'd known Leif all his life. Leif could be stern and demanding and blunt and sometimes autocratic; he could also be gentle and understanding when no one else in the world was. Leif could not possibly be a cold-blooded killer.

Okay, that was a fact that Jamie knew.

But then, what was Leif doing crawling over the balcony to accost Tracy in the dead of the night?

CHAPTER TWO

Once in the hallway, Tracy dashed for her own suite.
Once inside, she leaned against the door, gasped for
breath—and longed to kick herself.

What a fool! Trying to return via the balcony! But
then, Leif had that kind of effect on her. Oh, God! She
covered her face with her hands, furious with herself.
Leif should have had no effect on her—none whatsoever!
It had been seven years since she had seen him. Seven
long, long years.

She pushed herself away from the door, then, on second thought, turned back and twisted the top dead bolt.
She gazed at her hands, and they trembled, and once
again she was angry with herself.

Exhaling a long sigh, she walked through the posh,
nearly identical salon of her own suite to her nearly identical balcony. The breeze touched her cheeks, cooling,
reviving. Far below her, horns tooted and brakes
squealed. The night never died here. Little tiny play people seemed to move about despite the hour. There was a
very nice sense of normalcy about it all.

Tracy inhaled and exhaled again and leaned against the
building, trying to still her shivers. Nothing about her life
had ever been normal, but in the last few years she
thought that she had achieved a pleasant stage of accep-

tance—maturity and stability. Just seeing Leif Johnston had torn that all to shreds. If she hadn't been taken so completely by surprise . . .

Idiot! she accused herself with disgust. She'd been so meticulous and careful when delving into the life of her father's assassin! How could she not have known that Leif Johnston was traveling on this concert tour with her brother!

But she hadn't. Leif had become a very private person —not even the tabloids ever seemed able to get anything on him. Still, the information should have been somewhere! And it had been common knowledge that he had been close to Jamie Kuger—closer than his own father. It was natural that Jamie would have turned to Leif . . .

"Oh, God!" she breathed aloud, and all the hurt came back; all her feelings of shame and humiliation.

She spoke out loud again—maybe it was because the words seemed more assuring that way.

"You weren't that terrible, Tracy! You were very young, and what they did to you wasn't in the least bit fair!"

No, of course, it hadn't been fair in the least. She had been—in the eyes of her grandfather and mother—a most ungodly mistake. Arthur Kingsley was a rich, rich man. Tracy didn't even know his total worth—it was in the billions. When his daughter had become involved with a long-haired seventeen-year-old pop singer, Arthur had quickly seen that the affair ended. Tracy was born under very discreet circumstances in a clinic in Switzerland; a year later her eighteen-year-old mother had married Ted Blare, a young man with the impeccable type of family background that old Arthur could stomach. Yale all the way.

Tracy thought then how she loved Ted; he was a dear,

dear man, far more of a caring parent than either of the two who had biologically bred her!

She hadn't known anything about her real father, though, until she was eight years old. She was playing on her most beloved object—a grand piano—that Ted had bought especially for her despite her mother's protests. Protests she hadn't understood at the time but had come to comprehend fully on that fateful day.

She'd been supposed to pick up her toys, but had become entranced with a melody on the piano. She hadn't heard her mother yelling at her at all. Then suddenly beautiful Audrey had been standing before her like the wrath of God, screaming and swearing and telling her that she was just like her father—all she cared about was the bloody-awful music.

Ted explained the truth to her—more or less—saying that her real father had loved music and that he, Ted, had adopted her because she was the loveliest little girl that he had ever seen. He did it all so gently that she loved him all the more. But the seeds of curiosity had been sown in her young soul, and she could never forget that in her fury her mother had called her a "little bastard."

Jesse Kuger and his group went on to become very famous and immensely rich—and idolized by millions of women across the globe. Audrey was very bitter about it, and it wasn't until Tracy was eight that she discovered that one of her absolute idols was her own father. It was right after a group of her school friends had been over and they'd all been screaming with delight over the newest album by the Limelights. Tracy mentioned very casually that she had dreamt of Jesse Kuger falling madly in love with her and marrying her in a dream. Audrey had turned pale, and then she'd been furious all over again. She'd told Tracy that she was Jesse Kuger's daughter, and that if she had any sense, she'd dislike the man intensely.

There was no way that Audrey would ever be rational about the man, so Tracy's stepfather was the one to bring her to meet her natural father.

He was wonderful to her; he was all a child could dream of. At his massive estate in Connecticut she met his wife and her baby brother, and she received all kinds of presents. Except that she wasn't really wanted, of course.

She wanted to daydream that her famous and unique father could be a prince to marry her mother. But she adored her stepfather! And then, of course, there was Carol, Jamie's mother.

Jesse's marriage to Carol had only lasted ten more years, but by the time they divorced, Tracy had been seventeen and in total rebellion. Jesse had written to her steadily over the years—but never again had he seen her. He was just so busy . . .

She loved him; she hated him. Just as she resented and adored her mother. There had really been nothing for her to do but create her own separate life and seek out her father again herself . . .

Tracy started to shiver in the cool of the night; she turned away and reentered the suite. There was a bottle of champagne cooling in her salon, too, and though she felt as if she'd like something stronger, she decided champagne would be better than nothing. She uncorked the bottle, then sat back on the sofa with a little sigh, sipped the bubbling brew, and continued remembering.

She managed to get close enough to see him at a party to which she had obtained an invitation through her own merits—she had sold a ballad to a country-and-western singer and the song had risen high on the charts. In grati-

33

tude, the singer had urged her to come to a massive bash she was having in Nashville. "Everyone" who was "anyone" was supposed to have been there.

The champagne went down badly suddenly; Tracy felt a hot flush rise to her cheeks, and her palms went instantly damp.

She was tiny, but she'd always looked so mature. At seventeen she had passed for twenty-five. She wrote her songs under a pen name. And after everything, she'd had this vivid dream that her father would see her, cry joyously, and welcome her with absolute adoration.

The dream had been dashed when Jesse Kuger hadn't recognized her and hadn't given her a second glance. Crushed, still shy of her eighteenth birthday, she had reacted horribly. She'd wanted to hurt Jesse as badly as he had hurt her. And being so young and inexperienced, she hadn't cared how she set about to do it.

In the end, she'd been the one to pay because Leif Johnston had been there. Leif was slightly aloof, but charming—a center of attention. Striking in his manner, striking with his brooding dark eyes.

Leif—untouchable until now, so the gossip went. Since he'd returned from the service he'd been very private and very discreet, shunning the press—and living quietly with a beautiful blond classical pianist he had met in Paris. According to the gossip columnists, he and Celia had suddenly parted, and no one knew why. They only knew that he might be available again . . .

Tracy hadn't been bowled over by him at first—she'd been upset and furious and determined to get even with her father. When Leif had started to flirt with her, she'd been more furious still. So stupidly determined to get even! She hadn't known where the idea had begun, or if it had ever really been a solid idea. She'd never seduced anyone in her life. She'd coldly set out to seduce Leif Johnston just to be able to tell her father that she was his best friend's latest conquest.

"I will not think about it!" Tracy whispered aloud.

But it was as if a dam had broken, and she had no choice.

She couldn't hate Leif for what she had done herself; she'd lied about her age, and her first taste of martinis had certainly given her boldness.

He'd been a wonderful lover and he'd been stunned by her lack of experience. Quiet, pensive—and then irritated. But even then she'd played it well. Perhaps it hadn't been play—she'd been in awe, terrified of intimacy. Then she'd made her fatal mistake—she'd started to fall in love with him. Her game didn't mean anything anymore.

She'd spent a month with him. Secretly, they'd traveled to Connecticut, and in that time they'd shut out the world. There'd been no plan in Tracy's mind anymore; she was simply in love. She didn't want to get even with her father; she just wanted Leif. Someday she knew that she would have to tell him who she really was—she knew that. But she couldn't break the spell. Not then. She let herself believe that the right time would come. And she lived in the enchantment. Waking up beside him, sipping morning coffee on the terrace that overlooked the rose garden and the pool, curling beside him and watching movies late at night, clad in velour robes that could be so easily shed . . .

Enchantment.

Then her mother had finally reached her father, and, with Arthur Kingsley in tow, they had burst in upon a most intimate moment. Tracy had been furious and indignant, but not half so much so as those around her! Her

35

father had accused Leif of horrible things—and Leif had been the most furious of all, glaring at Tracy with those smoke-and-fire eyes, aware that he had been duped in Tracy's plot against her father. There was no way to tell him that it had only begun that way. She didn't have a chance.

Oh, God! It had been horrible! Tracy could still feel sick, recalling that night. Her father—Leif—

They'd come to blows. Jesse had been wild, thundering against Leif. And Leif had taken it for a while, trying to tell Jesse that he hadn't known, that he hadn't had the faintest idea—that Tracy had gone by her pen name and told him that she was twenty-three.

In frustration, Leif had finally decked Jesse. And her grandfather had come up from behind and decked Leif with his old baseball bat, and Leif had gone out like a light.

Well, she'd meant to hurt her father. And she had.

He and Leif didn't speak for a year after the incident. And protesting all the way, she'd been hauled back to grandfather's estate in Switzerland, her nightmare really just beginning. She'd expected to pay for the incident—never as seriously and painfully as she did in that cold retreat where she felt she had lost everything.

Automatically, she sipped more champagne. Maybe it had all done something—though that price she had paid had been so high. She'd seen her father right after Zurich, and afterwards they had been close, seeing each other somewhere at least every six months.

Until he had died.

Tears welled hot behind her eyes; she swallowed and did not shed them. He'd been dead almost a year. It still hurt. Tracy knew all his faults so clearly! She had borne the brunt of many of them. But she'd still loved him and now she had to find the truth. At first she'd been stunned, then so terribly hurt—then furious because he had been such a young man—barely forty-two—and because he'd had so much more to give the world. He'd been so full of life . . .

Her father's murderer had been shot down before he'd ever left the park. For Tracy that hadn't been enough. She'd dug into the man's past with the help of a private investigator. And when she'd found out about the money, she'd realized with horror that one of Jesse's love/hate relationships had been dangerous enough to bring about his death.

"Which one had him killed?" she whispered aloud.

"Me—remember."

Naturally, she screamed. Luckily, she was so stunned that the sound was nothing more than a pathetic squeal.

Leif was in the salon and the draperies were drifting softly behind him.

"How dare you?" she whispered, embarrassed that he had caught her so off guard, annoyed that all his emotions were neatly hidden behind the smoke-gray shield of his eyes.

He shrugged, moving easily into the room, plopping down on the sofa as if he intended to stay. Relaxed, long, jeans-clad legs stretched out on the teak coffee table, fingers laced behind his dark head as he settled into the plush upholstery. He shouldn't fit there, she thought; he was in worn Wranglers and a blue denim work shirt, and the room was far more conducive to a man in a tux.

But Leif fit. Here, in a park, on a horse, in costume, out of costume, Leif simply fit. He could be comfortable in any surrounding, with any group. He liked to be comfortable; he liked casual clothing. He looked wonderful in three-piece suits and tuxes, too. He would be forty in

May, she knew; he could have passed for thirty. He was lean and trim—and not a speck of gray yet to dust his dark hair. Only his eyes and his manner reflected his maturity. His smoke-and-steel gaze gave off a certain hard-edged confidence, a certain weariness; a look that somehow warned he was not a man with whom to trifle.

"What are you doing here? Sneaking in through the balcony," she muttered.

"You just sneaked into my suite."

"My brother's suite."

"It was reserved in my name, Miss— Just what name are you going by these days, Tracy? Your father told me you had it legally changed to Kuger—but you don't use it, do you?"

"No."

"Why?"

"It's none of your business. You didn't answer my question; you were after me for coming in through the balcony—why didn't you knock at the door?"

"Would you have let me in?"

"No."

"I rest my case."

"Good. Get out, then."

He didn't move. She grew acutely uncomfortable as he studied her with blunt curiosity, his unfathomable gaze moving at a leisurely pace from her eyes to her toes.

"You haven't changed, Tracy."

"I most certainly have. Drastically."

"Well, you've got that same nasty streak. Once upon a time you used me to get to your father. Are you using Jamie now to get to me?"

"Don't be ridiculous. I never expected to see you again. I had no idea you were with Jamie."

"But I'm at the top of your suspect list. How were you

38

planning on proving that I was in on a conspiracy to commit murder without seeing me?"

Tracy took a breath without answering him. She didn't know how she was going to prove anything—she only knew that she had to get to the truth.

He waited for several seconds, watching her. She wished that she could run into her bedroom and wrap herself in an all-encompassing blanket to ward off that scrutiny, but she didn't move. She didn't intend to show a single sign of weakness in front of him—ever. Not after the way that they had last parted—he furious, she screaming and in tears.

He took his feet off the coffee table, folded his hands before him, and sighed softly as he stared down at them.

"Tracy, you're being a fool when it's a dangerous time to be one."

"What are you talking about?" she demanded.

He hesitated a moment, then stood, coming toward her. Instinctively, she backed away, but he didn't appear to notice. His hands fell upon her shoulders. His hands! Seven years, and she remembered them so well! Oh, feeling them again . . . Fingers long and tapering, magic upon a keyboard or a guitar, magic upon bare flesh . . .

She almost screamed with the crippling memory of it. She didn't, because he was already talking.

"Tracy, I know, too, that there was something more to your father's death. I hired a detective, too. I know all about the money deposited into Martin Smith's account."

She inhaled sharply, staring up into his eyes. Years were swept away. She knew his gaze—dark, passionate, tense.

"If you know—"

"Tracy, you can't wander around making accusations —unless you want a hired assassin coming after you."

"I'm not making accusations—"

"You accused me."

"You belong in a list of suspects!" she cried out. And it was too much for her. She wrenched away from him and started for the door to the suite. "Leif, there's no need for you to leave by the balcony. Please, go by the front door."

She turned around and discovered that he was standing patiently where she had left him, still watching her, still waiting.

"Tracy, we're not done."

"We've been done for years."

"I wasn't talking about the past, but we can discuss that, too, if you wish."

"I don't wish."

"Fine. But come back here and sit down."

"Leif—"

"Tracy," he interrupted, "you can come back and sit down, or I can come over and insist that you sit down."

"I'm not eighteen anymore!"

He laughed bitterly. "You weren't eighteen then, either, Tracy."

"I was almost—"

"Almost, but not quite. You convinced me that you were twenty-three. I would have believed it until I died— if your grandfather hadn't threatened to have me locked up for twenty years on several counts of statutory rape! Which, at that point, was exactly what I felt I deserved. I felt like a child molester!"

"My grandfather wouldn't have—"

"No—he wouldn't. He couldn't have born the publicity. He decided to knock me out with a baseball bat instead."

"Dammit! I'm sorry! I had no control over what happened then! I was a minor. They dragged me out—they—"

"Yep—they dragged you out and whisked you away. And thankfully Jesse decided that he didn't really want me dead and he called an ambulance. Okay, Tracy, so your grandfather controlled you. He controlled your mother all her life, too. I'm surprised your stepfather is sane. But tell me, Tracy, does he still control you? You turned eighteen a month later. You never called with an explanation—or an apology."

"You're forgetting something, aren't you, Mr. Johnston?" Tracy queried softly. She felt like she was strangling. "You were married to Celia a month later. I didn't know if it was something you had discussed with your bride or not. I presumed, like everyone else, that you wanted to pretend it had never happened."

"Oh, it happened, Tracy. It most certainly happened!"

Tracy felt the blood drain from her face. Seven years hadn't really eased one bit of that horribly humiliating day. It suddenly seemed very unfair that such a miserable mistake of her youth should haunt her forever, that there was no going back. She could never explain the truth to him now; she could never tell him how sorry she was. And she could certainly never tell him that she had already paid far more dearly than he could ever know.

She made an impatient sound and inhaled deeply.

"Leif—has it occurred to you that being near you right now is a very difficult experience for me?"

"Tracy—it's not exactly easy for me! But I'm talking about life and death! Yours. Now get over here and sit!"

How much had the man changed? she wondered a little nervously. Or had he changed at all? The way he was staring at her, she didn't think she wanted to risk his temper, although she despised the fact that she was going

41

to obey him. She felt seventeen again—with someone else taking charge of her life.

"Tracy!" It was the softest whisper of her name; it was a warning and again recall came upon her in a staggering burst of lightning. Tracy! He had said her name just the same way that awful night when he had discovered himself betrayed—and when he hadn't wanted to believe it. Tracy! Is it true?

She lowered her lashes, set her jaw, and returned to the couch, sitting quite stiffly upon it.

And to her horror, he came to her, lowered on one knee to take her hands in his in such a grip that she couldn't wrench away; she could only meet his eyes. His encompassed her own.

"Tracy, listen to me. You can't do anything, and you can't say anything. You should have never said anything to Jamie—"

"He's my brother!" she burst out passionately. "He's the only one that I can trust in this!"

Leif shook his head impatiently. "Tracy! This isn't the way to go about it! Now you've gotten Jamie involved, and I'm willing to bet that you haven't the faintest idea of what you're going to do!"

"Leif!" With a gasp she pulled away from him, retreating around the back of the sofa and facing him again from that safe distance. "Jamie needed to know!"

He lifted a brow to her, then started down the hall and made a left. Tracy frowned, aware that he had gone into the little kitchenette. She trailed quickly after him, pausing in the doorway.

In amazement she stared at him while he switched on the drip coffeepot and rifled through the shelves for coffee and filters.

"What do you think you're doing now?" she demanded irritably. "Leif—it's close to four o'clock in the morning and you're—"

"Making coffee. You can help, or you can sit, because I'm not leaving until we've gotten this straightened out."

"Leif—"

"What?" He poured the water through the coffeepot, leaned against the counter, and watched her, a dark brow arched. "What is it, Tracy? Have you got Mom and Gramps stashed away somewhere? Should I expect another concussion?"

"No!" she retorted with a saccharine smile. "You can expect *me* to give you a concussion if you don't get out of my suite!"

"Ah, that's right. You are legal these days, aren't you? You're twenty-five years old. A quarter of a century. That's a long, long time—and yet it's not so long at all."

"Leif—"

He moved across the room quickly. To her annoyance, she let out a little gasp as his arms stretched out and his fingers splayed across the wall on either side of her head.

"Your father couldn't even find you for a year!"

She ducked to crawl beneath his arm and escape him; he caught her chin and held it so that her eyes were locked with his.

"Leif! My God, it's all ancient history—"

"Why weren't you at the funeral?"

"Because it was a zoo and you know it!"

"Ah, yes, it was a zoo! But your entire cast of suspects was present. Your grandfather was there, your mother, and your stepfather. Jamie's mother, Carol, was there, and Lauren—the second Mrs. Kuger, the grieving widow. And the surviving Limelights—Tiger, Sam, and me. And, of course, Jamie. Only Tracy was missing. Why weren't you with your mother?"

43

"Leif—let me go," Tracy breathed. She'd never felt so threatened, his palm upon her chin, his fingers long enough to crush her face, his eyes simmering with a brooding intensity that promised a torrential storm.

He sighed suddenly, releasing her, turning back to the shelves to find the elegant little hotel mugs.

"Black?" he asked her.

She was very surprised that he remembered. She nodded, and accepted the mug he handed her, gritting her teeth when she discovered his hand on her elbow, veering her quickly back to the salon, where she found herself seated at his side again.

"Tracy, you're going to have to accept something if you really want to catch a killer."

"And what's that?"

"You may be looking to your own family."

"And I may not!"

He shook his head at her, disgusted. "Tracy, you're being blinded! Tracy, your grandfather hated Jesse. I can still remember everything that happened when he found out about that affair. He was brutal. He didn't give the two of them a chance."

Tracy found herself setting her cup down and flying to her feet. "And maybe he was right! Look at my father's life! He went through women like he did shirts! He ignored me, then he ignored Jamie! He would have made a rotten, rotten husband—and my stepfather made a wonderful husband and parent!"

"I thought you loved your father."

"I did! Damn you, you have no right to question that! I loved him very much—but I have never pretended that he didn't have faults, and maybe my grandfather had a right to his feelings! Dad didn't stay married to Carol, and he probably wouldn't have stayed married to Lauren—"

"Did it ever occur to you that Jesse loved your mother? That they might have made it—if they'd ever been given a chance?"

He voiced the question so softly. She wondered just what Leif knew and what he didn't know. Almost everything, probably. He and Jesse were like brothers.

She sucked in her breath suddenly, wishing desperately that he were gone—that he had never reappeared. She had tried so hard. And surely, surely memory had become dim at times. She had loved him; she had hated him. He was here with her now, and though time had passed, he was still the same man. Still so attractive. Alluring in movement, in masculine grace, in the deep tone of his voice. Arrogant, confident—impatient.

"Sit down, Tracy."

"I will not—"

"You will!"

And she did, tense, rigid, inflamed, because he stood up, placed his hands on her shoulders, and pushed her back down.

"Leif! You just said it—I'm a quarter of a century old now! I don't have to tolerate this from you or anyone else."

"Where did you go, Tracy?"

"What?" she said, faltering.

He was staring at her so intently—as if her answer were of extreme importance.

"Switzerland!" she snapped back.

Something strange came to his gaze; a further cover of smoke. He stared at her then, guarded, careful, and she discovered herself then the one at a loss.

"Leif! Would you quit this, please!" She begged. "Why

do you care! You married Celia. You settled down. You—you had a baby."

He stood up and walked to the balcony and stared out into the night, not facing her. For a long moment he stayed there, back stiff, shoulders squared, hands upon his hips. Then he turned back to her, and the shields were in place. There was no telltale emotion of any kind to read from his hard-planed face.

"Tracy, tell me—have you got a plan?"

"Well, I—"

"You don't, do you?" he queried softly.

"No! Do you?"

"Yes, as a matter of fact, I do."

"And what is that?"

"A memorial service."

"Leif—you're crazy."

"No, I don't think I am. Jesse died almost a year ago. He was easily a man to be remembered and honored. Those of us who loved him did so deeply. And our lives became very tangled and entwined. My house isn't far from the city. To get everyone together as guests at a house party to end back in New York with the service might very well be the perfect occasion to try to figure out just who had the strongest motive to want Jesse dead."

Tracy shook her head. "They won't all come!"

He shrugged. "Jamie's mother will come—we're still pretty good friends, and Jamie will be there. The last Mrs. Kuger will arrive with bells on—life has been rather dreary for her lately, I hear. You'll be there; Jamie will be there. Sam and Tiger and I are still good friends—very good friends. They planned to come for Jamie's final concert anyway."

46

"No way, Leif. I won't be there. And you can guarantee that neither my mother, stepfather, or grandfather will show up!"

"And why won't you be there?"

"I can't. I don't ever want to go back into that house again."

"Don't be absurd."

"I'm not! Leif, you don't know—"

"I don't know what?"

"Never mind!"

"Memories you can't handle?"

"That's right."

"Or memories you want to relive?"

"Leif—get out of here. Just go."

"I am going, Tracy. Thanks for the coffee—and the hospitality." He started down the hallway, then turned back with a pleasant smile.

"Tomorrow night is Jamie's last concert on the tour, you know. We'll be here one more night. Sunday morning he's leaving with me for Connecticut. And by the way, Tracy, my plan is already in action. Your mother, stepfather, and grandfather have already agreed to come. You didn't know that, did you? Maybe you really did break the ties that bind you, Tracy. Good for you. But if you want to see Jamie, you'd better plan on a trip to Connecticut."

"Speak of binding ties!" she snapped.

He shrugged, and came back to her. He was smiling with a certain amount of admiration; there was just a touch of the gentle silver she had once known to his eyes.

She wanted to swear at him. The words didn't come, nor did she move when he touched her chin again.

There was no force to that touch. It was nearly tender.

Just his knuckle below her chin, lightly lifting her face to his.

"You really haven't changed, Tracy," he told her very softly. "You're still very, very beautiful."

He shouldn't have touched her, Leif realized. He shouldn't have come so near her—felt the brush of her nothing gown, stared into the liquid elegance of her eyes. He shouldn't have felt the softness of her flesh, because time didn't really heal all wounds at all; he felt as if he bled all over again. He hadn't—surely, he hadn't!—loved her all those years.

Maybe he had; maybe he hadn't. Maybe time had no bearing on things at all. Maybe it was just the moment. He wanted to slip his arms around her as if she had never been gone, touch her lips and feel the magic, hold her against him and never let her go . . .

Madness. There was nothing between them. Nothing except for mistrust and bitterness . . . and magic. He wanted her now. Desperately. To hold her, touch her, feel her hair cascade upon his naked flesh, the heat of her body meld with his own . . .

He forced a crooked smile to his face; forced his lids to fall, to break the spell.

"Very, very lovely, Tracy," he said lightly. Release her, fool! his mind cried.

She couldn't think of a reply. She couldn't make a sound. The cast of his eyes, the touch of his hand . . . Again, time slipped away and the traitorous sensation eclipsed all else. All she could do was stare at him, caught in the web of a strange spell once again.

He released her at last—and walked down the hall. She still didn't move nor speak. Until the door closed softly in his wake.

Then, swearing, she leapt to her feet. She bolted the door. And when that was done, she hurried to the sliding-glass balcony doors, drew them shut—and locked them.

CHAPTER THREE

It was almost dawn when Tracy had finally slept, so she shouldn't have been terribly surprised that it was well after noon when she was awakened by a phone call.

It was Jamie to tell her that he'd just ordered breakfast up from room service—would she come over and join him.

She hesitated just a second, then asked him, "Where's Leif?"

Jamie hesitated just a little bit longer than she had. "He's still in his room. Why?"

"No reason," she said quickly—and then again she paused. She couldn't avoid Leif—not if he was with Jamie. Nor did she want to create friction between the two of them.

"Tracy?"

"Give me a few minutes. You just woke me up. Okay?"

"Sure."

Jamie rang off and Tracy hurried into the shower. Last night she had been off guard—she simply hadn't known that Leif was with Jamie. Well, today she knew. And the past was ancient history. She wouldn't allow her emotions to control her; she would be polite and cordial and so calm that he couldn't get beneath her skin.

With that in mind, she swept her hair off her neck into

a neat little chignon and wore three-inch boot heels with a sweeping leather skirt and tailored silk shirt. She chided herself about her attempt at sophistication. After all, it had been her ability to appear mature and sophisticated that had been her original downfall. But she couldn't help wanting to feel taller. Jamie was tall, and Leif was around six foot three, and somehow his knack for staring down at her was intimidating. Not that she could wear heels high enough to face him eye to eye—she was only five foot four. But any little bit of help seemed warranted here. She was not a child now; she had paid vast dues to become an adult, and she was going to be treated as one.

Still, her hands grew clammy as she traversed the short distance of hall between her suite and Jamie's. She took a deep breath before knocking and was still exhaling it when Jamie instantly flung the door open.

"Wow," he told her with a flattering appreciation. "You really are a knockout."

"Thanks, Jamie." She grinned, looking over his silver-buttoned black cavalry jacket, tight black jeans, and head full of gold-blond hair—hair worn a little long at the neck, but thick, wavy, and very attractive with his soulful eyes and youth.

"So are you."

He grimaced. "I'm 'cute.' You're beautiful."

She inclined her head to him, grinning. "Again, thank you. Have you got coffee in here?"

"Sure—*voilà!* I ordered everything I could think of because I have no idea what you like. Isn't that something? You're my sister, and I don't know anything about you at all. I mean, are you a vegetarian? A health freak? Do you jog? What's your sign? Do you use sugar?"

Tracy started laughing at his rapid fire of questions while he led her to a table elegantly set before the windows of the balcony. He really had ordered everything. There were chafing dishes all over the table and baskets of toast, muffins, hard rolls, and bagels.

"Jamie—this is wasteful!" she chided him.

"But I'm immensely wealthy!" he replied innocently, reaching for a silver coffee urn.

"Coffee, madame! See—I don't even know how you take it!"

"Black," Leif replied from behind them before Tracy had a chance to form the word.

She spun around—defensive already. And then she was annoyed with herself that she could be so quickly unnerved. She would have never imagined that after all this time the mere sound of his voice could cast her into uneasy quivers that swept away all poise and control.

Get it back, get it back! she warned herself. And she didn't do badly at all. She glanced briefly at Leif, then smiled at Jamie. "Yes, black, please."

She accepted the cup of coffee, nervously aware that Leif was by then right behind her, reaching around her for the coffeepot that Jamie had set down. She didn't really look at him, but he was next to her, so she was very aware of him. He'd just come from the shower and he smelled wonderfully of soap and after-shave. His dark hair was still damp and very sleek. He seemed exceptionally tall, sinewed, and tan in a yellow polo shirt and dark cords.

She moved away from him, choosing a chair that looked out over the balcony. He seemed oblivious to her, too, sipping his coffee as he gazed out at the day, then sliding into the chair across from Tracy.

She felt his eyes on her, and despite her will not to do so, she felt her gaze pulled from the window to meet his.

She wanted to scream. Instead, she smiled pleasantly

and felt all the more uneasy. Last night had been different. He had stared at her, but it had seemed a more natural curiosity. Today it was as if he wondered something, or had a clue to something—something that did not endear her to him in the least. Did he have her on the top of *his* list of suspects?

"Gee," Jamie murmured, interrupting her thoughts. "Just when did you two meet?" he asked innocently.

Leif arched his brows, glancing Jamie's way, then looking back at Tracy. "Oh, years ago," he replied idly. "We met at a party." His steady gaze remained on her. "We really didn't know one another very long; her grandfather whisked her off to Europe shortly after we met."

"Wow. You've led an exciting life, Tracy!" Jamie said.

"Umm. Wonderful," Tracy managed to say, unable to tear her gaze from Leif's. He looked tired, she thought. He was leaning back, almost looking comfortable and casual in his chair, but the tiny lines about his eyes were evident in the sunlight, as if he hadn't slept well.

"What's he really like, Tracy?"

"What?" she murmured, disconcerted, drawing her eyes from Leif to look at Jamie at last.

"Arthur Kingsley—billionaire. They say he owns half of the U.S. interests around the whole world."

"I—uh—guess he does."

Leif was still staring at Tracy. "He's a very powerful man," he told Jamie. "Accustomed to buying anything he wants."

"What are they estimating you at these days, Mr. Johnston?" Tracy asked acidly. "A rather high figure, last I heard. And if you did nothing more than whistle Dixie through an entire album, it would still sell in the millions, so I really don't think you have a right to judge Arthur."

"Arthur? You call him Arthur?" Jamie asked.

I don't call him anything, Tracy almost answered. But she didn't want Leif to know that she had spent the last five years carefully severing the yoke that Arthur Kingsley had attempted to tie around her neck. She called him occasionally and she spent each Christmas with her family—but other than that, she kept carefully away.

"More importantly, Tracy, what are you calling yourself?" Leif asked her.

"Kuger," she told him.

"You are not using that name," Leif responded instantly.

"Why do I feel like I never know what's going on here?" Jamie complained.

"How do you know that I'm not using my name?" Tracy demanded of Leif.

"Guys—" Jamie tried.

"Because I've had detectives looking for you for the last year, too. I got as far as a remote town in northern Scotland, and then no one could get any further."

"I like my privacy," Tracy said.

"So much so that your mother didn't even know where you were?"

"What business is it of yours?"

"Guys—listen—everything is getting cold. We've got eggs Benedict, steak and eggs, French toast—I mean, this is some fluffy French toast we've got going here—"

"Dammit, Tracy, what do I have to do to get through to you! You were waltzing around a balcony forty floors up to get to your brother, so you know that I'm telling the truth—"

"All right! You're telling the truth about my father, but what has that got to do with anything else? It's none of

54

your business where I went, or what I did, or what I do, or—"

"It is my business, Tracy. You want to make me your number one murder suspect, and you don't want to admit that you're on the outs with your own family. Tracy! You have to accept that someone in your immediate family might very well be the conspirator!"

"Oh, God," Jamie groaned, sinking back into his chair. "I'm not hungry anymore."

Tracy looked over at Jamie and was instantly sorry. "Jamie," she murmured. "I—"

He shook his head. "I'm a big kid, Tracy." He stared at Leif then. "So what are we going to do?"

Leif stood up and walked over to the balcony, staring out at the beautiful spring day and Central Park, stretching out across the street. He shrugged. "I've got a few irons in the fire," he said softly. "It's just going to be a difficult thing to prove, because everyone involved could have easily come up with the money. I was telling Tracy last night that I thought a memorial service might be a good idea. Get everyone together and see where the discussions flowed."

"Get everyone together—where? Your house in Connecticut?" Jamie asked.

"That's what I had in mind—yes."

Tracy wasn't sure why, but little shivers suddenly went down her spine. Leif wasn't looking at her; he was watching Jamie. Leif was leaning against the edge of the window, sipping his coffee. His stance seemed negligent but she knew it really wasn't. Looking him over, she decided he really wasn't slender at all—his height gave him that appearance. Clad in the knit polo shirt, the breadth of his shoulders was very visible, as were their muscles. She swallowed, suddenly remembering that when he was shirtless, his abdomen had little ripples of tautness, that he was wired and taut as a drum and his grip was like iron. He'd fought in jungle warfare, and he'd never forgotten the movements—how to stalk, how to spin, how to remain on guard—and how to snap shut a trap.

"Is that why we're going there tomorrow?" Jamie asked unhappily. "And why Sam and Tiger are coming in tonight and going with us?"

"Yes," Leif said simply.

Tracy lifted her hands in her annoyance. "I still don't see what you're trying to prove."

"Who had a motive?" Jamie demanded.

"Everyone," Leif and Tracy replied simultaneously, bringing their eyes back to one another again.

"But I don't—"

"Leif, Tiger, and Sam inherited Dad's share of their mutual holdings," Tracy said.

"Right. The three of us are broke," Leif drawled sarcastically, "so we were after more money."

Tracy ignored him. "Then there's Lauren, the widow —she inherited the majority of his estate. And the last I heard, she's writing a book on his one great and real love affair—theirs."

"Don't forget Jamie's mother," Leif reminded her. "Sorry, Jamie, things never did go smoothly after that divorce."

"My mother didn't—"

"I certainly don't think that she did," Tracy said softly, simply because she cared for him. She owed Carol nothing—Carol hadn't wanted her around when she was a child.

"And then," Leif announced, sitting across from Tracy and staring at her again, "then we have Tracy's collection. Her grandfather—the great Arthur Kingsley. A man so irate that his daughter should fall in love with a penniless musician that he dragged her away and married her off to an accountant before the fruit of such an affair should appear. Only things backfired a bit because the steady and reliable accountant had a heart and a conscience. And we have Tracy's mother—who never really forgave Jesse for not panting after her the rest of her life. Then there's Tracy's stepfather, Ted Blare himself. Perhaps he couldn't bear the years of his wife yearning for the man she had lost."

Tracy was on her feet by then, her palms flat on the table while she glared across at him in a red fury. "Then there's Leif himself! Did he ever tell you, Jamie, that there was a whole year when he and Dad didn't speak to one another? Did he ever tell you that it became violent and physical between them and he was flattened out on the floor!"

Leif was calmly watching Tracy, leisurely lighting a cigarette, inhaling, exhaling, and pointedly returning her stare. She was barely aware of what she was saying; he knew exactly what she was spewing, and was quite ready for Jamie's natural question.

"Over what?"

Too late, she looked from Leif to her brother and saw his troubled frown. And, too late, she realized that she had practically spelled the whole thing out. She focused uneasily on Leif again and noted his satisfied smile and wondered suddenly if he hadn't been maneuvering her into telling her brother exactly what he wanted her to tell him.

He inclined his head slightly toward her and said quietly, "Well, Tracy? Go on. He wants to know why I might have wanted to kill your father."

What the hell was his game? she wondered. Should she call his bluff or what? She felt trapped, needed more time.

"All right, Tracy, I'll tell him."

He smiled very politely at her and turned to Jamie. "Your sister—"

"We had an affair," Tracy blurted out. God! She didn't want Leif telling the story. Not from his point of view.

His lashes shielded his eyes; it still appeared that he was secretively smiling, as if she had played exactly into his hands.

He looked at her then and lifted his hands innocently. "Tracy, I was just going to say that we had a little tiff at the party and your father and mother's family wound up involved."

Jamie was staring back and forth between them. "Well?" He demanded.

Tracy realized that her fingers were wound into the snowy starch-ironed tablecloth. She was shaking horribly and still so angry that her head seemed to ring. Her vision was blurred and something seemed to burn in the pit of her stomach. She wanted to strangle Leif. She wanted to do something—anything!—to erase the cool satisfaction that touched his smoky eyes and grim smile.

"Well, what!" she snapped at Jamie.

"Did you or didn't you have an affair?"

"I'll let Tracy answer that," Leif said.

She didn't really intend to do anything violent; it was just that her fingers were so tightly wound into that cloth. She must have jerked from emotion and not logic—but whatever her intent, the outcome was tremendous. The cloth wrenched away—and the steaming chafing dishes filled with Jamie's carefully planned breakfast goodies all went flying toward Leif.

He was up in a second, leaping away, so that only one

of the silver dishes flew against his thigh. Coffee, silverware, and plates went everywhere. Jamie yelped and backed away—and stared at Tracy with a certain amount of awe and amazement.

"You did have an affair, huh?"

Tracy barely heard him; she was staring at the utter disaster she hadn't meant to create. And then she stared from the chaos on the floor upward and into Leif's eyes.

He didn't say a word. He just looked at her with a cool gray assessment that was somehow more terrible than any oaths he could have flung her way.

He stepped over a chafing dish and came around the table, and she just watched him, unable to move. And then it was too late to move, because he was smiling at her distantly, but his hands were upon her shoulders like iron fists.

"Frankly, Tracy, I can't understand why you get so angry over the past. *I* was the one taken for an idiot. However, I'm glad you had your little temper tantrum now—it could be lethal later. And it's just as well—it was important that Jamie know now what happened for the same reason."

"Why?" Tracy whispered thickly, thinking she would give anything to go back just five minutes—just long enough to undo this disaster! Anything to avoid his hold on her now and his eyes probing into her soul.

"Because you are coming to Connecticut with us."

"No—I'm not."

"Sure you are, Tracy. Arthur is going to come, and Audrey is going to come—and Ted is going to bring her."

She shook her head vehemently. "They'll never come, Leif—you're crazy! Not after—"

"Oh, don't kid yourself. Your mother and I always got along fine. She called me and apologized after everything.

59

You didn't know that? Well, it doesn't really matter. They're all coming."

"I still don't believe you! There's nothing you could have said to convince them all to come to a memorial service for Jesse!"

His gaze fell over the mess on the floor; he stared at Jamie, who was still surveying them both in stunned silence. Then he smiled coolly back at Tracy.

"Yes, there was something. It worked like a charm."

"What—what are you talking about?" Tracy asked uneasily. She tried to wrench free from his hold, but it was too firm—her effort went barely noticed. Then he quite suddenly released her, but only to set his arms about her and pull her tightly to his chest with his chin resting atop her head, his hands locked just below her breasts.

"We do make a charming couple, don't we, Jamie?"

"I—uh—" Jamie began.

Tracy interrupted him, swearing rather elaborately, but once again her fervent efforts against him went unnoticed. He spun her around grimly; her fists were useless because they were too tightly crushed against his chest as he stared down at her. "I told them that you were living with me again, Tracy. And the amazing thing is that they believed it. So, I would say, most obviously, my love, that they have been kept in the dark about your movements the same as everyone else. I could tell that your mother was shocked—but, of course, I reminded her that you were quite of age now and could live anywhere you desired. I also said that we wanted peace among all of us, of course."

"You what!" Tracy got out at last, livid. Oh, so much for control and poise and sophistication. "You're crazy! I won't have any part of it! I will never go near that house again as long as I live!"

He raised a dark brow to her, pleasantly, but didn't release her. Her heels didn't help her at all; she felt small and powerless and she hated him for it. Just like she hated the way that he made her feel, holding her, after all these years. Holding her with what felt like latent anger, an anger that had simmered and brewed and waited and now.

He had her.

No, he did not. Because she would never go to his house. She would never live his lie.

"Why on earth should I do this?" she railed, near hysteria. "I don't believe my family had anything to do with it."

"Then you're a coward. You're afraid to prove that what you're saying is true."

"You'll never prove anything—"

"Tracy!"

It was Jamie who called out her name. She turned to him, unaware that Leif's grip eased enough for her to slide within his arms, yet remain against him.

And she wasn't really aware then of Leif's arms still about her, for one thing was true—Jamie had every bit of his father's haunting sensitivity in his features. He swallowed miserably as he stared at her, then spoke with a hoarse croak in his throat. "Tracy, maybe it's our only chance. I didn't know anything—you came to me. But now that I know, Tracy—by God! We've got to have the truth! Tracy, we're his children! We can't let his real murderer go free. And if that means my family or your family, we both have to know, whatever the truth is."

She shook her head, denying the pain that swelled within her. "Jamie, this is crazy!"

"It could work! Ah, come on, Tracy—you just admit-

61

ted it. You've already slept with Leif—how hard can it be just to stay in his house?"

"Oh!" Tracy gasped out, stunned by his casual acceptance of everything. Some blood brother!—standing there while Leif manhandled her and acting as if it were fine. How typically male, how typically—like her father, and Leif.

She wrenched away from the latter with a sudden spurt of fury and approached Jamie with fire flaring brightly in her eyes. He, too, stood way taller than she, but he backed away as she came near.

"Jamie, don't you dare ever assume that everything in life is casual. Don't sentence yourself to a life like Dad's, where nothing ever meant anything because he had too much! Oh, never mind! I'll never get through to any of you!"

She went flying out of the suite then, amazed that a simple breakfast could have gone so badly.

Why not? Leif had been there, and she had played right into his hands. She had said and done exactly what he wanted; he had her in a position where she would be pressured to play his game his way—to trap her grandfather.

Tracy didn't quite make it to her suite's door; she spun back and slammed back into Jamie's.

He and Leif were righting the chafing dishes. "This is just great!" Jamie was complaining. "The hotel will blame me for being young and wild when my sister threw the food at you!"

"I didn't throw food at anyone!" Tracy protested.

"Oh?" Leif inquired casually. "You could have fooled me."

"Yes, and you can fool anyone, can't you? You're try-

62

ing to sizzle my grandfather. Well, I'm sorry, I haven't vindicated you as yet, Mr. Johnston."

"Tracy, you don't believe that."

"No? I should believe my mother is a murderess?"

He shook his head and stooped to pick up the coffee-pot. "Tracy, I merely said—"

"You didn't 'merely' say anything. You were vicious."

"Wait a minute!"

Jamie paused in his endeavors and lifted his hand, a pained expression on his face. He smiled ruefully at them both.

"I'm just going to go lock myself in my closet for a while, huh? I—uh—well, I love you both, and I'm not so sure I want to be a part of this. Settle things between you, huh?"

He turned around, walked away—and pointedly closed the door to his bedroom.

Both Leif and Tracy were silent for several seconds. Leif continued picking things up—it was still going to look bad when room service showed up.

Tracy really didn't feel very guilty—he had been baiting her, and they both knew it. But in the stiff silence that followed her brother's departure, she swallowed hard and set to replacing the now ragged tablecloth. To her great discomfort, she paused, aware that Leif had done so, that he was quietly watching her.

"He's right, you know. This isn't fair to him," said Leif.

"This isn't fair to anyone," Tracy retorted sharply. She set a pile of silverware back on the table, then paused again, her fingers shaking. He hadn't ceased watching her —not for one moment—and she had that feeling again that he was after something more.

She looked up at him; shadowed smoky eyes shielded all his thoughts again.

"Well," he murmured, "I've got a few calls to make before tonight. Jamie has to be at setup by nine."

He didn't move though. Tracy lowered her eyes and went back to righting the positions of things on the table.

"You've been with him all through the tour?"

"It hasn't been that long a tour. Three months. Paris, London, Rome, Atlanta, Chicago, L.A., and New York. A nice roundup for his first time out."

She found herself looking at him again. "You always hated to tour."

"Yeah. Well, it was his first time out. He's only twenty. I wanted to see him come out of it as a level-headed human being. Jamie is a real nice kid. And talented."

"And everyone is comparing him to our father."

"That's natural."

"I suppose."

"How can it be that none of the tabloids have picked up on you?"

"I stay in the background."

"You're still working. I saw your last video. It was good."

"Thanks. And by the way, I'm the one who bought your last set of songs. You'll hear some of them tonight."

Her head shot up at that. "What?"

"Tracy—I am L & L Incorporated. I'm the one who bought your last set of songs. I gave them to Jamie— they'll be his next album."

"But—"

"You are T. B. Decker—among your other names. I do know that much. But you've also got one terrific agent—I was ready to beg, borrow, or steal for your address."

64

She gasped, stunned that he knew that much. "She never told me that you were looking for me."

He grimaced. "I never gave her a name, either. If you had known that I was looking for you, you would have dug yourself into an even deeper burrow. What is it, Tracy? You never wanted to be compared to your father? Is that why everything is under a pen name?"

She shook her head. She was afraid that she'd cry in front of him, and that was something she never wanted. She wished that she could explain. She didn't know if she could or not—or if the feelings were so deep that she simply couldn't ever share them with anyone. All of her life had been chaotic—all of it filled with trauma. She didn't want that anymore. She didn't want the things that came with fame and fortune—different lovers every week, failed marriages, children who were ignored.

"I don't care for publicity," she said simply.

He didn't refute her. And she found herself watching him as he watched her. And remembering. All the things she had cared about so much. The way he locked his jaw and dug his thumbs into his pockets when he was determined. The way his eyes could change from a glistening silver to a deep, dusky charcoal. The way his hair fell across his forehead and the way he could push it back impatiently.

The sound of his voice, the way he laughed, and even the way he could rage in righteous fury. The way that he could talk about the world, the past and the future . . .

The way that he whispered when he made love to her, touching her, enchanting her . . .

He is seven years older, she thought. And so am I.

She should have forgotten him completely, but that had been impossible. The Limelights had broken up for that year in which Jesse and Leif had been at total odds.

But they had gotten back together, and for the next three years their work had topped the charts. There had been videos and music scores—and no matter where she had traveled, she had seen him on television and in newspapers. When Celia had died, the event had been covered in newspapers and magazines the world over; not even in grief had he received any privacy from the media. One of the major weeklies had carried a haunting picture of Leif and his son at the church, the little boy gripping his father's hands—a little boy with his father's glistening gray eyes—placing a rose upon his mother's coffin.

"I'm very sorry about Celia," she said suddenly, remembering that picture.

"Thank you."

"How could you have traveled with Jamie? Where's your little boy?"

He smiled suddenly—the rakish smile that had stirred the imaginations of many a lonely heart.

"Blake is coming in later. He's been with my sister at home in Connecticut. They're coming in for the final show—I promised him that he could see Jamie's last show."

Tracy nodded. She suddenly wanted to run from the room and from Leif. She didn't want to see the sensuous smile that had captured her teenage heart so long ago.

"You'll meet him tonight."

"Oh, no. I'm not going to the concert."

"You have to. Jamie will be terribly hurt if you don't go."

She lowered her eyes instantly, wishing she had never decided it mandatory to seek her brother out and crawl from balcony to balcony in an attempt to meet him alone. It hadn't worked. She had drawn him into a murder investigation but he was inadvertently drawing her into a nightmare.

"It's not so bad—just stay in the wings," Leif told her. "Well, I've got to make those phone calls. Why don't you tell Jamie that it's safe to come out?"

"Is it?" she asked him.

He hesitated. For a second she thought he was going to come to her again. He didn't.

"Tracy, if you really want the truth, you'll do as I ask you."

"You're brutal."

"I don't mean to be. It's just that you want to open a Pandora's box. If you're going to do that, you have to be willing to accept the consequences. You think I'm wrong. I've no set decisions made. Prove to me that I'm wrong. I had to say what I did to your family. It was the only way to make sure that we would have a full house—and a full house is necessary."

He didn't wait for her answer; he turned around and headed for his room. Tracy watched him, then on impulse started after him, surprising herself when she caught his arm and spun him around to stare down at her once more.

"Leif, you're not telling me everything and that isn't fair. You want to use me to trap my family, but there's more to this, isn't there? You know something that—"

"I don't 'know' anything, Tracy."

"But—"

"There's more to this, yes."

"What?" she begged him.

He stared down at her so intently then, searching out her eyes, and she felt again that he was desperately trying to read her mind. Why?

But then he pulled away with dry skepticism, twisting

67

his jaw, shaking his head. "You play it my way, first, Tracy. We'll see where we go from there."

"That's not f—"

"Fair. Maybe not. But that's the way it's going to be. My way or not at all, for the moment. So what's it going to be, Tracy?"

She stepped back, frustrated, growing angry again. She crossed her arms over her chest and stubbornly narrowed her eyes at him.

"Why was it so important for you to know where I went after—when—after—"

He arched a brow with slow, bitter amusement.

"After you seduced me to get to your father?"

"Why was it important to know where I went?" she persisted.

"What happened between you and your family, Tracy? Why don't they know where you are? Why was it so easy for your mother to believe that you had been living with me?"

"That's none of your business."

"I think that it is."

"Why?"

He smiled and turned around.

"Leif!"

At his door he turned back to her. "Maybe none of it is important at all, Tracy. I don't know yet. But you'll never find out if you don't play things my way."

She locked her jaw tightly and stared at him.

"What's it going to be, Tracy? Are you going to move in with me for our game of charades?"

She wasn't sure that she could do it. She would probably reach his house and break down screaming on the lawn, unable to go inside.

"Tracy?"

"All right," she said coolly.

"Good."

His door started to close; he came back around the corner, smiling sardonically.

"Just remember, Tracy—you've got to make it look good. Don't throw food at me in front of the others, huh? But then, like Jamie said, it should be easy. After all, you've already slept with me."

The door closed then. Her fingers closed around the coffeepot—and it was all she could do to keep herself from throwing it against the door.

She concentrated and loosened her fingers. She had to learn to control herself! She had just agreed to go back to the scene of both her sweetest and most bitter memories.

To find a murderer, she warned herself. The murderer who had taken her father's life.

She shivered suddenly, acutely aware that there was danger involved. In many, many ways.

CHAPTER FOUR

From the wings of the concert hall, the sound of the music was so loud that it was almost deafening, yet Tracy was glad that she had come. It was wonderful to watch Jamie, yet it was painful, too. Certain inflections, certain words were so like his father's. Their father's.

But Jamie was his own man; he was singing his own tunes and those that Leif had bought from her. And he was doing them well. He not only had musical ability—a nice husky tenor—but a definite showmanship that would take him far.

"The kid is great!"

Sam Nagel shouted the words in her ear, and she turned to grin out her agreement, then paused, studying Sam. Her first instinct was one of warmth—Sam, the oldest Limelight at forty-four, was as bald as a buzzard, husky as a teddy bear, and adorned as he had been forever with a huge gold hoop earring in one ear. She'd always liked Sam—he had bright blue eyes and was quite handsome in his unique way, easily prone to good-natured affability and prone to giving lots and lots of hugs. Right before her father had died, she had seen Sam when he was with Jesse and they had all worked together on Jesse's last album. She really liked Sam.

Except now she wasn't able to look at anyone without silently demanding, *Did you kill my father?*

"Fabulous," Tiger stated then, giving Tracy a quick hug. 'Tiger' was really Jim Smith. Maybe the simplicity of Jim Smith had caused him to adopt the nickname years ago—or maybe it was because he had a natural platinum streak in his dusty-blond hair. Tracy didn't really know. He had always been "Tiger." She hadn't seen Tiger in seven years, but Tiger, too, resembled somewhat "A Picture of Dorian Gray." He was the shortest of the old group at about five-ten and he looked like something out of a Civil War flick with his drooping but elegant mustache and over-the-collar curling hair, but he, too, could have easily passed for thirty. Had they all sold their souls to the devil? Tracy wondered whimsically. Even her father, Jesse, could have passed for a kid on the street the day he had died.

It was really impossible to talk while the concert was going on. Tracy turned back around to watch her brother, and she was surprised at her own feelings of absolute pride. The audience was wild—and Jamie was brilliant, standing entirely on his own. When his song ended—one of the softer ballads that had been her own creation—the cheering seemed louder than the final drumbeats that had preceded it. Jamie, sweaty but beaming, stood and began to talk.

Sam and Tiger were into a discussion on Jamie's equipment. Tracy idly glanced around and saw that Leif had been cornered by a reporter in the wings. She couldn't help but watch him, nor could she control the physical reactions that rose within her. She felt shaky as if breathing had suddenly become a little more difficult, as if her heart had forgotten how to beat in its proper fashion. Leif was striking—had always been, would always be. So

71

straight, so tall, so dark, and with those wonderful smoky eyes. Tonight he was in a soft leather fawn jacket, no tie, but a chocolate silk shirt and light trousers. She smiled, thinking that when she had been eight and in a childish state of adoration over Jesse before she had learned who he was, the Limelights had performed in tricorns and frock coats. Then they'd gone through a Nehru jacket stage—then coats and ties—then whatever anyone felt like wearing.

"Oh, my God!" Tiger groaned suddenly. "What a thing to do to us!"

Startled, Tracy gave him her attention. He was looking at her, but staring over her head. She followed his gaze and saw that Jamie was reaching out a hand to the wings entreatingly.

"What'll we do?" Sam asked.

"Ask Leif."

"Ask Leif what?"

He was with them, hands in his pockets as he came between the two other men to smile down at Tracy. "I don't know how he got back here"—he cast his head in the reporter's direction—"but I had to promise him an interview later. Will you mind waiting?"

She shook her head, wondering why he had asked her. She had ridden over with him and Jamie—she'd return with them both when they were ready. And it was more than obvious that Jamie would be inundated by the media.

"Leif!" Tiger persisted. "Did you know anything about this? He's calling us out there!"

Leif frowned and shook his head and realized that Jamie was onstage, his hand still outstretched. And the audience was chanting; thousands of feet were stamping in unison.

Jamie crooked a finger at Leif.

Leif crooked a finger back at Jamie.

Jamie shook his head, smiled at the audience, then shrugged and walked into the wings.

"What are you doing?" Leif demanded. "I promised to manage the tour for you—not perform on it!"

"Ah, Leif, come on! When will we all be together again? Probably never. Listen to them out there. Please—it will be an historical event."

"He thinks we're history," Sam groaned.

"We are history," Tiger said.

"Please, Leif?" Jamie begged.

Leif stared at him a long moment and Tracy saw all the things that passed between them—the depth of affection, the give and take. Again, despite herself, she was glad that Jamie had Leif.

"All—right," Leif said at last.

Jamie screamed out some kind of cry of triumph, then went rushing back out. Sam and Tiger looked at one another and grinned, and followed him. Leif was following behind them, but suddenly he caught Tracy's hand and started dragging her with him.

"Leif!" she cried out in blind panic, fighting the pull of his long fingers around her wrist. "What are you doing?"

"The old stuff, Tracy. We always hired vocalists. You know all the parts—come on."

"No!" she cried, still panicked. "Leif—"

"Tracy, I know you know all the vocals. I know that you worked with your father. The old songs—the new ones. You know by heart everything that your father and the Limelights ever did."

"But I don't—"

"Just this once, Tracy. I dare you. Come on. Feel it. If

73

you do, maybe you'll understand your father better—and your brother."

"But they'll know, Leif! I've kept my privacy—"

He suddenly pulled her against his chest. She felt the power of will, the force of his eyes. It seemed that for long moments she didn't even know what she said; she found herself lost in thought. Every man had a unique scent. Usually subtle, usually clean, but a scent as individual as eyes and faces and minds. And just like a face, like eyes, like strong, tapering fingers, it could be something that seeped into the memory—and beckoned one back.

"Tracy, you can't hide forever."

"That's not—"

"Tracy, I didn't plan this, but it might be good."

"Leif—"

It was a shriek that she cut off abruptly because she couldn't escape him—and she was suddenly just behind the footlights with the globe strobes ricocheting all around her.

On stage, with her brother and the Limelights.

Minus only Jesse Kuger . . .

It seemed that pandemonium broke out; Tracy had never heard such a cacophony of sound. Sam went up behind the drums, Tiger took over from Jamie's bass player, Leif was at the keyboard, and Jamie had the lead guitar.

And Tracy had a mike stuck into her hand; she was ridiculously center with Jamie on one side of her, Leif on the other.

They hadn't discussed what they were going to do; it was instinctive, like stepping into comfortable, worn jeans. She heard the count from Leif and instantly knew that they were doing "Sunset Paradise"—the Limelights' first top-of-the-charts single, a song nearly twenty-five years old.

And still as fresh as a new day.

Her father's song. His first.

And to Tracy's amazement, she did feel it. The roar, the adulation of the audience. The beat of the music that shivered through the floorboards, that echoed all around her, that permeated her entire being. It lifted her above herself. It was chilling, it was wonderful—it was being outside of her body and into a magical chasm. This was it; it was what they had lived for—what, Jamie, too, meant to make his life.

Perhaps it was good that she was so awestruck; when her harmony and solo parts came, they came naturally to her. She knew the song so well. Anything that Jesse had touched she had made her own. She was his blood, and she had strived so hard to touch him . . .

"Sunset Paradise" moved into "Man with a Mind"— Leif's song. Then Tiger's lighter "Red Letter Lady."

On and on . . .

Until her father's "When Night Comes"—a poignant piece on life and death, soft and haunting. A memorial to the man, if ever there could be one.

And that was it. Tracy, suddenly confused, stepped backward, refusing to take part as they bowed, accepting the hysterical laud and praise that came their way. Leif led the way off; Tracy followed him blindly. Jamie was still on stage, his concert having been handed back to him. He was talking again with his pleasant banter, Tracy was vaguely aware—he would do one more number, and then it would all be ended.

But for Tracy the awesome thrill departed as quickly as it had come. The feeling was something like an all-consuming lust for gold. She understood it—yes! The invasion of the heart and soul—the horrendous power. But she hated it; despised it. Despised what it had done to Jesse. He had become something quite similar to a god, and in so being, he hadn't felt the need to conform to conscience or consideration. No one love could mean anything—because love was something captured by the moment, taken, discarded, abused. She didn't want any of it! She didn't want the publicity—she didn't want the tabloids digging into the circumstances of her birth, or her life, or—her affair with Leif.

And, she realized, it was all going to happen now. Because Jamie was out there telling everyone that she was Tracy Kuger, his sister, Jesse Kuger's daughter.

She slammed into something hard suddenly and realized that it was Leif's back. She was very close to tears and ready to light into him vehemently for what he had forced her to do. She wanted to plummet her fists against his back in sheer rage and frustration, and she was so upset she might well have done it.

Except that his back wasn't there anymore. He'd let out a little cry and stepped into the wings, and it seemed that a little tornado was racing toward him—catapulting suddenly and winding up in his arms.

"Daddy! Daddy! You were neat!"

"Was I, Blake? Well, if you thought so, it was worth it!"

The anger drained from Tracy; she stepped backward, feeling as if she had stepped into a frozen void. It was as if she watched a movie, a performance, a play—some action that evolved before her with no connection to her. Leif had the little boy up in his arms; the child had his arms wrapped around Leif's neck and Leif wore the most tender smile Tracy had ever seen curve his lip. The boy's large gray eyes, as deep as his father's, sparkled hints of silver with eager love and total affection.

"When did you get here? Where is Aunt Liz?"

"Right there—talking to Tiger."

Blake Johnston suddenly looked past his father and saw Tracy. She saw his blunt and curious, innocent child's stare, and for an instant the pain that assailed her was incredible, as if she'd received a physical blow against the chest. He was just about the same age as . . . the same age . . .

As her child would have been—their child—had it lived.

In that moment, in that bitter realization, she knew that half the hostility she had harbored against Leif all the years had been borne of that simple fact. None of the events that had taken place between them had been his fault.

But after she had been taken away, he had gone right back to Celia. Gone right back to her and married her. And produced, nine months later, a beautiful little boy.

While Tracy had been virtually held prisoner by her grandfather. Hounded to have an abortion. Told over and over again that she had never meant a thing to Leif— hadn't he proven it? He had gone on to marry Celia.

She'd refused. Absolutely refused. Even when she had seen Leif's wedding pictures plastered across every morning paper, she had fought for the child. She was a "mistake" herself—she wasn't about to let her infant perish for being nothing but a victim of her own vindictiveness.

In the end, it hadn't mattered. Arthur Kingsley had paid for all the medical care one could buy in Switzerland —and her child had died anyway.

But here was Leif's other son. A first-grader, now, surely. Bright and solid and beautiful and staring at her.

77

He clapped his hands together suddenly. "Tracy! You were great, too!"

She felt so brittle that if she smiled her face would crack like a china plate. Mechanically, she smiled back anyway.

"You're Jamie's sister?" Blake asked. "I didn't know that!"

Leif chuckled softly. "Of course! If she's Jesse's daughter, son, she's Jamie's sister."

"Oh. I guess. I didn't know."

"Well, you're only six years old!" Leif said lightly. "You're not supposed to know everything yet."

"Do you know everything?"

Leif chuckled. "No, Blake. We never get to know everything. But we do get to know more and more."

He turned around at last. "It seems Blake knows you." He paused, continuing a little dryly, "Jesse talked about you—quite frequently. But you don't know Blake. Tracy Kuger, Blake Johnston. Blake, Miss Tracy Kuger, Uncle Jesse's daughter."

Blake stuck a hand out over his father's shoulder, still watching her with unabashed and blunt curiosity. "How do you do, Tracy?" He said very politely and solemnly.

She discovered that she could talk after all, that she could give him a deep and natural smile.

"Very well, thank you, Blake. How are you?"

"Super! I missed my daddy, but we're back together, and it's really okay, you know, because I know that Jamie needed him."

"Hey, Leif!" Tiger called out suddenly. "Leif, the press is tearing up the place back here. You want to take a minute and say something so we can get out of here."

"Uh—yeah."

Leif turned around, setting Blake down. He gazed up

78

at Tracy questioningly, then looked back to his son. "Will you stay with Tracy for just a minute and then I promise I'll be right back?"

Blake nodded solemnly. Leif walked away. Tracy felt a little hand fit snugly into hers.

"I'm sorry about your daddy, Tracy. I loved Uncle Jesse a whole lot. But you mustn't worry about him, you know. He went up to heaven to live with the angels, and my mother is there, too, so I'm sure he won't be lonely."

Tears pricked her eyes and Tracy decided that it was only because it had been a horribly traumatic day and a worse night. She knelt down beside Blake Johnston, smiling a little to note that he had a small and very stubborn cowlick in his hair—exactly the same as his father's. While Leif was dark, Blake was a soft blond—but the cowlick was still the same.

"Thank you, Blake. I'm sorry about your mommy, too, and I'm very glad that she and my dad will be together."

He gave her a very encouraging grin and squeezed her hand. She squeezed his back, thinking what a nice, normal little child he was. He seemed to know that his father was famous—but he didn't seem to think that he should be especially privileged because of it.

"Do you know my Aunt Liz?" he asked her.

Tracy shook her head. Blake dragged her over to where Tiger and Sam were talking to a tall brunette woman. She turned at Tracy's approach, and Tracy saw another version of Leif's deep gray eyes. Liz also resembled Leif in her coloring, her elegant height, and in her slow, charming smile.

"Tracy? I'm Liz. Glad to meet you at last." She chuckled lightly. "How strange! Leif has been searching high and low for you over the last year—and here you are!"

Tracy smiled weakly, startled to hear that Leif's search

79

for her had been that intensive. She liked Liz instantly. She seemed to encompass all kinds of easy warmth and grace.

"It's nice to meet you, Liz," she said, extending a hand.

But then she had to stop to wonder if Liz knew anything about what had happened all those years ago, and if she did know, what did she think? Or was Tracy blowing it all out of proportion herself? Maybe no one would really think anything of it at all . . .

"Ah, here comes Jamie! Show's over!" Liz said.

Jamie came in off the stage, dripping wet with perspiration, grinning from ear to ear. He gave Tracy a sloppy kiss first, hugged Liz, then swept Blake off the floor, while effusively thanking Tiger and Sam for coming on stage with him. Blake giggled away, and then it seemed that everyone was talking at once.

"Jamie—go take a shower so we can get out of here!" Liz begged at last. "Oh—look. That man from the weekly has Leif over there. He does so hate interviews—but he looks calm. Jamie—go get changed, please. Then give him a few words, too, so we can go somewhere private!"

"Gotcha, Liz!" Jamie saluted her neatly, then started toward the dressing room. He turned back once.

"Tracy—was I great?"

He asked with such eager enthusiasm that she nodded.

"You were great, Jamie."

He blew her a kiss. "So were you. Your songs are fabulous! And you sing like a lark. And—"

"Jamie, get out of here!"

Liz laughed happily behind Tracy, then linked arms with her. "Come on—let's go save Leif."

Saving Leif was the last thing Tracy had on her mind,

but with Liz hurrying her along, she had little choice but to keep up. They came upon Leif and the reporter against one of the outer walls just before the dressing rooms. Leif looked calm, but he was eyeing the man carefully, though his stance was casual. He answered each question slowly, taking his time, weighing his answers, while still appearing casual and idle about the whole thing.

"You actually disbanded two years ago, right?"

"That's right."

"Why?"

Leif shrugged, glancing at his sister and Tracy over the man's head, arching a brow and grimacing. He turned his attention back to the eager reporter.

"Well, because we really started out as street musicians when we were kids. Tiger and Sam were a little bit older, Jesse was sixteen, I was fifteen. Two years ago we celebrated twenty-five years together, and we just decided it was time to call it quits."

"What about the times that you split up before?"

Leif shook his head. "We never split up before."

"Sure you did! All the rags had this thing going about some massive fight going on between you and Jesse—"

"The group didn't split up. We held off recording for awhile."

"What was the fight about? How did you two finally make it up? Was it over a woman?"

Tracy felt her cheeks burn, but not a muscle in Leif's face twitched, nor did he glance Tracy's way.

"Jesse and I had a little blowup, yeah. It was over a song. We solved it by keeping our distance for a while, that's all."

"What about before?"

"There was no 'before.' I was drafted into the service, but the group didn't split up then. I wrote songs when I could, and we carried on long distance, you might say. Obviously, we didn't do any concerts then, but we were still a group. When I came home, we toured for a year, then we worked in the studio for a year. It was like that frequently."

"Are you planning on forming a new band with Jamie Kuger? And what about Jesse's daughter? We've never heard much about her before. Why? Who is she really? Can you—"

Leif reached around the man for Tracy's hand, pulling her next to him in a protective gesture. "Tracy—this is Mack Arnold. Mack—Tracy Kuger. The real Tracy Kuger."

"Miss Kuger!" Mack offered her a fleshy hand. "What a pleasure! What have you been doing all your life!" He laughed at the scope of his own question. "It's rumored that you write music and songs—under a bunch of pseudonyms. Is that true? How—"

"Mack! You've gotten to see the lady—let her breathe!" Leif jumped in. "She writes—and she keeps pseudonyms because she likes her privacy. So let her keep it, OK?"

Mack didn't get any choice—Leif smoothly introduced his sister and his son, then promised to send Jamie out to talk to him. Tracy was glad that he had defended her. Mack Arnold might well have ripped her to shreds in a matter of seconds. But she was still ready to kill Leif for pulling her on stage, and she didn't feel any kinder toward him when he smoothly got them away from Mack and into Jamie's dressing room. Her brother's backup musicians were all there and Jamie dragged her around like an exotic prize. She understood—he was special to her, too—maybe more so since it had taken them so long to reach one another. She just didn't like the thousand-

and-one questions everyone asked her now that they knew she was Jesse's other child.

Champagne flowed freely in the dressing room. Tracy sipped some idly, trying to steer questions away from herself and keep her comments on her brother's performance. Naturally, people asked her where she had been, how and when she and Jamie had gotten together—and just how well she knew Leif, since it seemed they were all so comfortable together.

After all the years she had struggled so hard to maintain her anonymity, become totally independent—and nearly invisible! All her determination to stay out of the public eye was ruined. Here she was, dragged back into it all because Leif had fed her to the wolves!

The desire to throttle Leif rose in her again. She glanced his way through the crowd and saw that he was managing to carry on easy conversations. He laughed at something someone said, offered more champagne. She saw him give a pretty redhead a friendly kiss on the cheek just before the girl left. The kiss bothered her, and she was highly irritated with herself for the stab of jealousy she felt. But he looked good that night—exceptionally good. Tall and lean, both relaxed and elegant, and somehow not quite approachable—an intriguing man with a casual manner, yet whose hard eyes veiled a thousand secrets.

At long last, Jamie disappeared with his group in tow. Blake was happily playing at the mirror with Jamie's brushes, Leif idly stretched and rubbed the back of his neck, and Liz asked Tracy if she would like more champagne.

"I'm really a little sick of champagne," she murmured.

"Poor baby!" Leif laughed. "Too much Dom Perignon, huh?"

"Leif, be nice!" Liz chastised. "And tell me—what are we going to do? With Blake and me—I mean. I told you, didn't I, that I couldn't get hotel reservations? The place is full—with groupies trying to get close to Jamie, I think!"

"Blake can sleep in with me. And Jamie can, too. Then you can have the other bedroom, Liz. Oh, wait—that's not necessary at all. Tracy—you wouldn't mind giving Liz your extra bedroom, would you?"

"No, not at all," Tracy murmured, but she did. She felt as if she were being sucked into a whirlpool. She hadn't wanted to see Leif, she hadn't wanted to go to Connecticut, and she certainly hadn't wanted to go on stage—but she had done it all. She was falling deeper and deeper into a vortex of the past, and it was frightening.

And to make it all much worse, Leif was staring at her again. Gray eyes charcoal and smoke, probing, somehow frightening. What was it that he was looking for when it seemed that his eyes burned into her soul, stripped her, ran her ragged, and then raked so tensely over her once again.

She lowered her head to avoid his gaze. Blake started to talk to Leif about his latest schoolwork, and Tracy felt herself shivering.

Had Leif ever told anyone about the fiasco between them? No one seemed to know. He had forced her to tell Jamie—but he had defended her smoothly before Mack Arnold's barrage of questions.

Tracy could just imagine the truth in the paper! That he and Jesse had fought over Jesse's daughter. Because Jesse's daughter had been piqued at her father for forgetting her face . . .

Tiger stuck his head into the dressing room suddenly,

grinning and offering Liz a ride back to the hotel. "We've still got a room reserved for dinner?" he asked Leif.

"Yes. Did you get a room okay?"

"Sure—I planned ahead. Liz?"

"Yes, I'd better get back with Blake. It's getting very late for him."

Tracy swirled around to Liz. "I can go back with Blake, Liz! You're welcome to stay here and take your time—"

"Oh, no, no!" Liz protested. "This was Jamie's big day —all of them in a group, but very especially you. Blake— come on, young man. We'll get to ride in Tiger's sports car!"

Blake hadn't appeared pleased about leaving his father until Liz mentioned Tiger's car, then his eyes lit up. He gave Leif a massive hug but a quick kiss and slipped his hand into his aunt's to leave. At the door he paused.

"Bye, Tracy."

"Bye, Blake."

The door closed behind them and Tracy was alone with Leif once again. He didn't say anything; he just paced around, a bit like a bored panther on the prowl. Tracy stared at him for several seconds, her tension brewing, since it seemed the room had grown much much smaller with just the two of them in it.

"You've just wrecked my life, you know," she told him.

He started, turning to her. "I beg your pardon?"

"I didn't want to go out on that stage."

He shrugged. "You're rather dramatic, I'd say. One appearance can't wreck your life." He leaned against the dressing table, staring at her as he crossed his arms over his chest in a dry manner. "You did all right out there.

You've done your father's things before—with your father, I imagine."

"That's different—"

"Tracy, you loved him, but you're down on him. Being out there was the only way for you to understand him."

She shook her head vehemently. "No, Leif. I'll admit —it is a power trip. All those people screaming. But it's no excuse for a man to live with a total lack of consideration—"

"You loved him anyway."

"Yes! But that doesn't mean that I didn't despise his life-style. He hurt people, Leif. He—oh, never mind! I don't have to explain this to you. And thanks to you, I have lost my privacy, my secrecy! I didn't want to go out there—and I damn well don't want to go to Connecticut! I haven't done anything that I wanted to do since you walked back into my life. Damn you, Leif! I'm not going to go to Connecticut. I'm not going to be manipulated any further."

She sped toward the door and started to open it; it slammed shut before it had opened more than an inch.

He'd closed it.

She spun, pressing her back against it. He was right there, his palm still flat against the door as he held it and probed deep into her eyes with his own, his ever-knowing gray gaze intent upon her.

"I thought you wanted the truth, Tracy."

"I do! But I don't see where you're going to get it for me. I might as well be on my own. I was before—and we came to the same conclusions."

He shook his head. "We take it together from here on out, Tracy."

"Why?" she fumed. She hadn't the strength to push him aside. "Leif, my God, you're using me!"

"Maybe that's fate. You used me."

"I—"

She didn't finish—the door was suddenly pushed open from outside. Leif frowned and moved back—just in time for Tracy to come catapulting into his arms from the pressure outside. Instinctively she threw her arms around him to keep from toppling to the floor. Instinctively, he steadied her, his arms around her waist.

"What the hell—" Leif began, cutting himself off when he saw that it was Jamie. But right behind Jamie was the group of photographers that had sent him rushing to his dressing room for a safe haven.

Five of them, at least, were crowding in the doorway, and Leif had his hands at Tracy's waist, Tracy's fingers curled around his nape.

Flashbulbs started going off, blinding the three of them. "Hey, wait a minute!" Leif snapped. Then he caught sight of Tracy's startled and furious eyes and he began to laugh, setting her from him and walking to the door.

"Excuse us, will you, guys? You got your pictures."

"That's her, huh, Leif, isn't it?" One of the men called out. "Jesse's girl! How long has—"

"Tracy Kuger, George. And—none of your business. Good night!"

He closed the door firmly, grinning in a rather pleased fashion.

Tracy stared at him furiously. "You just made that man think that—that—"

"That something was going on. Yes, precisely."

Tracy swore at him in no uncertain terms. Jamie uncomfortably shuffled his feet.

Leif ignored them both, stating it was time for them to head back to the hotel.

CHAPTER FIVE

Leif's late-night "private" dinner turned out to be quite a fiasco to Tracy's way of seeing things—there was nothing private about it. Jamie had invited six dates and the guys in his band had invited another twenty, so it seemed. The dates had invited friends, and so on. With all these people, the press managed to get in, and it seemed that there were a hundred people in a space that had been planned for twenty. As quickly as she could, she escaped to the elevator and up to her own suite.

She found that Liz was already there, opening a bag of Oreos for Blake, to be served with a pint carton of milk.

"Tracy, I hope you don't mind. That just seemed like too much to bring Blake into, so I hedged everything and came on up!" Liz apologized.

Tracy shook her head, sitting down on the sofa to doff her boots and smiling.

"I don't blame you. It's awful down there!"

"Did you see the bald girl with the sequins glued to her scalp?" Liz asked.

Tracy started laughing. "Yes, I did. I'm afraid that she's one of my brother's dates."

"Oh."

"Tracy, would you like an Oreo?" Blake offered.

Tracy smiled at the little boy. "No, Blake, but thanks

for the offer." He gave her an engaging grin, and she felt as if her heart toppled a bit. Those wonderful eyes! If his father were ever to look at her that way again . . .

"Okay, Blake, I think it's way, way past bedtime for you!" Liz announced.

"But I was going to sleep with Daddy—"

"Daddy won't be up for a while. You can come in with me, okay?"

Blake didn't refute Liz; he simply ignored her. He came over and sat down next to Tracy. "You and Jamie don't look too much alike. He's so tall. And he has yellow hair. Yours is dark."

"Well," Tracy said, "brothers and sisters don't necessarily look alike. Jamie has our dad's hair—I think I have my mother's."

"But you both have blue eyes," Blake noted wisely. "I mean, really blue eyes. You have pretty eyes, Tracy."

"Thank you, Blake, so do you. Just like your dad's."

"What?" Liz said suddenly.

Tracy looked up to discover that Liz was staring at her with a curious frown.

"His eyes," Tracy said, "are just like Leif's."

"Oh?" Liz came over to stare down at Blake, which Tracy found rather peculiar. Surely Liz knew what her nephew's eyes looked like!

Blake was already turning to another subject. "Aunt Liz, I'm not sleepy. Can't I wait till Dad comes up?"

"No."

"But—"

"Hey," Tracy interrupted, "I've got an idea." She glanced at Liz for approval. "I've got some bubble stuff in the bathroom. Want to take a warm bath? Maybe that will make you sleepy."

"Oh, neat! Can I?" Blake asked his aunt.

Liz gave up with a shrug. "If Tracy is willing—"

"Tracy is very willing," Tracy assured her. She stood on her stocking feet and reached for Blake's hand. With a little sigh, Liz sank down on the sofa. Tracy led Blake off to her bedroom and they walked through it to the bath. She sat at the edge of the tub and ran the water hard, creating a burst of bubbles for Blake to play in.

At six, it seemed that Blake had no inhibitions. With a little cry of delight, he stripped away his sneakers and jeans, T-shirt, and He-Man underwear. Tracy lowered her head with a nostalgic little smile as she watched him —he was so perfect! Such a little body, a bit on the skinny side. But perfect. Long, long legs, squared shoulders, a sturdy little chest.

He slid into the water laughing as bubbles floated above him.

"Do you have any toys?" he asked Tracy.

"Bath toys, hmm. Let me ask Liz."

She came out to Liz. Liz guiltily jumped to her feet and provided Tracy not only with a little sack of plastic toys, but with Blake's toothbrush and a Masters of the Universe set of pajamas.

"Tracy!" Liz called, when she was just set to return to the bathtub with her booty. "Mind if I order up a drink?"

"Not at all."

"Want something?"

"Sure. Kahlua and cream."

Tracy returned to Blake. They played sea monsters with his toys, and she began to worry that her idea hadn't been so terribly brilliant—Blake seemed more wide-eyed awake than ever.

But though he stayed that way while she dried and dressed him and told him to brush his teeth, he suddenly left the bathroom while she was still hanging towels.

She came out to find him curled up on her bed and sound asleep. Smiling, she adjusted his weight to pull down the covers and tuck him in. Then she went back out to join Liz in the salon.

Their drinks had arrived. Liz had her bare feet up on the coffee table and was sipping her drink. She arched a brow to Tracy and asked, "Did he conk out?"

"Yes. He's sound asleep."

Liz nodded. "I expected it. Kids are so funny! They go a hundred miles an hour and you think you'll never make it—then *wham,* they're out like lights."

Tracy sat down and picked up her drink, smiling as she sipped it. "He's a wonderful little boy. Very unaffected."

Liz smiled. "He is a nice kid. I envy Leif."

"You don't have any children?"

Liz shook her head, smiling ruefully. "No, and it seems unlikely now that I ever will. The old biological time clock, you know. I'll be forty next year."

Tracy smiled encouragingly to her. "Well, I'd say you've still got a little time. I've another half brother who is only two, and my mother is forty-three."

"Yes, but she'd already had you. Besides"—Liz laughed—"I'm not even seeing anyone seriously at the moment!" She shook her head in weary wonderment. "It's really not terribly fair, you know! I admit, I was a lot like the guys way back when they got started. I can still remember it. Leif and I were just kids when Dad went to London to oversee the construction of the new hotel. The next thing I knew, Leif, Tiger, Sam, and Jesse had gotten together. Everyone thought they were 'cute', that it was a phase. Some phase! They lasted twenty-five years! I was just on the fringes, but being there, I wasn't about to settle down. And now—well—I get to be a wonderful Aunt Liz to Blake, but probably never 'mommy' to anyone!"

"I wouldn't give up yet," Tracy replied cheerfully, for lack of anything else to say. She smiled. "Blake's resemblance to Leif is remarkable."

"That's impossible—" Liz began, but cut herself off quickly.

"Why?"

"What? Oh, why? Well, I—uh—just don't see the resemblance, I guess," Liz murmured. She stood and walked around the sofa, going to the balcony, walking back and yawning. She smiled at Tracy again. "I really hope you don't mind being put out like this! How strange, though—after all that time that Leif spent looking for you, you pop up out of nowhere!"

Tracy shrugged, but asked Liz, "Why was Leif looking for me?"

"He was concerned after Jesse's death. For you and Jamie. I don't really know quite why he seemed so frantic —maybe it was just that he and Jesse had been so close for so many years. It unhinged him for a while, I think. Well, I don't know, who wouldn't be? He lost Celia one year, and Jesse the next. Of course, he'd always known about Celia."

Tracy tensed at Liz's words, her brows knitting across her forehead. "I'm sorry, Liz. I'm lost. What do you mean about Leif's always knowing about Celia?"

"Why, her heart condition, of course. Oh, they did everything, but she wasn't eligible for a transplant—something about the nature of her heart's weakness. But he knew how ill she was; they both knew when he married her." Liz sighed. "I miss her dearly—she was a lovely woman. So good for Leif! They met right after he came out of the service, and she soothed him through a lot of nightmares. I don't know if you remember it or not —so much that is pure trash has been written up about these guys—but she just walked out on him one day. No one understood it. Anyway, she'd found out about her condition, and she'd left him because she'd loved him so much. She came back—to explain. And that was when Leif insisted they marry anyway. Oh, well, that's all in the past now. And I'm awfully glad that you're here and that you're coming to Connecticut. I've always known about you—and Jesse really did adore you, you know. Well, I guess I'll go pick up my nephew and remove him from your bed!"

"No, no, Liz, leave him! That's a king-sized bed—we'll be fine in there."

"Oh, no, that isn't fair—"

"I don't mind at all. Leave him."

"Well, then, thanks, Tracy. Then I'll be turning in—I feel like I've been awake for a month! Good night."

"Good night, Liz," Tracy told her.

Liz disappeared into the suite's second bedroom; Tracy finished sipping her drink, still puzzled by Liz's insistence that Blake didn't look like his father.

Then she remembered that Blake's father had made a travesty of her life that night. She winced, wondering what the morning papers would say. Then she shrugged, clicked her glass down on the table, and stood, stretching. She wandered over to the balcony and stared out at the night, still horribly wound up by the events of the night.

She shivered suddenly, feeling queasy inside. Celia Johnston had been sick all along. Celia had left Leif because she loved him so much—and Tracy had moved in because she'd been such a brat! Tracy winced, wishing once again with all her heart that she could go back and undo the past. But she couldn't.

She turned around and walked quickly back to her own room. Blake hadn't moved; he was still curled in a little ball on her bed. She smiled, quietly collected her things, and went into the bathroom for a quick shower. She left the bathroom light on and just halfway closed the door over, thinking that Blake might awaken a little frightened and disoriented in the night.

Then she lay down on the other side of the bed, several feet away from him. It hurt to be there; the light reflected on his beautiful blond hair and she couldn't help but think that her own son would have been his age and that, as Jesse's grandson, he too might have had a wonderful cap of blond curls.

Then she was ashamed of herself, because Blake was Celia's son, and Celia had not survived to see him grow.

And then she was thinking about Leif again—all these years later.

She felt as if time and events hadn't really passed between them at all. Seeing him again—she might never have been away. But she had. Eons of changes had taken place. Still, it was just the same. Looking at him, feeling his touch. Knowing his scent, just as she recognized a sea breeze or jasmine, the musk of a forest, or the whisper of pine.

She had come to see Jamie—because she'd felt absolutely compelled to do so—but nothing was going as she had planned. And every hour seemed to drag her more and more deeply into something for which she was not at all prepared.

She wanted to know who had conspired to kill her father. With a total sense of grief and outrage, she had to know. Leif, it appeared, wanted the same thing. They had been working in parallel positions, but he knew more than she did, and she was frightened, because she felt that she was rushing head-on into a nightmare.

And you're agreeing to it all, like an idiot, she warned herself! Leif had told her mother that they were living together; she hadn't disputed him. He'd pulled her onto a stage, and she had gone. He'd implied to half a dozen photographers that they were having an affair—and all that she had done was call him a few unkind names!

How was he getting away with it?

She sighed softly and tightly closed her eyes. She didn't know. She wasn't sure if she was so terribly desperate to know about her father or if . . .

Or if, after all these years, she wasn't still compelled by a look that went right through her, a whisper that sent shivers up her spine, a voice that beckoned her, even in anger.

Fool! Maybe she was already trapped, and just didn't realize it. She glanced at the clock by her bed. It was almost five. She groaned softly and closed her eyes, determined to sleep.

Leif quickly discovered that neither Liz nor Tracy was in his and Jamie's suite; he naturally assumed that Liz had Blake in Tracy's suite.

Naturally, the door was locked, and Leif found himself staring down at the street again as he crawled from balcony to balcony once again wondering if they weren't all crazy.

He was startled and experienced just a bit of panic when he opened the first bedroom door and saw that his sister was sound asleep—without Blake. He softly closed her door, then hurried on to the next, his heart beating a little erratically. In the next room, however, he did find his son—sweetly sleeping with his thumb in his mouth and his little rump curled next to the woman beside him.

Tracy.

Leif moved quietly across the room, staring down at the two of them. Tracy had an arm around Blake's tummy, and Blake was very contentedly clinging to it with one hand. There was something entirely innocent and entirely endearing about the two of them. Tracy's silky dark hair feathering across the pillow, her encompassing flannel gown adding to the innocence. Blake, golden, small against her, so trusting.

Leif eased himself down to sit on the side of the bed— it was a massive thing, plenty of room. For a moment he smiled, entranced by the sight of the two of them. He looked at Tracy's face, at her skin, so smooth and clear, at the elegant lines and planes of her features. Her lips, full and sweet and slightly parted as she breathed.

Then his jaw twisted and hardened as he began to think. He had to make her talk. One way or the other. He knew that she didn't ever intend to tell him anything— but if he didn't have just a little more to go on, he couldn't pursue the accusations he intended to make. He believed with all his heart that she knew nothing about his suspicions.

And if he was right? What would she feel then about her mother, grandfather, and stepfather? If she realized what they had done to her, mightn't she be willing to accept the fact that one of them had most probably conspired to murder her father.

He sighed softly, thinking that he could be wrong.

No—he wasn't wrong. It had taken him years to realize the truth—but then, it took years for children to grow and change, and he hadn't been in the temperament to suspect anything at first.

He closed his eyes tightly, fighting back the urge to reach over his son's body, grasp her shoulders in fury, and shake her awake—to demand to know the truth.

Chills settled over him. Maybe she knew the truth. Maybe that was why it was so easy for her to be here now, asleep beside his son, so tenderly, so naturally.

She stirred slightly and he sensed that she was about to waken—and that she'd probably scream, finding a man in her bedroom. He placed his palm over her mouth just as her eyes opened and then widened in alarm.

"It's just me!" he whispered.

She didn't scream; she shook off the touch of his palm with annoyance. " 'Just you' can get out of here!" she whispered vehemently.

"I came for Blake."

"Why? He's fast asleep—he's fine."

The light reflecting from the bathroom touched upon her eyes; they were so very blue, deep and stunning. She was wearing her hair a little shorter now; there was still an abundance of it, thick, rich, and dark against the pillow. He swallowed quickly, and he swallowed down pain. How bitterly he had resented her for what she had done. He'd felt such a miserable tangle of emotions; horror that he had fallen prey to a seventeen-year-old, and that girl the daughter of his best friend. Anger at the absolute fool he had been; fury—against her, for having used him.

And still . . . the caring.

Love was something that began in caring and grew. They had been passionately involved, totally committed to one another for that fantasy interlude.

Admittedly, he hadn't been much of a bargain in his twenties. He'd lived in the fast lane and he'd learned its dangers and its fallacies. He'd been in bed with scores of women whom he would never recognize if he were ever to see them again. But not only had that all been years before he had known Tracy, he had never known anything like the feelings he had experienced with her. The wonder of her innocence, something that made her seduction of him of all the more sweet. The touch of her, the feel of her, the scent of her—they were all things that had lived with him. Things that had plagued him—despite the massive guilt he had endured at first.

He had loved Celia. Tenderly, dearly. They'd lived together before she had left him; she had been soft-spoken, sensitive, gentle. He'd never in a thousand years have hurt her; losing her had been like taking away a part of his soul—the better part. But even loving Celia, he had often dreamt troubled dreams of Tracy.

"Will you go away, please," she asked him with a yawn, casting her arm over her eyes to shield them from the light that exuded from the bathroom. "It's almost morning. And you've done enough for one day! You've destroyed my life."

"Oh, I did not, Tracy."

"You did! My picture—"

"Shush! Whisper!"

Tracy bit her lip, remembering that Blake slept between them. She wasn't done with Leif—but she was determined to keep her voice down.

"You had—"

In a like whisper, Leif interrupted her flatly. "It was necessary."

"Necessary?"

"Go back to sleep, Tracy. I want to leave here by noon."

She yawned again, and he was convinced she wasn't really awake at all, only halfway so.

"Where's Jamie?" she asked him, a sleepy slur to her voice.

"In bed."

"With whom?"

"Himself."

"Thank God. I'd hate to see him turn out like my father and you."

Irritated, Leif found himself looking at Blake again. His son slept soundly, curled to Tracy. Curled so trustingly that it caused Leif another pang. His son, and Tracy. Tracy looking so soft and feminine and lovely and very vulnerable in her tousled state . . .

He cleared his throat and remembered her words. "I resent that. I was a very faithful husband."

Tracy struggled to open her eyes again; his tone had a bitter and chilling quality to it that dragged her back to awareness. But in the poor light, she could read nothing at all in the dark, dark mystery of his eyes or the shadowed line of his mouth.

"And your father wasn't that bad. He didn't marry your mother because your grandfather wouldn't allow it. But he stayed with Jamie's mother for ten years—"

"During which he cheated," Tracy interrupted wearily.

"How do you know?"

She hesitated, but then she was so tired that it didn't seem to matter. "I don't know. But I think that my mother saw him during that time. Oh, God! Would you just go away, please?"

"How could you have known that? You only saw him once during those years, and that was when Jamie was a toddler."

Tracy rolled around, presenting him with her back.

"There were times when he was supposed to see me. When he was supposedly coming. He never showed up—but my mother disappeared. Now—will you please leave me alone?"

Leif didn't say anything else. But he didn't leave, either. He'd suspected himself that Jesse had seen Audrey now and then over the years—it would explain why the two of them had been close enough to come after Tracy together when they had realized that their little runaway was with him.

He opened his eyes again, about to speak. He didn't; he closed his mouth instead, aware that Tracy had let out a shuddering little sigh and that her breathing had become a deep and easy pattern. He started to rise, when Blake's little eyes suddenly opened.

"Daddy?"

"Yeah," he said softly. "I'm here, son."

Blake closed his eyes again, but his hand slipped into Leif's and held tightly. Leif tried to extricate himself; the little fingers closed more tightly around him.

Leif shrugged and leaned back, one hand in his son's, the other cast behind his head for support. He lay there next to them both, awake, for a long time. Thinking over the past. All the sins, all the travesties—all the lies.

It all felt as if a storm were brewing, with high winds to sweep away the shadows and the webs. He had coiled a tension in him, so that he was very glad of it all.

He wanted the truth, naked, cold, and brutal. It was the only way that any of them could ever go on.

He had meant to slip away from his son's hold eventually, but he didn't. Dawn was breaking over the city, and he slept.

"Some hot and heavy affair!" Jamie complained, laughter in his throat. "Will you look at that! Ma and Pa Kettle is more like it!"

Tracy fought her way out of a fog of sleep to blink and see her brother standing at the foot of the bed, grinning down at her. She struggled up to her elbows with a frown furrowed into her features, then saw that Leif—fully clothed except for his shoes—was curled up on the other side of Blake. He was already awake and staring at Jamie with his features harsh in a mask of weary irritation.

"Jamie—didn't anyone ever tell you about knocking?"

"Now that from a pair of people who crawl from balcony to balcony! Rude, I do say."

"Jamie—is Leif in there?"

Liz, a little more refined than Jamie about her entrances, appeared tentatively at the door. She chuckled softly then. "They do look like Ma and Pa Kettle, Jamie."

Tracy stared at the lot, then slammed her pillow against Leif's head; he caught it, and gave her a more deadly glare than he had offered Jamie.

"For God's sake—"

"Hey, Ma and Pa, thought you all just might like a glance at the morning paper!" Jamie announced.

The paper landed on the bed; they both reached for it—Tracy grabbed it.

The headlines were worse than she had expected. "Jesse's Girl Makes Shocking Appearance In Leif's Arms!"

She emitted some kind of oath and continued to scan the paper, feeling her temper soar ever higher. Speculation went on and on, the consensus being that she and Leif had been very heavily involved for some time.

101

She threw the paper at him. "You son of a—"

"Watch it, Tracy—my six-year-old is between us!" Leif snapped back heatedly.

"That's right—what kind of a father are you?"

"Well, there's the hot—where's the heavy?" Jamie queried.

"I must confess," Liz said. "I'm completely confused."

"Oh—they're pretending to have an affair again."

"Again?" Liz demanded, shocked.

"Jamie—you have a mouth like a bullhorn!" Tracy railed, really furious with him.

"Hey—" Jamie protested.

"Tracy—" Leif began.

"Get out of here! All of you!" Tracy demanded.

No one moved; Leif reached for her and she wasn't about to let him touch her, so she flew out of bed—and slammed herself into the bathroom.

She didn't know how long she just sat in there on the commode, fuming, swearing to herself—occasionally slamming a fist against the tile wall. Then she decided to take a cold shower, praying the water would cool her off enough so that she could behave rationally.

She stayed in the water a long time; she still felt flushed and hot when she came out. She wrapped herself in one of the hotel's huge white towels, brushed her teeth and her hair—and then realized that she hadn't brought anything into the bathroom with her to dress. It wouldn't matter—she was certain that her unwelcome visitors would have departed by then. Leif wouldn't remain in her room—he would have taken Blake out of there by then.

She slammed out of the door—only to instantly discover that she was wrong. Blake was gone, but Leif wasn't.

Tracy took a deep, deep breath, clutching the towel tightly behind her back. "Leif, get the hell out of here," she said as calmly and disgustedly as she could manage.

He was leaning against the foot of her bed, resting comfortably on an elbow. His hair was tousled and he looked completely comfortable and unaffected by her demand.

"Tracy, first off," he warned her, and she realized that there was a very real and slow-simmering fury held in leash by the control of his tone, "don't you ever hit on me where Blake is concerned."

"Hit on you! I don't want anything to do with either—"

"Secondly, little girl, you were the one to loop Jamie in on this. What happened to that impassioned speech about what was done to your father? That you have to know?"

"I don't see where you are doing me any good in the least, Leif. I may not have a plan, but yours sucks egg yolks. And I really don't want to discuss it here and now."

He inclined his head slightly, then moved with a slow-and-easy, controlled motion to unwind himself from the bed and onto his feet. He walked over to her, no smile on his face just speculation in his eyes. Shivers instantly began to cascade all over her; she felt more than naked, more than vulnerable.

He stopped before her, placing his hands upon her still damp shoulders. She started to shake away his touch, but grit her teeth instead. Because at her movement, the towel began to drop.

"Tracy," he told her very softly, "come hell or high water, we are going to go through with this!"

"With this?" she cried out passionately. "With what? We're not getting anywhere! All you're doing is planning a big party! What do you think is going to happen? All of a sudden someone is going to leap to their feet and yell, 'Hey! It was me! I paid to have Jesse Kuger murdered because—'? All you've done, Leif, is made a mess of my life—"

"I didn't do that for you, Tracy. You did it all by yourself."

"Oh, you are a hopeless case! I still don't know that you didn't kill him. You claim you were best friends. I saw the fight that you two had; it was vicious and it could have been lethal and—"

"And it was all over the fact that you sashayed stark naked into my bedroom and my bed like a little slut just—"

His words broke off because she slapped him. He touched his cheek, eyes narrowing, then his grip came to her shoulders once again, lifting her to her toes, knocking her against him—minus the towel, alas, because she lost her hold and it fell to the floor.

Tracy gasped in a great breath of horror.

Leif broke off completely, and for several seconds they just stood there, frozen.

Frozen—and burning, Leif thought, swallowing quickly, locking his jaw. Oh, God. This wasn't fair. Tracy. Tracy, in all her glory. So beautiful. The same. Matured. Slim and yet curved.

Naked.

And he could remember, oh, he could remember. So clearly that he could retrace each pattern his fingers had ever traversed over her. The silk of her hair, the satin of her skin, the full curve of her breasts, the tautness of her nipples . . .

The love in her eyes. The laughter. The beauty that had been—before the fall. He'd loved her.

He was still in love with her. Fascinated, enchanted. It was her beauty; it was herself. But a man, he told himself for at least the thousandth time, couldn't stay in love for seven long years.

But if he hadn't, this moment he had fallen all over again. She was his. He'd entered her, she'd entered him. And he had never, never escaped, and right now, it would seem the most natural thing in the world to reach out and hold her, let his trembling fingers curve over the fullness of her breasts, play upon the rose crests until they tautened at his touch and she sighed that soft whisper of hers that was like an enticement all in itself . . .

She'd probably jump out of the window before she let him touch her again, he reminded himself bitterly.

And he was forgetting his whole damn point of being here, and if he didn't move, if he didn't speak quickly, he'd make a complete fool out of himself.

He jerked a little convulsively, digging his fingers into her shoulders, forcing his eyes to meet and remain with hers, as if nothing, nothing had ever happened.

What an idiot! If she felt the pulse of his body . . .

He started up again, halfway shouting.

"Tracy! That is the truth, and you know it as well as I do! God alone knows what else you're trying to hide! I didn't kill your father—and so help me, you know that! Tracy, damn you, don't fight me on this—help me!"

She gasped for breath; she knew that she was a lobsterish shade of red, and she could feel all the power and heat of his body against her nudity like a torch. She discovered that she could only gasp his name, pressing nearly hysterically against his chest so that he might set her down upon her own feet once again.

"Leif—"

It was then that her door went flying open once again. And it wasn't that she was really exposed to anyone else —Leif's body shielded her slim form. It was just the way they looked—his body shielding her totally naked one.

"Whoops—sorry!"

She never saw him—she only knew that it had been Tiger's voice. The door slammed again, and he was gone.

"Let me go!" Tracy strangled out.

He released her, watching her with sudden amusement easing his fury away, and he very unhurriedly went to the floor for the towel and bluntly surveyed the length of her while he too slowly handed it back.

"You do the most convenient things," he told her pleasantly.

"Convenient!" she started to shrill, fumbling to cover herself with the towel.

"Completely," he said agreeably. He turned around, apparently ready at last to vacate her room.

"Leif!"

He turned again, arching a brow. "Is that an invitation to stay?"

"No! But I'm telling you now—you're trying to hang my family, and I will not let you! Maybe I don't believe that you would have killed my father—but neither did they."

"Your grandfather is a totally unscrupulous man, Tracy," he said softly. "And I just might prove that to you. Are you so afraid that I'm right?"

"No. I'm afraid that you're after something else, Leif. Oh, yes, maybe you do hope to discover who wanted my father killed. But there's more here, too, Leif—"

"Maybe there is, Tracy."

"What?" she shrieked.

He shook his head. "The only way you get to know is

by playing along, Tracy. And maybe, just maybe, you know already. And maybe that's why you're running scared."

"Scared of what?"

He shook his head again. "I don't trust you yet either, Tracy. Not completely. Don't forget—I did know you as a lying little con artist."

"Damn you—"

"Tracy, get dressed, will you? This is beginning to remind me very uncomfortably of another place and time in history. You were a con artist, but a very beautiful one. Passionate and seductive, and entirely convincing."

"Leif! Damn you, I won't—"

The door slammed on her words; she was alone at last.

"I won't play your game!" she breathed furiously in his wake. "I won't, Leif, I won't!"

She walked over to her door and locked it, thinking that she would never be around any of them without a locked door again.

"Rude! Didn't any of them ever learn any manners!" she muttered out loud.

She went to the closet then, quickly deciding on a sweater dress. She staunchly decided that she was going to get dressed—and take the first flight out of Kennedy, no matter where it was going.

But even as she slipped her shoes on, she knew that no determination could take her away now. Leif was after something, and she had to know what.

She sighed softly.

She also had the strangest feeling that if she tried to run, Leif would come after her—and find her this time, no matter where she went. She was part of something that she didn't understand. She was bait for him, too.

Why? What were they trying to lure out into the open? Would she survive the promised explosion? Worse still, she thought, shivering, would she survive another bout with Leif?

CHAPTER SIX

They were all in Jamie and Leif's suite—Tiger and Sam, Liz and Blake, and, of course, Jamie and Leif. Tracy entered the room in a slow, simmering boil, wondering if she wouldn't just erupt and tell them that they should all go to hell.

But no one really noticed her when she came in other than to smile and say good morning and offer her a cup of coffee. They were all sitting around the breakfast table, sipping coffee, and reading various papers with reviews on Jamie's performance.

Tracy slid into the remaining seat—between Leif and Blake—and accepted the coffee that Sam poured for her.

Leif chuckled softly. "Hey, Jamie, L. Bordon out of Toronto says that you're a 'genius.' How does that sit?"

"Quite nicely, thanks," Jamie said, grinning, in return.

Tiger gave him a little buff on the back of the head. "Don't go and become an egotist on us. Ted Bailey of the Chicago paper says that you need to learn some control. Work on that—huh?"

Sam chuckled. "Most of these papers are saying that Jamie's great—but they're more into this romance thing between Leif and Tracy."

There is no romance thing! Tracy wanted to scream. But before she got the words out, Leif turned to her with the most startling facsimile of a tender grin and reached over to massage her nape. "I knew you didn't really want it, Tracy, but what difference does it make, huh? None, really."

She almost slapped his hand away—but Blake spoke up before she could do so, asking wistfully, "Does a 'romance thing' mean that I can ask her to cut my waffle for me?"

"Oh, Blake, I'm sorry," Leif said instantly. "I didn't realize you were struggling there, son."

Tracy did snap out then, but not in the way she intended to at all.

"I can cut waffles!"

The whole table stared at her, of course. Jamie, with the silliest grin that made her want to slap him; Tiger, she noted, with a knowing smile. And she began to wish that a giant pterodactyl would swoop down and carry them all away.

She didn't get much of a chance to say anything to Leif; he threw his paper down as she was cutting Blake's food and said something about packing a few remaining things. Tiger and Sam exited to their own rooms for their things, and Tracy was left with only Blake, her brother, and Liz.

And Liz was still staring at her.

She smiled sheepishly and awkwardly when Tracy caught her gaze and pretended to be interested in folding her napkin. "I don't suppose that the traffic will be too heavy today. And we'll be getting an early start." She looked up at Tracy again. "Have you ever seen Leif's house in Connecticut, Tracy?"

"Yes," Tracy murmured, wishing she could deny it.

Blake gave her a wonderful smile. "You've been to my house?" He asked her, excited.

110

"Uh—briefly, a long time ago." She smiled at Blake, but felt acutely uncomfortable. Liz suggested that, since he had finished his waffles, he run back to Tracy's room and pick up his things so that they could get going on the road.

As soon as Blake disappeared, Tracy folded her hands on the table and looked pointedly at Liz. "There's nothing going on, Liz. Well, that's a lie. Your brother is after something, and I'm not sure what. I did know him years ago—very, very briefly—and things were an absolute disaster. That's all there is to it."

Liz shook her head ruefully. "It's none of my business."

Tracy smiled grimly and shrugged. "It was a rather well-kept secret, until recently." She gave Jamie a look that was meant to sizzle, but he was undauntable.

"Tracy—you're the one making the big deal out of things."

Liz folded her napkin again. "And all three of you think that somebody else was in on Jesse's murder, right?" she asked.

"Uh—yes," Tracy admitted. "You knew that?"

"I know my brother."

Jamie pushed his chair in. "I guess I'd better get a few things packed, too."

Liz shivered when he was gone and leaned closer to Tracy. "Tracy, as I said, it's none of my business, but I can see that you're upset. Still, I think that you should go along with Leif. If someone did conspire to kill your father, you and Jamie could be in danger, too."

Tracy took a deep breath and shook her head, touched by the concern in Liz's silver eyes.

"Leif is after my family, Liz. He's trying to hang one of them—in more ways than one."

111

"What do you mean by that?"

Tracy laughed. "I don't know really. I just know that he's suspicious about something and that he intends to use me to get to the bottom of it. That isn't terribly fair."

"Whoever promised fair?" Liz sighed. "Tracy, for your safety, play along. A young woman alone is easy game."

"Oh, I'm wonderfully easy game! For Leif," Tracy muttered bitterly. "I don't even know what he's up to!"

Liz poured herself more coffee and laughed. "All the more reason you should go along with him! You know Leif."

"No—I don't."

"Well, I'll give you a hint. Fight him, and he growls and fights back like a lion. Say a few soft words, and he's a kitten. Go along with him and you'll get him to talk to you."

Tracy lowered her lashes and sipped her coffee. She wasn't sure she could manage even a few soft words for Leif at this point. But thirty minutes later, when they were all ready to leave, Tracy remembered Liz's words. She'd been about to insist that she would ride with Liz and Blake when Leif asked the bellhop to pack Tracy's things in his trunk.

She didn't protest; she smiled sweetly and demurely slid into the passenger seat of his silver Jaguar.

Tiger and Sam, ahead of them in the souped-up Mercedes, waved that they were starting. Liz and Blake crawled into her powder-blue Rolls and waved, too. Leif turned his key in the ignition. They weren't really planning on following one another; they would just start off together and meet when they stopped for coffee at a little place just outside of Mystic.

Tracy was silent as they started off. She slid comfortably back in the very plush seat and pulled the rim of her red and gray felt hat low over her eyes. She sensed that he was watching her—waiting for her to tear into him. She merely smiled, because it was nice to have him be the tense one for a change. She didn't intend to say a thing; he could wait the entire trip.

"Tracy?"

"What?" She made an elaborate point of yawning.

"Listen, what I'm doing—"

"You're just going to do anyway, whether I agree with you or not. You just go ahead, Leif. Could you turn on the radio, please?"

"I've got tapes. What do you want to hear?"

"Anything but the Limelights," she said sweetly, closing her eyes once again.

He didn't reply, but opened the glove compartment and pulled out a tape. She was somewhat surprised that he managed so smoothly, since the Jaguar was a four on the floor, and the car didn't miss a beat. The tape was a set of Croce ballads, soft and easy.

Tracy kept her eyes closed, determining to feign sleep. Liz had been right, she decided with amusement. Leif was all set to go to battle. Well, she wasn't going to take up arms—not now.

But "feigning" sleep wasn't such a wonderful idea. Once they were out of the city, the traffic was light on the highway. Leif drove competently and smoothly. The air was on and the windows were up and the music was like a cushion against her thoughts. She really did fall asleep.

When she woke up, it was to discover herself in a rather precarious position. She frowned as she opened her eyes because she couldn't see much of anything—her hair was tangled all over her face. She blinked and tugged at the wayward tresses and realized that the car was still and Leif was talking and her head was on his lap and her fingers were curled over his thigh. His hand was lightly resting on her head and he was telling Jamie that she had conked out as soon as they reached the bridge.

She struggled to sit up, wishing that she didn't so easily turn to lobster red. Leif's hand trailed down her back as she sat, and she stared at him with blue fire sizzling in her eyes, forgetting for that moment that she had determined to be sweet. He was laughing—as were Tiger, Sam, and Jamie, who were just outside the open driver's door of the Jaguar.

"Better brush your hair before we go in," Leif warned her, but subtle humor was in his eyes.

"Glad to have you with us again, Tracy!" Tiger said. "Guess we'd better get on in and help Liz and Blake hold down a table!"

Jamie winked at her and followed Tiger and Sam.

Tracy started to swear beneath her breath, and Leif burst into laughter. "Careful, luv, your claws are showing." He reached down to the floor where her hat had fallen, then to her temple, where her hair still fell in disarray. There was something about his gaze, something about his touch that held her still.

"He's a brat," she muttered.

"Jamie? Not really; he's not a bad kid at all. There— tug down that brim of yours and we're all set."

Tracy pulled her hat low. Leif came around and opened her door and took her hand when she stepped out of the car. She started to pull it away. His grip tightened and she noted that he was watching the others as they came to the restaurant door. She bit her lip and went rigid, but ceased her useless fight for the retrieval of her hand.

"Leif, I give up. I'm not sure which, but you're planning on hanging either my mother, my stepfather, or my grandfather. Why the charade for Tiger and Sam?"

He glanced her way, pausing to open the door for her. "I'm not ready to hang anyone."

"You're convinced that one of them is guilty—or something."

"All of them are guilty—of something."

"You're not making any sense."

"I haven't vindicated anyone. Does that help?"

She laughed suddenly. "Leif, what are you planning—an Agatha Christie finale? We'll all gather in the grand salon and recreate the crime?"

He smiled at her, his eyes light and silver, and a mystery.

"Hercule Poirot, at your service, ma'am."

"Oh, Lord, save us," Tracy murmured, and she went on through the door. He moved his hand to the small of her back to guide her, and she felt a trickle of exciting warmth that frightened and appalled her. She still cared for him, she knew. Still found it terribly easy to fall under his spell.

It was a small family-run Italian restaurant, very dark and quiet. They had a table in a little alcove, and apparently Leif was a valued customer, because homemade wine came their way, and an aromatic collection of pastas and delicacies. They'd really only intended to stop for a snack, but the food was delicious and they lingered a long while over the various courses, coffee, and dessert.

Tracy was quite impressed with Blake's table manners. For a six-year-old, the little boy was extremely patient in the company of adults. *Was I ever good?* Tracy wondered, and she knew that she hadn't been. She hadn't been that much older than Blake when she had become a terror, rebellious and confused.

115

Once again, she found herself between Blake and Leif with Liz on the other side of the little boy. She was careful to talk to him during the meal, so he wouldn't feel left out. But being there, she began to wonder just what she had missed out on in her determination to stay apart from what was—in a strange way—her heritage. They were all so very close and easy together. Jamie was close to Leif, close to Blake, close to Liz, and even to Tiger and Sam. Like family.

She might have felt the same. If only her father had recognized her that night! But then, maybe she couldn't blame Jesse. She would never have left that night from Leif's if she hadn't still been seventeen and legally bound to her mother and stepfather.

One of them might have killed Dad, she reminded herself, but with little conviction. Surely not Leif! Nor Tiger, nor Sam! Twenty-five years of their lives they had given to one another! Much more than many a marriage.

Then who? Cold chills crept over her. Not her mother or her grandfather, and certainly not her stepfather.

Jamie's mother did it, she decided. And immediately she admitted that her decision was based on the fact that she had never really liked Carol—because Carol had never really liked her.

"Lauren," she murmured, unaware that she had spoken aloud.

Her father's last wife. A sophisticated beauty with very little real interest in music. Tracy didn't think that Lauren would have lasted long with her father had Jesse not died. She had never understood that Jesse's need was not for an audience, but for the music itself.

An elbow suddenly slammed against her rib. She looked up, startled, to find Leif staring at her.

116

"No, I don't think that Lauren is coming in until to-morrow," he was saying, as if she had asked a question.

"Tracy—your folks will be there today, though, huh?" Tiger asked her from across the table.

"They—will?" That same damned elbow slammed against her again. "They will. Yes, they will!" she stated more firmly.

Sam said something to Tiger about the green lasagna; Tracy slammed her elbow against Leif's ribs and was rewarded by a sharp gasp and a groan. He leaned over to whisper in her ear. "Claws, my darling! Retract those claws!"

"You slammed into me!" she whispered back. "Twice!"

"Those were love taps!"

"Love taps my—"

"Your what, my love?"

"Oh, stuff some garlic bread into your mouth, will you please?"

Smiling elusively, he moved away. Tracy noted that Sam was watching them with a bemused expression. He caught her gaze and returned it innocently, crunching into a massive olive.

Leif paid the check and they left. Tracy was amazed to see that it was getting dark. There was still some day-light; it was one of those strange times when the sun could still be seen in the west, while the moon rose in the east.

The others piled into their respective cars; Tracy paused at the passenger's door to the Jag while Leif held still for a moment, his key in the lock, but his eyes on the sky.

Then he stared across the top of the car to Tracy. He smiled at her sardonically. She wasn't sure if he was rueful, or if he mocked her, or if maybe his driving emotions were not a bit of each.

"Liar's moon, Tracy," he said softly.

She frowned, feeling that rare warmth sweep through her again. That whisper, that soft, low, guttural whisper. It always touched her so that it took an absurdly long time for her to register the meaning of his words.

"Liar's moon," he repeated. "Remember?"

And, of course, she remembered. That shadowed sliver of a moon, haunting and glowing, giving and taking, when they had been together before. Gentle light, tender light, light to hide a host of sins.

She started to shiver.

"I don't know what you're talking about," she said curtly. "Can we go?"

His lashes lowered and raised. "You know exactly what I'm talking about, Tracy. Are you still lying to me?"

"Me!" she gasped out. "So I'm the one you're trying to hang? You're crazy!"

He shook his head impatiently. "I'm not trying to hang you either, Tracy. I just want the truth, and one of you has it."

"What truth! You won't even tell me what the hell you're talking about. You keep talking in riddles and you're making me insane!"

His key turned in the lock at last. "Get in the car, Tracy. You've got to face your own dragons soon."

"My dragons?"

"Your mother, my love."

"Quit that!"

"Quit what?"

"My mother isn't a dragon—and I'm not 'your love' and I never was and never will be."

Leif laughed, revving the car as she stepped into it at last. "She's very beautiful—but a beautiful dragon. And your grandfather—definitely. And as to the other—yes, you were, my little delinquent, once upon a time, my love. Such a fool is man!"

"Turn the tape back on," she told him.

"Want to take another nap? Your mom will just love it if we arrive at the house as we did at the restaurant."

"You're cruel!" Tracy accused him. "You never let it rest! My God, aren't you ever going to forgive me?"

He shook his head, but she couldn't read his thoughts —his eyes were on the road.

"Forgive you—I was never really angry with you. You were terribly young and terribly hurt—all you wanted was your father's attention. It was myself I had a hard time forgiving."

She didn't have a chance to reply to him; he reached forward and turned up the tape player.

Night seemed to fall in a single curtain, and they drove on in silence. Tracy didn't close her eyes again; she sat stiff and straight, feeling a coldness settle over her as they came closer to the scene of her personal disaster.

They turned off the highway. The Jag choked and roared and moved smoothly into gear.

Leif's arm came around her; she started, but his fingers moved firmly over her nape, easing away the rigid tension there.

"Afraid to go back, Tracy?" he asked her softly.

"You can never go back," she replied.

He was silent for a second. "But you can try," he murmured quietly.

His hand moved back to the wheel. It was dark, but by the green glowing light from the dashboard she could see his fingers, clearly defined in their tight grip around the

119

wheel. Long, tanned, and very strong. Sure when he drove, when he played, when he touched a woman.

They turned again, down a long, curving driveway, through an acre of foliage, elms and oaks and chestnuts. Then the house rose before them, a restored colonial with massive white pillars, a beautiful, gleaming hardwood porch. Another tug tore at her heart; she had loved the house. It had every modern convenience; it was planned to be comfortable, planned for a family, for children to play, for people to live.

Leif parked the Jag in front of the porch. The front door swung open and Tracy tensed again. She hadn't really believed that Audrey would come, no matter what Leif had said. But her mother was there. Ted was at her side, although Tracy didn't see any sign of her grandfather.

Audrey and Ted started down the steps as Leif crawled out of the car and came around to open Tracy's door. Tracy had to remind herself that she was twenty-five—that she had torn away six years ago and lived on her own, that Audrey could do nothing to her, that the horrible scene could not be repeated.

"What a—lovely—smile," Leif murmured, close to her ear.

Lovely—plastic. Audrey Blare was a beautiful woman. Exquisite, really. She was small like Tracy, extremely well shaped, like a perfect little Dresden doll. Her eyes were enormous and a true emerald, her softly cut hair was a lightly frosted auburn that highlighted the striking color of her eyes. Her face was delicate and oval and unlined and she might have been Tracy's sister rather than her parent.

But marring her beauty was—her smile. It was plastic

120

and so strained that it gave her a drawn and weary appearance that belied all the youth about her.

"You are cruel!" Tracy swore in a furious whisper. This couldn't be any easier for Audrey than it was for her.

"Tracy!" Audrey called.

"Mum, how are you?"

Determined to somehow change the horrible restraint of the occasion, Tracy gave her mother a tremendous hug and a huge smile. Then she hurried past her to where her stepfather waited silently on the step.

"Ted, it's so good to see you."

Ted Blare, a handsome man of medium height and build with steady dark eyes and a lopsided, easy smile, hugged her back—but stared at her reproachfully when they parted.

"Tracy . . . I wish that you might have given us some hint. This—this has been quite a shock for your mother."

"Oh, well, mother has endured a number of shocks," Tracy said nervously. What exactly had Leif told them? And for God's sake, why wasn't she stopping this charade now?

She lowered her eyes, frantically telling herself that it was because she was going to prove Leif wrong. He was going to have to look to a source other than her family to find the criminal who wanted her father dead.

"Audrey, Ted."

To Tracy's surprise, Leif shook hands with the two of them easily. By their actions, she suspected that her mother—and maybe Ted, too—had seen Leif a number of times that she did not know about.

"Thanks for coming," Leif was saying, and she almost jumped out of her skin when she felt his hand rest at the small of her back, casually, easily. "I thought that it

121

might be nice for Tracy and Jamie if we all remembered Jesse this way."

Audrey murmured something, but Tracy barely heard her. She realized that the other cars had driven up, that the porch and the steps were suddenly filled with kisses and hugs and greetings.

Only Jamie hung back a little; Jamie and Blake.

Tracy shook off Leif's hand to reach for her brother's hand and draw him forward to introduce him to Audrey and Ted. She realized then that Jamie was shy; almost painfully shy. But Audrey suddenly decided to shake off the rigidity of the evening, too, and pulled Jamie from his shell with her inestimable charm.

"Oh, and Blake! Mom, Ted, this is Blake Johnston, Leif's son."

She thought that the two of them stood like pokers for a minute, but then she laughed, remembering that her mother had never been brilliant with small children—she didn't like people until they were old enough to drive.

"Hey, Mom—you've got a two-year-old. Blake is all of six—you can deal with that."

"Hello, Blake," Audrey said. Tracy thought she still seemed ridiculously stiff. But then, they were in a horribly awkward situation. She was a guest in a house where she had once charged in to drag her seventeen-year-old away.

"How is the baby?" Leif asked Audrey.

"Oh, Anthony is just fine."

"Big and beautiful," Ted said with enthusiasm. "I waited a long, long time for him, but he's a wonderful boy!"

It was Ted's natural and pleasant pride that seemed to make the atmosphere bearable again. They all entered the house. Leif asked them if their room was okay, if they had been taken care of properly.

"Oh, the room is wonderful, Leif. You know that this is an absolutely marvelous house, and Katie is the most competent household manager I've ever met. I've envied you her for years."

"We spent the day out by the pool, getting tan," Ted added.

Tiger passed them by at the door, with Sam on his heels. Tracy swallowed sharply as she saw that they had rushed up to hug the woman standing there, Katie Carnie, Leif's housekeeper.

She had forgotten about Katie.

For a moment she stumbled, but Leif's arm swept around her waist, leading her forward. Her turn came; tall, gray-haired Katie, with sky-blue eyes and the sweetest smile in Christendom, didn't blink or hesitate.

"Tracy, luv!" she said only, giving her a little hug. " 'Tis so lovely to have the house full. Blake—where's that young man of mine now. There you are! Leif, the bar's all set up in the back—snacks are on the trays for thems that are hungry!"

"Thanks, Katie. Ask Havis and the boys to get all the bags when they get a chance, will you?"

Tracy didn't realize that she had held her breath until she gasped a large quantity of air into her lungs and discovered that she was dizzy. She couldn't go through with this; she couldn't go any further. Everyone else was chatting—talking about their lives. She couldn't talk; she couldn't be easy. Not now—not now that she had seen Katie. Katie had been wonderful the time that Tracy had lived with Leif. And as long as she lived, Tracy would never forget the sight of her huge blue and horrified eyes when her grandfather had hauled her out, screaming and kicking, in nothing but a blanket.

"Your grandfather is out by the pool Tracy," Audrey told her suddenly. "You worry him terribly, dear, you know. Go tell him hello."

To her amazement, Tracy found herself turning to Leif for support. Then she wanted to kick herself, because he smiled sardonically. He offered her a hand, though, and walked her through the living room and family room to the French doors that led out to tiled patio and pool.

But at those doors, he pushed her forward.

"What are you doing? You're not coming—"

"Oh, no. Meet your dragons alone, my love!" he told her cryptically.

"I should tell my 'dragon' the truth!" she snapped to him, only to discover that he was no longer behind her.

She stepped out into the night. Colored lights fell over the pool, misting it in tranquil beauty. Far to the opposite side of the large kidney-shaped structure sat Arthur Kingsley, billionaire.

Tracy hesitated, then firmly stepped around the pool.

He was just sixty-six, still a giant of a man, broad shouldered, with snow-white hair, a hawk-nosed face. He saw Tracy coming, but didn't say a word—nor did he rise from his lawn chair.

"Hello, Grandfather."

His gaze swept over her disapprovingly. "I'm shocked, Tracy. I can't believe you're with Leif Johnston again."

Tracy sat on the chair next to him and leaned over to plant a kiss on his cheek. "Love you, Grandpa," she murmured, and it hurt a little inside to see him close his eyes and cherish her touch no matter how gruff he looked on the outside.

She sat back. "I can't believe that you came," she said softly.

"I only came," he told her sternly, "to warn you that I would cut you entirely out of my will and leave every blessed cent that I have to your baby brother if you don't cease this foolish alliance immediately."

Tracy lowered her head and smiled. "Grandpa, I don't care where you choose to leave your money. I think that you should frivolously spend it all—it's yours."

"Humph!" he muttered. "I mean it, Tracy."

"So do I. I can support myself nicely, thanks."

"Tracy, you're setting yourself up for heartache! These musicians . . . Tracy, your father was a philanderer. He would have made your mother's life a tragedy! Different cities, different women, night after night!"

She didn't tell her grandfather that she did consider her mother's life a tragedy. "Grandpa, Leif doesn't play any more. Not on the road."

"I've given you warning, Tracy. Now you think about it. Leave him or I cut you out without a cent."

Tracy sighed. "Grandpa—"

"Don't answer me. Just think about it." He was silent for a minute. "It's good to see you, Tracy. I worry about you. Christmas isn't enough. I—I always thought that you'd come home."

Tracy stood again and smiled down at him. "I can't live at home. I love you, but it's true. You want to rule us all. Sometimes I think that you're Henry the Eighth come back to life."

"Tracy Blare—"

"Kuger, Grandpa. I use my father's name."

He waved a hand impatiently in the air. "You use a dozen names—like a chameleon—just so that we can't find you!"

"Well, I'm here, and you're here. We're all here," she murmured a little hysterically, and then she felt that she had to escape him, had to escape them all. She kissed his cheek hurriedly. "See you in the morning, huh, Grandpa?"

She started off in the general direction of the house. She could see the lights, she could hear laughter and conversation. She wondered if they might be talking about Jesse, if enough time had passed for those who had loved him to laugh and talk with nostalgia and ease.

One of them had probably hired his killer . . .

No. Lauren wasn't here yet, nor was Carol. One of his wives, yes. Her mother had never gotten to be his wife—just his lover.

"Oh, God!" she whispered miserably out loud, and she knew that she couldn't go back to the house. She veered around it, heading for the maze and the rose garden that flanked the left side of the pool.

She hurried down the first path, blindly determined just to escape them all. It was amazing how easily she tread the path, though—without faltering. Straight through all the flowers and brush without a hitch, until she came panting to the center, where pines cast a natural arbor over a fountain of dancing nymphs.

She gripped the fountain, staring up at the moon, breathing as deeply as she dared. The moon hung there alone now, a crescent shadowed and hazed. A liar's moon. Leif's term. They had laughed about it once, but then the lies had become very tangled webs, and the fact of it was no laughing matter anymore.

"A shadowed crescent, Tracy. Beautiful, deceitful. Touching us all."

She almost screamed; she spun around instead, thinking that she should not be so surprised to see him here.

From the heavy shade of a pine he walked toward her, eyes silver with the moon and the night, his height towering in the shadows. He came before her and took her cheeks between his palms, studying her eyes.

She should have run then, but she didn't.

"Why didn't you tell him the truth?" he demanded. "Arthur is a billionaire, and an infant you barely know will inherit it all."

"You're horrid!" she said. "You were eavesdropping."

"It's one way to learn things that I have to know."

"And what did you learn from that?"

"That he doesn't control you, Tracy. Not anymore."

"It's really none of your concern."

"It's a lot of money."

"I'm a very good songwriter," she said coolly. "I earn my own way."

His palms, against her cheeks, moved slightly. Stroking her flesh, as he gazed down at her, silver brooding and perhaps bemusement marking his eyes, touching his slow smile.

"You remembered the rose garden—and the maze. Step by step you came here—so directly. You had the path charted in your mind."

"I—uh—once you know it—"

"I know. Once you know certain things, they are charted by heart."

She felt that the air had grown thin; that she could barely stand. She had been here before. In this very place. As lovers, they had stared up at the moon; in a fantasy world, they had absorbed the scent of roses and lain on a bed of pine.

You can never go back, she had told him.

You can try.

Or perhaps you never really left.

"Once you know certain things . . ." he murmured again, and a tender smile just slightly curled his lips as he leaned downward, bringing his mouth just a breath away from hers. Warmth welled and flared within her until she quivered with the memory, hot from some inner well, aching for his touch. In harmony with her desires, his palms left her cheek and his arms swept around her, bearing her down beside him on a bed of pine.

"Without a falter or a lapse, I remember you, Tracy. I remember the night you first came to me. The way you looked, shedding your clothing, clad in moonlight, rhythmic, slow, and so sensual. I nearly died a thousand deaths waiting for you to reach me. I remember the fullness of your breasts, the curve of your spine, the way your hair looked, dark and splayed across my pillow. Just like the maze, Tracy. I could touch you again and know exactly where I was going."

She stared up at him, unable to refute him, disbelieving that they could be in the rose garden together again, a bed of pines beneath him, his hands upon her, firm and secure and tantalizing, his mouth . . . brushing hers, at long last.

She curled her arms around his neck, felt his tongue part her lips and then her teeth, then create a cascade of shivering heat inside of her as it filled her mouth, stroking and playing, and drawing her into a heated return of the fevered hunger. She clung to him, eager to touch the hair at his nape, know his shoulders again with her fingers, press against him and feel the pliable steel of his chest, hard against her. The touch of his hands, in her hair, on her cheeks, stroking her throat, cradling her breasts . . .

The soft scent of the roses haunted her, the all-male scent of his body came to her in subtle wonderment, and

128

she could have stayed there forever, just knowing his touch—a touch that remembered her, and charted her form as surely as she had charted the maze.

He drew his lips from hers and lay beside her, smiling as he stroked her hair, breathing a little too heavily and staring at her with a desire barely held in check. He opened the buttons on her blouse one by one; she felt his hands on her bare breasts and she gasped suddenly, remembering where she was . . .

And who she was with.

"Leif—we're—we're—out in the open."

"We're in a maze," he told her dryly.

"But—but—my grandfather—your son—all of them—"

His lashes were lowered; she saw a tick in his cheek, but he spoke with no vehemence, rather too casually. "You're twenty-five years old now, Tracy. This is between you and me and no one else. If your grandfather were to have a problem now, he knows damned well I'd throw him out of my house."

She inhaled and exhaled, staring at him.

"I really was more than a little bit in love with you, Tracy."

"Celia—"

"I loved Celia, too, that's true. I can't deny it. And I suffered the agony of the damned—feeling that I had seduced not only my best friend's daughter, but a minor at that. You were too young and it was wrong. You're an adult now, Tracy. The decisions are all yours."

She could only stare at him, longing to touch him, afraid to do so. She smiled ruefully, staring into the smoky gray depths of eyes that were wise and wary, and sometimes charcoal with anger, sometimes silver with laughter, always deep with a fascination she could never deny.

"I'd wondered if things might have changed—if you mightn't have grown obese and ugly. There were times I nearly prayed that I could see you so and forget you. I still want you, Tracy, in that same way."

She was ready to touch him, ready to fall into the wonderful heat and passion of his arms and pretend that the liar's moon had forever glowed above them.

But he closed the buttons on her shirt, smiled and stood, and reached a hand down to her. He drew her close to him and gave her a wicked smile as he pulled her taut against his chest once again, stroking the lower crescent of her breast.

"My room, Tracy? Have you got the courage? Have you really got enough courage to give us a chance again?"

He released her and left her alone in the center of the maze with the roses and the fountain and the nymphs and the . . .

Liar's moon. Shadowed and glowing—and frightening, because there was some truth that he sought that she didn't understand.

Run! Leave! she warned herself.

But she stared at the moon again and knew that she would go to him. There was one truth that she knew— she wanted him now, with all the hunger, all the need . . .

All the love and desire that she had learned before. As thoroughly charted against her heart as the maze was against her mind.

CHAPTER SEVEN

There was a deck that led from Leif's second-story room out over the patio; and there were steps that led from the far right of the pool to that deck.

Coming from the maze, Tracy noted that her grandfather had gone in, and she smiled a little bitterly, knowing that it wouldn't have mattered to her if he had still been there or not. She passed the tiled pool area and climbed the steps to the deck.

The doors were open. The breeze caught the drapes, billowing them about in the moonlight. Tracy came to the doors and paused, remembering a long ago time when she stood here, frightened, unsure, yet determined and moving by instinct alone.

Leif was not in the room. She didn't need light to know that he was not here yet. He was a father, she reminded herself, of a six-year-old. He might well be putting his son to bed. He was also the host this evening. He might be seeing to the welfare of his guests. He might be doing one of half a dozen things.

But he would come back here. And he would wonder if she would come to him or not.

She came in, noting that little had changed. The doors opened into an antechamber. Victorian furniture created a beautiful little nook—a loveseat and matching chairs, a tea cart, and bookcases. To the right against the wall was a grand piano, to the left a stereo setup.

Straight ahead was an archway that opened into the bedroom.

Tracy moved silently over the carpet, pausing there again. Nothing had changed. His bed was framed by an antique headboard and footboard in golden oak—an English set that he had picked up at a Paris flea market years and years ago. She knew he had refinished it himself, that he liked to work with his hands on wood, returning it to luster himself.

Nothing had changed.

But everything had. He'd been married; he'd lost a wife. Celia had lived here, had slept in this bed. She felt so distant to Tracy, though. She had never known her.

Tracy closed her eyes for a minute, dizzy.

Jesse, too, was lost to them all. Jesse, who had raged in here—furious with Leif, furious with himself. He'd fought Leif, knowing sickly all the while that he'd been at fault himself.

"Ah, Dad!" Tracy murmured out loud, wincing. Careless, insensitive—for so much of his life! But age had brought him wisdom. In those final years he'd admitted so much to her! How he was horrified by his own treatment of his children. How he was grateful that they could still love him. How he had been blessed with special friends. How life was all so much a greater thing once a man learned to care.

He had told her that Leif often plagued him about her; she had told him that surely he understood—she didn't want Leif to know anything about her at all. She didn't really want to ever hear his name again.

Jesse, it seemed, had respected her wishes.

But he'd once told her that she shouldn't be so hard.

"I think he might have been the only one who really cared about you that night. Cared about your feelings. Oh, he was mad—shocked, humiliated, and betrayed. But he was still trying to understand, to protect you. I was busy hating myself for not even knowing you—so I had to blame you, and Leif. Your grandfather was horrified about the scandal and he'd never forgive me. I think your mother saw only her own lost youth. You, grown and beautiful and more sultry and sweetly beautiful than she had ever been herself."

Tracy's fingers curled around the molding. She couldn't think about her father. It would either make her cry or go mad, because he shouldn't have lost life just when he had really gained it.

She didn't want to cry or bewail the past. Or even think about the future. She was older now. Seasons had come and turned and changed, and it was all up to her. Leif wanted her still.

And she . . .

Wanted Leif. It was her choice; no one could stop her now.

She smiled, surveying the room again. She remembered them together—the silent way he could move about the room; his silhouette in the moonlight; the hard, sleek lines of his body, beautiful in nakedness, easy, natural, strong and proud.

Tracy took a breath, then hurried across the room. The bathroom was to the far rear, with a wonderful dressing room just before it, complete with two gorgeous skylights.

She hurried through the dressing room, though, hastily shedding her clothes, rushing into the shower. She curled her hair high above her hair to keep it dry and met the pulse of the jet spray with a growing beat in her heart.

133

Her fingers curled around the soap—his soap. It gave her a sense not so much of coming home, but of being exactly where she belonged.

Seconds later, she stepped out and toweled herself dry, acutely aware then even of the feel of the terry towel. She wrapped it about herself, then let it fall to the floor. She stepped out of the bathroom and walked deliberately to his bed, pulling down the comforter and sheets and crawling beneath them.

Her heart began to pulse and beat like a lark's as she waited. Waited and waited, and began to doubt her sanity.

She wondered how long it would take her to leap from the bed, dash back to the bathroom, and retrieve her clothes . . .

It was then he came.

Like Tracy, he entered by the deck. He had been outside, perhaps feeling the night breeze, perhaps watching the moon with its haze and its shadows.

He came to the doorway and stood still, framed by the floating curtains, blocking the moon. She saw his form only at first, tall, hands upon his hips, legs spread slightly, feet firmly upon the ground.

He stood there a long time. She knew that he stared in at her, that he saw her past the loveseat and the archway, that he knew she was curled in his bed.

He came through at last, walking slowly, silently.

He paused at the archway, dropping his shoes.

Then he moved, still slowly, fluidly, to the bed. He was dressed in jeans and a blue plaid flannel shirt; he didn't disrobe, but swept down beside her suddenly, encompassing sheet, comforter, and all into his arms.

His mouth burned atop hers. His kiss stole her breath, ground against her, went deeper than the ocean, lasted hot and wet and hungry for eons and eons, until hers came around in return, until she feathered his dark hair through her fingers, clenching, unclenching.

He drew from her and ripped the covers away. And stared. Against the liar's moon she saw the handsome contours of his face—hard, granite, somewhat savage with desire . . . and memory. She lay still, unflinching, feeling the heartbeats of time that passed between them.

He savored the memory and the reality. Her breasts rose and fell with the rush of her breath, and they were fuller, the nipples darker, dusky rose and taut, than they had been. With his eyes, he devoured those gold and satin breasts, gazed down to the slim line of her ribs and torso, to the delicate molding of her belly. His gaze traveled farther to the haunting crevices of her beautiful feminity, and her hips and thighs and legs that stretched forever in shapely beauty.

And her eyes rested upon him, blue and questioning, innocent and sultry.

He touched her at last; his fingers against her abdomen. A shudder shook him, a groan that was an echoing thunder of his heart, of the pulse of his desire. His hand, his fingers, splayed, encompassing more of her bare flesh, stroking with fascination, knowing again the feel of her breasts, the quiver of her thighs when he touched her.

"Leif—"

He curled his frame against her, pressing his lips against her throat, the hollow of her shoulder, the valley of her breasts. He took a nipple carefully into his mouth, then sucked hard on it, then swept the tender flesh with the gentle balm of his tongue and filled his mouth again.

He rose above her, seeing her eyes. Huge and dark and everlastingly blue, still a torment that beguiled and enchanted a man and sent bursting through him a shaft of desire that burned and demanded.

He rolled from her and stood and shed his shirt in the moonlight. She loved his shoulders, touched by that glow, hard and lean and sinewed. The color of him was gold; the sight of him cast her into a wonder that she knew could never go away. His chest was richly touched with short dark hair. She ached to feel the coarse and fascinating curls in her fingers, rough and arousing against her flesh. But as he stood before her she could only look and note how his sensuous chest hair angled and narrowed and became a thin line at his belt.

Then he shed his jeans and stood naked in the moonlight, all masculine beauty and ever golden still.

He came down beside her again. She cried out something inarticulate and curved around to him, burying her face against his chest, feeling the hair play against her cheek and nose and lips. She rubbed her mouth there, loving the feel of him, loving the beat of his heart, the ragged sound of his breath, his touch, his fingers through her hair, at her nape . . .

He set her from him. She felt the hardness of his body, taut, rigid, strained. He seemed to thirst for the touch of her, her movement, her scent. She felt his mouth against her flesh, his teeth, his tongue. The length of his body. The roughness of his palm sliding against her, the deliberate exploration of his fingers, intimate between her thighs, causing her to shudder and ache, and throb ever more greatly with the heated rush of desire.

"Leif!"

His eyes were above her, the lean hard length of his body was strong between her thighs. The pulse of his sex was hard against her belly and she was both ecstatic and frightened, on the crest of a great wave, hungry as she

136

had never been before, whispering words that rushed from her heart.

"Please . . . please . . ."

Her hands rested around his throat and shoulders, her eyes stared into his smoke and silver ones, still savage now, intent, as passionate as the quivers that racked his muscled length.

"Take me," she whispered, "fill me, pour into me . . ."

His eyes closed; his head buried against hers; his fingers laced around hers, and he penetrated into her, so slowly that she gasped a little breath with each second of thrust, dying a little inside with the exquisite invasion, then crying softly as he stiffened and moved in a sudden completion, seeming to be so deep and strong inside of her that he touched her heart.

He stared into her eyes and loved them. He touched her lips quickly with his own, touched again, kissed long and deep, and drew away again. His hands slid beneath her, lifting her. His urgings brought her legs about him, wrapped tightly around his back, forming them together.

Pleasure rose in her. Sweet like wine; rich and fragrant and delicious. She was acutely aware of the feel of his dark hair against his cheek, the intimate sensation of her breasts crushed hard to his chest, the rhythmic motion of his hips, thrusting, grinding, bringing them together again and again in an ever greater need. He spoke to her —words so blatantly sexual that her body heated further. Their bodies became slick and melded closer, their breathing deepened and rushed, and joined with the heady pounding of their hearts. The hazy moonlight fell upon them, and they were beautiful—so attuned to one another there could have been music.

Tracy closed her eyes and ran her fingers along his

137

spine, feeling still the magnificent tension that kept him within her body, strong and kinetic then, reaching. She opened her eyes and saw his face; eyes closed, head back. Cheeks drawn and taut as he arched, filling her explosively one last time, reaching, reaching—touching that perfect chord, causing her to shudder as the crest of sensation came upon her, drenching her, sweeping her, bringing a ragged little cry to her lips.

He fell against her, sweeping her into his arms, carrying her weight against his own. They lay there in absolute silence, both fighting for breath as the seconds passed, as minutes elapsed, as they rode down upon the ebb of perfect sensation.

For a moment she was very content just to be there; just to feel the damp sleekness of his body, slick from the heat that so slowly cooled from their flesh. Content to feel his arm about her, to know the breeze upon her, to feel the glow of the moon, like a balm, like a blessing. Then she winced, thinking that it was a spell again, and that spells could be broken.

This—this was how they had lain when the door had burst in on them. He had held her just like this, wrapped her protectively to him in his mass confusion over the intrusion. Stared down at her in incredulous disbelief . . .

Tracy, is it true?

The question; the slow shield over his eyes, the growing fury, the hard grate of his teeth when Jesse had slammed into him, and he had rolled to defend himself from his best friend's blows.

A little sob shook her suddenly.

"Oh, God. I hope we're not here in vengeance," she whispered.

He stiffened, like rock.

"I'm not, Tracy. Are you?"

She shook her head vehemently, wishing she had never spoken, knowing that she had to speak again.

"Leif—were you planning this all along? You said that you wanted to find my father's murderer. Is that really true? Or . . ." Her voice faded away.

The tension in him eased and he stroked her hair with a soft sigh. "Tracy, no, I didn't plan this. How could I? Too many years had passed. Long years, vast changes. No, I didn't plan this. I knew when I saw you again that I wanted you again." His thumb grazed gently over her cheek. "I was a little bit in love with you, though. I never could forget you."

A little bit! he thought ironically. I was bewitched, entranced, totally captivated. I'd have happily lain down my life for you, and thought it only a small token. Tracy . . . the magic was there again, but he swallowed back any thought of words, of giving away those feelings. He couldn't trust her; he couldn't trust himself. Time would have to tell, and he would have to take the gravest care.

He knew then, with all his heart, that he would not lose her again. Whatever it took—he would not lose her again.

She swallowed, wincing, curling her fingers against his chest. "You—you did forget me. You married Celia instantly."

He was dead still for a second, then he gently moved her from him and rose. Naked, he walked over to the open doorway, where the draperies still drifted in the night breeze. He stared out, running his fingers through his hair, then leaning against the window frame and idly crossing his arms over his chest.

"I did love Celia. But I didn't forget you. I went mad trying to find out where your grandfather had hid you.

139

Jesse and I were at awful odds. I just wanted to see you again. I wanted you to know that I had been angry because I had been so stunned—being dragged out of bed like that was not a thrilling experience. But it was worse on you. If you really wanted to disappear, that was fine. But . . ."

He hesitated, shrugging. "I did stay that little bit in love with you, Tracy." He stood again, framed in the draperies, hands on his hips, his bare back to her. Then he spun around suddenly, coming back to the bed, bracing his arms on either side of her and staring down at her.

"What about you, Tracy? What were you feeling?"

She froze; she couldn't tell him the truth. She couldn't tell him that she had hated him with all her heart—that she had, indeed, been a prisoner, young and miserable and pregnant—with the fact that he had married immediately following their affair being crammed down her throat daily.

"Tell me, Tracy!" he said suddenly, intently.

She shook her head. It wasn't that she particularly wanted to deceive him; there was just no sense in giving him the truth. No sense in telling him that she had been wretchedly pregnant—and that she had held her child only once before it had died. That, at eighteen, she had stood in a tiny cemetary outside of Zurich with a light dusting of snow falling all about her while the tiny coffin containing the child who had not survived a full day was lowered into the earth.

She couldn't tell him that from there she had begun to sever the strangling ties her mother and grandfather had laced around her. That she had found Jesse then; that she struck off on her own.

"I don't know what I felt. It was a long, long time ago," she cried.

"Not so long. Not so long that you didn't remember me. Not so long that we didn't wind up together again—with rather astonishing speed."

"Leif! What does it matter? You were married to Celia! There was nothing that could have been said or done!"

"Liar's moon, Tracy! Damn you, don't lie to me now!"

"Leif! I don't know what you're talking about?"

"Why won't you tell me the truth?"

"What truth? Why are you always talking in riddles?"

"Tracy—"

His teeth grit suddenly, his fingers knotted the sheets into his fists. Startled and wary, Tracy grasped at the comforter, drawing it to her chest, inching toward the bedpost, out of the circle of his arms.

"Leave me alone, Leif. Until you feel like telling me what you're talking about. God, I knew that this was a mistake."

He didn't reply. His eyes glittered hotly in the moonlight, and she felt a sudden and desperate urge to escape him. She tried to push past the bar of his arm. The comforter fell away from her hold, and she didn't notice it in her grim determination to be free.

"Leif, let me out of here. This was—"

"Where are you going?" he queried softly.

"Away!" She looked back to his eyes. The frightening glitter was gone; he was smiling as he shook his hand, moving his arm of his own accord—but encircling her wrist with his fingers.

The blanket was gone; her breasts were bare and silver shadowed in the moonlight. And dusky rose nipples peaked out evocatively from a tangled curl of her hair and he knew that he could never let her go again.

"Stay, Tracy."

"Leif—"

141

She stared down at his fingers, so tightly wound around her wrist. She looked into his eyes again, and the sexual message was staggering. It caught her unaware, off guard, vulnerable. Her lips parted slightly in her effort to breathe; a cascade of liquid heat swept through her and she felt the power of his will and tension travel like a rushing stream from his body to her own.

He smiled. His lips touched hers, and she sank back to the pillow again beneath the hard weight of his lean form.

In the morning Leif slipped into the room beside his own, which he had intended for Tracy, and quietly returned to his own with her luggage. She was still sleeping.

He smiled as he watched her, feeling a tug at his heart, painful and sweet. Some things changed; some things didn't. She still slept the same, hair an absolute silky tangle, lips just so slightly parted—and her arms wrapped tightly around a pillow now that he was gone. He pulled the comforter over her shoulders lest she feel too cool from the morning air.

Minutes later, he was downstairs in his trunks, quickly plunging into the pool. He swam a dozen laps, then floated on his back. The air was cool; the pool was heated. The sun was overhead, and it seemed an incredibly beautiful morning. None of his house guests was stirring yet; he was alone.

He glanced at his watch and saw that it was eight thirty at last. He left the pool, grabbing a towel from a shelf behind the tiled patio wet bar, then entered the downstairs through the back door and quietly followed the family room to his office at its left.

He sat down and picked up the phone, dialing a number he now knew by heart.

Rob Dorry answered on the second ring. "Hi, Rob. Leif Johnston. Just checking in. Anything new?"

"Yeah, Leif, a couple of things," Rob replied. He was a clean-shaven, quiet young man who always wore three-piece suits. His office was a clean, neat place with an attractive array of plants and bookshelves—not a thing like the grubby holes television had led Leif to imagine would serve as a P.I.'s office.

"In which direction?"

"Both directions," Rob told him. "First and most importantly, you were definitely right about the cop who shot Martin when he was coming out of the park right after he stabbed Jesse Kuger."

"You're sure?" Leif said, his heartbeat quickening.

"Positive. He's been driving around in a Mercedes, and a month ago he bought a little condo facing the park. Do you know what kind of money you need to do things like that in N.Y.C.?"

"Have you talked to him?" Leif asked. "Never mind, maybe I should do that myself. I'll—"

"Well, here's the bad news. Neither of us can talk to him. Seems he fell off a roof the other day. The man is dead. His partner thinks he must have tried to follow a few hoods escaping from building to building—and might have been too fat and out of shape to make the leap."

Leif grit his teeth to keep his voice level; he'd been so damned close! "When did it happen?"

"Saturday."

"You think he might have been pushed?"

"Anything is possible—but it seems that his partner was down in an alley, so there were no witnesses."

"I'll be back in the city for Jesse's memorial service. It's planned for three in the afternoon. I'll stay Monday and see if I can't talk to the partner myself. If I haven't anything else to go on by then," Leif muttered. "Anything else?"

"Yes, well, I finally tracked down Jesse's old secretary. She'd taken off with her little inheritance to live in Hawaii. Arthur Kingsley did see Jesse two weeks before the stabbing. And it seems that they had a horrible row over something. She said she fled—went to lunch—because the walls were vibrating."

"Kingsley," Leif murmured.

"But he may not be your man. Or woman. According to the reigning Mrs. Kuger's manicurist, Lauren Kuger was all upset about the same time. The manicurist was convinced that the marriage was on the rocks."

"That doesn't necessarily mean anything. Broken marriages usually end in divorce—not murder."

"Lauren Kuger got a lot of Jesse's money. A lot more than she might have with alimony payments."

"Granted. Anything else?"

"Yep. Jesse did see Audrey Blare any number of times over the last years—his doorman at the penthouse recognized her picture. They kept a nice hot little affair going. Sporadic—she saw him a couple of times a year. But it seems their little secret was a long-lived one."

"That's not a shock. What else?"

"Well, I'm still trying to discover what your friends Tiger and Sam did with a hundred thousand dollars between them. That's a tricky one—I don't have a legal leg to stand on when I try to pry into their affairs."

"I know. Just keep at it, okay?"

"You're the boss, Mr. Johnston."

"Thanks—"

"Don't hang up. I've got more."

Leif tensed, sitting straight up in his chair, feeling a sick, dizzying sensation sweep through him.

"I've found what you're looking for. I've even found a legal way to dig it up. When can you head overseas with me?"

He thought he would black out for a minute, he was so astounded. And furious all over again. His hunch had paid off—in one way at least. But he wouldn't know the truth one way or another until he could see for himself.

He hesitated a moment, though. Instinct and emotion urged him to fly out on the next plane; caution warned him not to. Lauren and Carol were both coming in today —he had just gotten his house guests assembled.

He had just gotten Tracy back into bed with him. Where she belonged. At his side.

"Tomorrow. Make the arrangements and give me a time. I'll meet you at Kennedy. I'll have to turn around and fly right back, though."

"Sure thing. I'll call with the flight information."

Leif slowly set the receiver back into its cradle. He sat back, wondering why he should be so shocked. He had suspected the truth for some time.

Because I told her not to lie to me! he thought, fighting down the sick rage. Of course, he didn't know what he would find yet.

Yes, he did. It would be empty. He was sure of it, and he felt sick, and he wondered what she knew . . .

"Leif?"

Startled, he looked up. Lost in thought, he hadn't heard the door to his office slide open.

It was Audrey. She came in and closed the door behind her, smiling. She was dressed in designer jeans and a sexy top that bared her left shoulder and hung becomingly to

145

a wide red sash belt that emphasized her slim waist and trim hips.

She stared at him and he realized that he was still in his trunks, hair wet, shoulders slick.

"You still swim every morning," she said, smiling and walking around to sit on the edge of his desk, amazingly like a coed.

Leif sat back, idly folding his fingers before him.

"Yes, I still like the water."

She leaned over to help herself to a cigarette from the pack on his desk, moving as sensuously as a kitten. She offered him another of her brilliant smiles and he noted grudgingly that she was still as lovely as she had been when Jesse had first met her, when they had all been kids, eager to face the world, convinced of their immortality.

Lovely . . . and very practiced in her charming wiles. He discovered himself feeling very sorry for Ted Blare— the silent husband. Well, Ted had received great benefits from Arthur Kingsley's money. Maybe he wasn't all that "long suffering."

"Give me a light, Leif?"

He found his lighter and lit the flame. Her eyes touched his again and he smiled.

She's got it, too—Tracy has it. That movement, that sensual appeal. She's just a great deal more discriminating about its use.

Audrey inhaled and exhaled. "I thought you had to be crazy to invite us all here, Leif. I'm glad you did, though." She was silent for a minute, then her voice sounded a little strange. "You and Tracy really are back together?"

"Yes."

"Yes, well . . ." Audrey attempted another smile—a weak one this time. "I guess I just wanted to make sure

146

that you and I were at peace. That you understand . . . Tracy didn't always just look mature, she was mature. But she was still—still my baby, I guess."

"It was more than that, Audrey, wasn't it?" Leif inquired politely, watching her reaction carefully. "You didn't want her involved the same way you were. Marrying Ted—and hanging on to Jesse anyway."

She jumped off his desk as if she had been burned. "Jesse and I were dear, dear friends—"

"Oh, Audrey, please."

"He told you?"

Leif shook his head. "Jesse wasn't like that, and you know it. If he had a confidence, he kept it. I just—know. It doesn't matter, Audrey. He's gone now. We all loved him, and he should be left at rest."

Audrey nodded. She started, a little dazed, toward the door. Then she turned back. "Well, I do love Tracy too, you know. She's my daughter."

"I know."

Audrey offered another smile. "I really hope it's a new beginning for you, Leif. I mean, I hope you two don't hash over the past all the time. You'd probably be happiest if you never mentioned bygone days at all."

"Really?" Leif came around and sat on the edge of his desk, smiling at her. "Is there something that all of us shouldn't admit? I rather think that facing the truth is best."

"Now Leif—"

She started back at him, grinning like a beautiful little gamin, planting one of her delicate little hands against his chest. She sighed softly. "Leif, Leif! I was terrible, and of course, it was terrible for Father to slam you with that bat, but we felt it imperative to get her out of there! You were tearing Jesse to pieces, and you were so wild and"—

she paused, swallowing, and allowing her red-tipped nails to slide down his bare chest—"you always were so powerful. Dad was just frightened that you'd kill Jesse, you know."

He caught her hand and smiled grimly. "Arthur would have loved it if I had killed Jesse, Audrey."

"Leif! What a terrible thing to say!" She stared at him with wide-eyed innocence. "Really! Oh, stop looking at me like that! I had every right to tear my daughter away from you. I knew you, Leif. I knew it would be impossible to count the women you'd had in your life if I stayed awake nights on end. I—"

"Audrey, give it a break, please." He laughed bitterly. "I happen to remember a night when Jesse didn't show up for a date with you. It was long ago, Audrey, but I remember it. You were peeved—and decided I might do instead. But Jesse was my friend and I turned you down. Maybe it bothered you just a little that your daughter had something you hadn't managed to take?"

"Bastard!" Audrey hissed coolly, slamming a palm against his chest.

"Hands off, Mrs. Blare, please," Leif said lightly.

"Maybe you're the one who can't handle it!" Audrey purred in return, coming just a shade closer.

And it was then that Leif looked over her head to see that the door had opened again. Tracy was standing there, just inside the room, dressed in a high-cut swimsuit that was stunning on her, enhancing her long supple legs and beautifully curved form. She stared at him coolly over her mother's head, and he wondered as his heart sank what she was thinking.

She didn't slam out of the room, though. She was extremely poised. "Mom, Leif, excuse me, I see that you're busy. I should have knocked."

She smiled at them both and departed.

"Great!" Leif muttered.

"Maybe she'll leave you of her own accord this time," Audrey said sweetly, and when he gazed her way with acute annoyance, he realized that she was enormously pleased about the situation.

She turned to leave. He grasped her arm and pulled her back. "Audrey, what are you trying to hide?" he demanded. "What is it that you don't want Tracy telling me?"

Audrey jerked her arm back. "Nothing!"

She ran out of his office, slamming the door in her wake.

Leif followed her more slowly, determined to find Tracy. He straightened his shoulders wearily, certain she would be aloof—certain that explaining her mother's presence so close to him wasn't going to be easy.

And equally certain that no matter how distant and cool she tried to be, he'd warm her back to his side by nightfall. He had to.

Because he'd have to leave her by morning. Leave her, because, one way or the other, he was going to drag the truth out of someone.

CHAPTER EIGHT

Tracy didn't really know what she felt; or, rather, she didn't feel anything at all. A numbness settled over her while a rational voice warned her that there was certainly nothing between Leif and her mother. But it still bothered her deeply. They knew one another well and had known one another for years. Just what had been the subject of that secret conversation in which Leif had looked like a tiger, batting at cornered but protected prey, and her mother had appeared like a little temptress trying to wile her way out of . . . something?

For a moment she wished that a great hole would open up in the earth and swallow them all. But then she felt a quickening sensation sweep through her—something so strong that she paused, gripping the wall as she blindly headed toward the kitchen.

She was with Leif again—sharing his room, sharing his life—and though the obstacles before them were tremendous, she believed with all her heart that he cared for her.

And she knew that none of her memories were faulty. He was unique and special to her. The sight of his lean naked body, glowing and golden as he moved, stirred her, and when he came to her she really knew what love meant—what it meant to be held . . .

To be a woman, and have a man. To be loved.

She drew in a ragged breath and started walking again, drawn by the delicious smell of brewing coffee. She paused once she had entered the huge old colonial kitchen with its window loveseat, hanging racks of copper pots, and center butcher-block island. Katie was there, working cheerfully over the stove while she gave instructions to a gardener.

The man tipped his hat to Katie, nodded an acknowledgment to Tracy, and went on out back. Katie turned around and gave a brilliant smile, left her pot of simmering eggs, and poured Tracy a mug of coffee—black.

"Good morning! You're an early riser, too, so it seems, Miss Kuger."

"Too?" Tracy smiled back weakly, glad that Katie could be so natural to her—not as if she had never known her before, but as if nothing that had happened had been . . . humiliating. She was suddenly certain that Leif had forewarned Katie about the events now taking place—a wise move, since it enabled Katie to be perfectly natural about her appearance here, since she was supposedly "living with" Leif.

"Your brother's up—he's out in the parlor. Open the western door and you'll hear him!"

Tracy arched a brow and Katie laughed. "Go on through, dear. Breakfast will be ready in about thirty minutes—buffet style in the dining room, since people will be coming and going at different times."

Tracy thanked her and went on through the door that led to the front of the house. As soon as she opened the door, she heard Jamie. He was sitting at the piano, idly playing.

She came in and leaned against the shiny black Steinway, smiling at him. He returned her grin, but didn't speak at first. He sang out an old English pub ditty that

151

Tracy knew, too—one of her father's favorite old bawdy tunes.

Jamie patted the bench and scooted over. She set her coffee mug on a coaster and joined him. They didn't talk at all for a long time; one of them would start one of Jesse's old favorites, the other would join in.

" 'Danny Boy'!" Jamie said jubilantly, and Tracy laughed and joined him, loving the ivory keys as he did, loving the pulse, the excitement of creating melodious sound.

At last they stopped and stared at one another, and laughed again.

"He taught us both the same things."

"He taught you more. You lived with him—I never did," Tracy reminded him.

Jamie shrugged. "That's true, huh." He looked at her peculiarly for a moment. "You meant an awful lot to him, though, Tracy. He talked about you all the time. Why—why didn't you ever try to meet me before?"

She hesitated, thinking that it had all been a loss—and her fault. Then she tried to answer him honestly.

"Jamie, my life was mass confusion. I was always being tugged one way or another. When I was finally legally responsible for myself, I just wanted some peace, some time to sort things out. I liked working as a songwriter and I could support myself decently. I own a little townhouse in Zurich, and I have another small place up in northern Michigan. Maybe it was running away—but I really did value my freedom and my privacy. I should have made an effort to see you again, though. I'm sorry. Can you forgive me?"

He wrapped his arms around her and gave her a big hug. "As long as you don't disappear again, huh?"

152

"I didn't disappear. I met Dad all along—until he was killed."

Jamie nodded and started fingering the keys idly again. "You back with Leif for good?"

"I—I—"

"None of my business, I know. Hey—Blake!" he said suddenly.

Tracy followed his gaze and saw that Blake had come in and was staring at them, smiling a little shyly.

"Come on over here, my friend!" Jamie said.

Blake looked a little hesitantly at Tracy; she smiled her own encouragement to him, and that won him over. She lifted him up between herself and Jamie, and when she started to show him a scale, she was startled to see his little fingers move over the keys with a wonderful dexterity.

Bemused, Tracy stared at Jamie. "I forgot—the child is Leif's son." She looked back to Blake. "Did your dad teach you how to play the piano?"

"Some. And Jesse taught me some."

"Hey! And who else?" Jamie demanded.

"Oh, yeah, sorry. Jamie taught me, too."

Tracy laughed. "Well, I guess you've had teachers coming at you in all directions! Do you like the piano?"

"Yeah, I guess. I like the drums better, though."

"The boy is a symphony in himself," Jamie told her dryly, and Tracy thought she might well agree. "Let's all do a three-way 'Row, Row, Row Your Boat,'" Jamie suggested, and they did, playing the piano with a very strange accord in three different keys.

They made such a racket, of course, that some of the others joined them. Only when they finished and started laughing did Tracy turn to see that her mother, Leif, and Tiger had come into the room.

Tiger was chuckling, too—vastly enjoying the scene of the three of them together. "Now that's something I've never heard before!" he announced.

"You can hope that you never get to hear it again!" Jamie told him, grinning from ear to ear.

Tracy looked up at Leif; he wasn't smiling. He was staring at her as if he longed to wrench her from the bench, shake her—and demand an answer.

To what?

She didn't like the smoldering, dark, and somehow dangerous cast to his eyes; she glanced away—and was even more disturbed to meet her mother's glance.

Audrey was ashen—very, very pale and still.

"Mother?" she murmured. "Are you all right?"

"What?" Audrey seemed to shake herself out of a trance. "Oh, I'm fine. I was just listening. You all reminded me so much of Jesse then—" She broke off with an awkward little laugh. "Ah, well, the Kugers are at it again!"

She turned, as if she wanted to run out of the room.

Leif caught her arm, drawing her back around. Tracy suddenly felt very defensive—her mother appeared to be frightened. Leif was giving her a cold smile that chilled even Tracy, far away from his touch.

"The 'Kugers,' Audrey?" he inquired politely. "Blake is a Johnston."

Audrey pulled her arm away. "I was referring to Tracy and Jamie." She ran on into the kitchen, and Leif didn't stop her.

His speculative, dark smoke gaze fell on Tracy again, and she realized that she wanted to shake him and tell him that she was sick of his baiting her mother—and hanging her family, no matter what his denials.

She didn't shout, though—there were others in the

154

room. But everyone was suddenly silent, suddenly aware of the tension.

It was only broken when Katie peeked her head into the room. "Breakfast in the dining room, all. Help yourselves, and do enjoy!"

Katie disappeared. Jamie said that he was starving; he tickled Blake, then ducked down to let the little boy ride on his shoulders to the dining room.

Tracy found herself left alone in the room with Leif, and suddenly she didn't want to be there at all. He walked over to her slowly; she felt like bolting out of his reach, but then, too suddenly, he was there, touching her, his hands idly upon her shoulders, thumbs stroking her nape so that she was caught in the hypnotism of his touch.

She stiffened, wary of his effect on her. He was still in damp bathing trunks. She could feel his bare chest behind, breathe his subtle, masculine scent, and feel all the power in his muscled body as he towered over her. She wanted to turn and bury her head against his taut abdomen—she equally wanted to strike him for his ability to be cruel in his quest for the truth.

His fingers paused against her.

"Well, I'm glad you're not annoyed. I was afraid you were going to think that something had been going on."

"Oh, I do think that something was going on. I'm just not sure what—except that you're browbeating her over something, and I think you'd better stop—now."

His fingers tensed. For a second she felt their power and force, and her heart beat too quickly, because she knew that he could also be cold and totally implacable when he chose.

"It had better stop—now—Tracy?" he inquired coolly. Then he was suddenly down beside her, his face hard and

155

lacking all tenderness, just a breath away from hers, his fingers clamped around her wrists.

"No, Tracy, you be forewarned—now. I'm going to dig until I get the truth. And if I discover that you've lied to me again, Tracy, if you've kept anything from me, you'll very, very seriously regret it."

She tried to wrench from him; he wouldn't let her, pinning her as ruthlessly with his eyes as he did with his hands.

"Let me go!" she commanded harshly. "I'm out of this, Leif! You play out your charade alone! If I'm going to tell the truth, I might as well start with telling my mother! That you made this entire thing up. That we're not—"

"Sleeping together," he interrupted her, so mockingly and insinuatively that a hot flash seemed to burn like an inferno inside of her, rendering her suddenly breathless—and furious.

"Let—me—go!" she repeated. "I swear to you, I intend to leave this fiasco of yours!"

His fingers eased suddenly; he smiled at her and released her, standing.

"Maybe that is the best idea," he said agreeably, and stood. "Excuse me, will you? I think that I'll shower and dress. Oh—maybe you'll want to wait breakfast for me. I'm going to take my brutal browbeating against your poor aging and powerless grandfather in a matter of minutes."

He left her. Tracy saw that her hands were shaking; she knew that she would wait. She knew that she would be with him. She wanted to hear what he had to say to her grandfather. And yes, she wanted to be ready to jump to his defense.

She gazed at her fingers. They still trembled like leaves

in the wind. She slammed a hand against the piano. "I hate you, Leif! Honest to God, I hate you!" she whispered.

But when he had been next to her, she had wanted to touch his chest. Curl her fingers into the hair there, feel his muscles ripple beneath her touch. She'd been with him; they'd made love. And it only made the yearning greater. To know him again, feel his hands on her, his lips, his . . . body. Moving in hers, with hers . . .

She let out a strangled little sound and leapt to her feet. She would not be sleeping with the man again!

She stalked on into the dining room, attempting desperately to smile with all negligent ease.

Leif was right back and to Tracy's surprise, he wasn't dressed at all for a casual day with guests in his own home. He was in a light, attractively tailored suit, complete with tie and vest. Very striking, very arresting.

He smelled of soap and after-shave and was completely compelling when he came upon Tracy at the buffet table, catching her elbow, steering her out through the glassed-in family room to the patio and pool beyond.

"Leif, I don't want—"

"Oh, but you do. Arthur is sipping decaf and munching on an English muffin right under the umbrella with your stepfather. We'll have a lovely breakfast."

"Lovely. I mean it, Leif. You watch your step or I'm out of here!"

He gazed at her with innocent surprise and something dangerous sizzling behind it.

"That's right. You're going to deny—us."

"I should, yes."

"Ah, but then I could be stunned and hurt and graphically describe the occurrence in question not twenty-four hours ago."

"Do what you like, Leif," she said coolly. But she was no longer tugging against his hold. He knew it; she knew it. He was smiling, she was stiff.

"Gentlemen, may we join you?" Leif inquired politely of the two men at the wrought-iron table.

"Please do," Ted said cheerfully. But Tracy thought that her stepfather seemed uncomfortable, too. Arthur muttered something to Leif and gave Tracy a very stiff good morning.

In the next ten minutes, Tracy felt herself foolishly lulled into a belief that Leif did intend to be pleasant. He discussed the weather, Jamie's concert—and asked polite questions about Tracy's baby half brother, Ted's pride and joy.

But then he finished with his food, sat back, and lit a cigarette. And cast an affectionate and possessive arm around the rear of Tracy's chair, idly rubbing her neck with his fingers, as a lover might do.

Tracy reddened; to throw off that touch would be very obvious. After all, there was nothing wrong with it. It was casual, not a public display.

She didn't have time to think about it long; Leif struck then with his trump card, a tight smile still on his lips.

"Arthur, I understand that you and Jesse had quite a row just before he was killed. I was just mentioning it to Tracy—out of idle curiosity, you know. What on earth did you two find to argue about twenty-something years after the fact?"

For a moment, she was afraid that her indomitable grandfather was about to have a heart attack.

"Leif!" she cried out in stricken reproach, rushing

around to Arthur's chair, kneeling down beside him. "Grandpa—"

But he didn't notice her. He waved her away, white and ashen, staring at Leif much as her mother had done before. And he seemed frightened—angry, but frightened. She gazed at Leif's face and saw the merciless expression in his eyes.

"Who the hell ever told you that Jesse Kuger and I had a row over anything?" Arthur Kingsley demanded.

Leif smiled, and it was a smile more threatening than any scowl Tracy had ever seen.

"His secretary mentioned it to me. I was curious—I didn't know that you and Jesse had seen each other recently. Not since the day you came here and dragged Tracy away after knocking me out."

"Please, must we—" Ted began.

"Leif," Arthur interrupted coolly, "I probably shouldn't have struck you with the bat. You've just got a lethal strength; you were a jungle fighter—Jesse never was. Granted, he attacked you. But you could have killed him. None of us had any idea that you didn't know Tracy was Jesse's daughter—or that she was a runaway child. We didn't know that she had duped you and lied."

"Grandfather! Stop discussing me as if I weren't here!" Tracy snapped, outraged—and humiliated all over again by the easy way these two were talking about her life.

She saw her stepfather's eyes. He had always understood—so much better than those who should have. "Really, both of you," Ted said smoothly. "That was all so long ago."

"Yes, it was." Leif stood. "Sorry, Arthur. I didn't mean to upset you—I was curious."

"Leave the past alone, why don't you, Leif?" Arthur demanded.

Leif shrugged and started around the table. Tracy was astounded that her grandfather actually appeared to flinch.

Leif paused, arching a brow. "More coffee, Arthur?"

"No, no!" Arthur Kingsley rose, too, a tall man, still robust for his age. "Excuse me, I've some calls to make. May I use your office, Leif?"

"Of course."

Arthur hurried toward the house. Leif stared at Tracy with his puzzling, wary scrutiny, then started after him. He paused.

Tracy sank back into her chair—exhausted. "What is he after?" she whispered, unaware she had asked her stepfather the question.

Ted reached across the table and squeezed her hand. "Honey, you should know. I mean—sorry—never mind." He stood then, too. "I think I'm going to take the car out for a spin. Want to come?"

She smiled up at him. "Sounds heavenly! Let's go!"

They avoided the others and slipped out of the house. Tracy hoped grimly that Leif would worry over whether or not she had really deserted him. But even as she laughed and chatted with her stepfather, she knew that he wouldn't worry in the least. He would know that she would be back.

They stopped at a little country inn for lunch, and Ted showed Tracy all the pictures of her little baby half brother. She enjoyed them and vowed that she would spend more time with Anthony. She loved him—he'd been a darling, darling baby. It was just that she couldn't spend too much time near any of them. They were incapable of loving her without smothering her.

Tracy and Ted didn't get back to the house until three in the afternoon. Katie let them in and informed them that two Mrs. Kugers were in the parlor—Jamie's mother, Carol, and Jesse's widow, Lauren.

Tracy wished she could run up the stairs and ignore them both. She sighed, aware that she couldn't be so rude, especially because of Jamie. He'd been very polite to her mother—she owed him the same courtesy.

"Let's go say hello, shall we?" she suggested cheerfully to Ted.

"I wouldn't miss it," he said. He seemed amused.

Tracy poked him in the ribs. "And what are you grinning about?" she demanded.

He lowered his voice. "All the cats are here. I'm willing to bet that there will be all kinds of hissing and clawing before this little party of Leif's comes to an end!"

"With two Mrs. Kugers, I guess so," Tracy agreed.

"Two Mrs. Kugers, and your mother," Ted said softly.

She glanced at him sharply and saw that his expression was a little sad. Tracy suddenly hoped fervently that he didn't know his wife of twenty-six years had cheated on him through many of those years with the father of her illegitimate child.

They were at the foyer entrance to the parlor. Tracy saw only Tiger and Sam, Jamie, and Lauren and Carol in the room. There was no sign of her mother—or Leif, for that matter. A little flutter touched her heart, and to her vast dismay, she realized that she was upset that Leif wasn't there, ready to rush over to her and demand to know in breathless tones where she had been.

"Tracy! There you are. Mum—didn't I tell you that she grew up to be absolutely gorgeous!" Jamie walked over to her.

Tracy stepped into the room, accepting Carol Kuger's hand as Carol stood to greet her, her smile only slightly stiff.

"Tracy, dear, how are you? I'm so glad that you and Jamie have gotten together. How nice, for you both."

Carol was a pretty woman, very tall and slim. She hadn't Audrey's startling allure, but she was nevertheless very attractive, and at the moment she sounded sincere. Maybe that was because Jesse was gone. Perhaps to Carol's way of seeing things there was no longer any reason to resent Tracy.

"Carol, it's nice to see you. And yes, I think that it's been wonderful to get to know Jamie!"

Carol smiled deeply at the praise.

Tracy turned around quickly to greet her father's widow, Lauren. Lauren was only a few years older than she was. They knew each other very little, because once she had grown up, Tracy had met Jesse away from his home life when they had seen one another. But once she'd had dinner at their house, and once Lauren had come along to lunch.

She was very slim and very nervous, with pansy blue, nearly violet eyes. She'd been a high-fashion model when she met Jesse. She had been totally dependent on Jesse—jealous even of his music.

But then, she had very little to worry about now. Jesse's death had left her rather incredibly well off.

"Lauren, how are you."

"Well enough, thanks, Tracy." She smiled uneasily, sat again, and hastily lit a cigarette taken from an ivory box on the table.

Jamie was quick to offer her a light, then quick to introduce Ted to Lauren.

"We met. At Jesse's funeral," Ted said, but he smiled at Lauren and sat beside her, and Tracy was somewhat bemused, because her stepfather's easy manner seemed to have a settling affect on even Lauren.

"How strange that we're all here!" Lauren said, studying the smoke from her cigarette. "Frankly, I was glad of Leif's invitation." She smiled again, and Tracy thought with a little unease that she was dazzling when she chose to be. "I've been so utterly disoriented and lost and lonely since Jesse that—well, even though I thought that a house party was a strange prelude to a memorial service, I was just thrilled. To see Tiger and Sam again, and of course, Leif. It really is so nice for us all to get together. Nice to see each other, nice to talk, nice to remember Jesse. But leave it to Leif." She offered Tracy a strange smile. "Leif is always so—thoughtful."

Thoughtful, hmm, Tracy thought. Yes, Lauren was young and Lauren was beautiful. And with that fragile-lovely-helplessly-feminine smile she was making a definite statement to Tracy.

Lauren was on the prowl again. And she was after Leif.

"Where is Leif?" Tracy tried to ask casually.

"Oh, he took your mother for a ride out to a new restaurant that just opened—she wanted to see the decor. It had been written up in one of those architectural magazines she's always been so crazy about," Tiger told Tracy.

He sounded cheerful. It seemed that even Tiger was looking at her strangely, though. Pityingly. Was she becoming absurdly paranoid?

Maybe, maybe not. But though Ted kept smiling, too, Tracy thought that he wasn't terribly happy about the situation either.

"I imagine they'll be back shortly. Leif said something about dressing for drinks at seven and dinner at eight," Carol told her.

163

"He was looking for you," Jamie said suddenly.

Tracy glanced across the room at her brother. He was staring at her hard, trying to tell her something. She smiled, because Jamie could be so darn loyal. He was trying to tell her with his blue eyes, so like her father's, so like her own, that Leif hadn't walked away from her—that he'd wanted to see her, that whatever he was doing with her mother, it was entirely innocent.

Oh, Jamie! she thought wistfully. You are wrong! There is nothing innocent about that man whatsoever! He is more dangerous than a cage full of lions.

She didn't say anything, of course. She smiled.

Then she sat back, because the "cats," as Ted had termed the two Mrs. Kugers, were at it. Subtly, of course. Talking about Jesse. Remembering him. Lauren claiming to have known him best, sweetly, of course. Carol smiling just as sweetly and saying, "But, Lauren, dear, we all heard that you were planning a divorce!"

"Who told you that!" Lauren demanded, flushing.

"Why, Jesse did, of course," Carol said, plucking her olive from her martini and smiling with a guise of understanding. "Well, he had to call me now and then, dear. We had Jamie's future to discuss, you know."

Tracy decided that she had listened to all that she could. She excused herself, saying that the drive had made her sleepy and that she was about to take a shower and a nap.

Lauren stopped her before she could leave. "I hear that you and Leif are a twosome, Tracy. How extraordinary! Are any congratulations in order?"

"I beg your pardon?" Tracy said, narrowing her eyes with a frown.

Lauren gave her a throaty laugh. "Are you going to

run off and elope or anything like that? Or, better yet, plan a huge wedding?"

"At the moment, Lauren, we haven't planned anything," Tracy managed to say evenly.

"Good," Lauren said, waiting just a second too long to add, "I wouldn't want to have missed anything." She grinned at Tracy, then very quickly lowered her exquisite violet eyes. She inhaled and exhaled, then looked at Tracy again. "He's such a striking man. The two of you must be beautiful together. If you were only a bit taller, Tracy, they could vote you one of the ten handsomest couples in the world."

"Umm. Thanks, Lauren." Taller, Lauren? As tall as you are?

She tried to smile, but all she could do was wonder with a horrible ache how she had ever wound up in all of this—in the tangle of Jesse's life, her mother's life—even her grandfather's life. She, with all her simple dreams of one love, one commitment. Partnership to last forever.

Leif is not like my father! she cried inwardly. No, a voice replied. Jesse was never merciless, never brutal. Never so determined, never so implacable.

Tracy waved to all of them and walked away. Upstairs, she sighed, hating herself as she hesitated with her hand on Leif's door. Jealous of her mother, jealous of Lauren. She wasn't doing well at all. She wanted to strangle Leif, but . . .

But she didn't want Lauren to have him, or her mother —or any other woman. She swallowed hard and leaned her forehead against the cool wood of the door.

There was nothing going on between Leif and her mother. Yes, there was.

But not sexual! Tracy swore to herself. Really!

165

And Lauren? Lauren had just gotten here. Lauren had been married to Jesse. Lauren was not going to remain a grieving widow all her life. She liked action and excitement and publicity, and she might very well be here simply because . . .

Well, there were three surviving members of the Limelights. Apparently, Lauren had missed them all.

Especially Leif?

She closed her eyes tightly and decided she wasn't going to think about it anymore. Not now.

Tracy pushed open the door. She took a long shower. She found aspirin in Leif's medicine chest and took two. With her towel still wrapped around her, she came out into the bedroom and stared at his bed.

I should leave, she told herself. Carry through and leave—now. Let him grill the people that I love all by himself. She came over and sat on the bed, telling herself that she shouldn't be there—conveniently—for him when he returned. Her head was aching; she lay down. She stared up at the ceiling and she knew she wasn't going to leave. She didn't trust Leif, and yet she did trust him. She believed that he cared.

Then why had he gone out for a four-hour lunch with her mother?

She knew him; she had to believe in him. Un-unh. She didn't really know him at all. How much of Leif had she ever really had? A month, once, years ago. And now—just a matter of days.

Tracy sighed and curled up, hugging a pillow as she closed her eyes and willed the thunder in her temple to cease.

Maybe she should leave, but she wasn't going to. She would be there to stand against him in this raging battle that he had going against her mother and her grandfather.

And she would be there, too, because she simply couldn't let him go. Not without learning if what they shared could be forever. If it could really be love.

CHAPTER NINE

It wasn't that he didn't desperately want to know which of the "loving" survivors had hated Jesse so coldly that he or she had hired a killer to take him out. He did. It was a fever inside of him; the last thing that he owed a friend of a quarter of a century.

There was just another obsession driving his life, too. A personal obsession—and he had to know the truth. Strangely, he felt, too, that if he solved the one mystery, he would solve the other also.

And Audrey was simply the easiest prey.

It hadn't been at all difficult to get her to go out with him; he had expected a struggle. But just as she was an excellent seductress, she made an easy mark for a seducer. And another point stood in his favor—they had known one another for years. Sporadically, as enemies, as friends—as two people very closely involved with Jesse.

He'd found her alone in the parlor, leaning against the window and holding back the drape—and staring outside, where Blake played in the paved circle behind the driveway on his bike.

"Audrey."

Startled, she turned back to him, nervously smiling, allowing the drapes to fall back into place.

"I'm sorry."

"So am I. We shouldn't fight. We've been friends a long, long time."

"Friends," she murmured. "I doubt if you thought that I was much of a friend once."

He grinned and lifted his hands, palms upward. "That was the past, Audrey. We should let it lie. It's over."

"I don't think we can ever escape the past, Leif."

"Not escape it, Audrey. Just live with it."

She stood very still, gazing at him again. And even if she didn't really trust him, it just wasn't in Audrey to leave a man alone. Not that she was really promiscuous; she just liked to flirt.

She came over to him, skinny heels against the tile of the floor. "Leif, you look good enough to eat. Oh—that sounded, uh, indecent, didn't it?" She ran her fingers over his tie, making an unnecessary adjustment. Then she stepped back and sighed softly. "I swear, Leif," she sighed softly, "Leif, you are a striking man. As striking as—"

She paused, and he didn't fill in the name for her. They both knew she was thinking of Jesse, and despite himself, Leif felt a tenderness for her creep over him. Audrey had really loved Jesse. She'd just never had the strength to fight her father.

"Jesse's gone, Audrey," he said very softly.

"Yes, he is." She looked sadly up at Leif. "I sound terrible, don't I? Ted is a wonderful husband. Still, I can't quite accept a world without Jesse in it."

"Neither can I."

He reached out a hand to her. She came against his chest, and he smoothed back her hair. They both broke away.

"Thanks, Leif."

"I've got an idea, Audrey. Let's both escape this for a

little while. There's a wonderful new place that opened. Are you still heavily into those design magazines? This one was featured on last month's cover. It's a wonderful place."

"I would like to get out of here . . ."

And so he had found Liz, to tell her where he was going and to ask her to see that his other guests were taken care of. And on the way out, he had called Blake over, giving him a big hug and promising to play ball with him later. And he had watched Audrey waiting for him while he talked to his son.

At the restaurant he had ordered wine right away. He'd seen to it that they consumed quite a bit before ordering. They laughed and talked about silly things in the past. And only when she was completely at ease and their meal completed did he lean back and smile, sadly, bitterly.

"How can you do it, Audrey?"

"What—what are you talking about?" she asked, moistening her lips, instantly on the defensive.

He leaned toward her, casually resting his elbows on the table, but capturing her gaze as if his own eyes were spears.

"Ignore your own grandson. Lie." He sat back, lifting his palms in an irritated and baffled manner. "Why did you do it?"

Her eyes lowered. She tossed her napkin on the table.

"Really, Leif—"

"Yes, really, Audrey. It took me years to be suspicious. But here I am, married to Celia. And you knew why Celia had left me, because when she came back, I told Jesse, and Jesse told you."

"I don't know what you're talking about."

"Yes, you do, Audrey. You could come into my house

170

with Jesse and your father because Katie would never have thought to stop you. You had the law behind you—and my own sense of guilt!—when you immobilized me and spirited Tracy away. But you had no right—none!—to keep from me the fact that Tracy was pregnant."

Audrey wouldn't meet his eyes. She was breathing too quickly, grasping at her wineglass and sipping quickly.

"Let me go on. Celia walked out on me because she knew about her heart—she knew she could never have children. I told her that I loved her, not her procreation capabilities. And the next thing I know, old Arthur Kingsley is calling me with an apology for the way things went, telling me that Tracy is in the west going to school and never wants to see my face again, and he's really sorry about trying to cave my head in. He's heard about Celia, and he's real sorry, but you know, money talks, maybe he can help. The next thing I know, Celia and I are both thrilled to death because, thanks to Arthur, we won't have to wait on a list for years and years to adopt an infant—Arthur knows of a young Swiss girl who wants to give her baby up for adoption."

Audrey was shaking her head. "You're crazy!" she told him.

He found her hand on the table. He wound his fingers tightly around hers, drawing her eyes to his again.

"Tracy was pregnant, wasn't she, Audrey? I adopted my own son!"

"No!"

"Audrey!"

"No!"

"There's a little grave in a cemetery just outside of Zurich, isn't there, Audrey. It reads, 'J. Kingsley.' But if I went there, Audrey, the grave would be empty, wouldn't it?"

"No. I don't know. Leif—leave me—"

"I am going there, Audrey."

"All right! All right!" she screamed suddenly. "Yes! Blake is your son, your biological son!"

"How could you—"

"Easily! Very easily, Leif! Because you're just like Jesse. He ignored her all her life. He ignored me—he made promises he didn't keep. Anywhere you went, women were ready to climb into bed with you. I didn't want that for her. Can't you see—can't you understand? My God, if it hadn't been for Tracy, I might have been able to cut it off! I might not have had to see Jesse again and again and—"

Her voice just paled away. He was sorry for her, but he couldn't let up.

He took a deep breath. "Did—did Tracy know?"

For the first time that day Audrey actually misunderstood him. She started laughing, hollowly—a sound that was so painful it might have been a cry.

"Of course she knew."

Men! What did he think—that Tracy had spent nine miserable months of pregnancy and not known it?

She was startled, the near hysterical laughter catching in her throat, when he pushed his chair back so violently that the legs rasped against the floor, like the nerve-jangling sound of nails scratching down a blackboard. Audrey stared at him and swallowed sharply and just caught herself from screaming out as he clenched her arm, practically dragging her from the chair, his mouth a line as tight as wire, the violence of his temper barely held in check.

"Leif, what—where—please—"

"We're just going back to the house, Audrey, that's all."

172

"What are you going to do?" she asked, shivering and watching the thunder in his dark eyes.

"I don't know yet."

"Leif, you're—hurting my arm!" Audrey gasped. He didn't hear her. They just kept going until they reached his car and he packed her into it, slamming the door when she tried to speak again.

Leif folded his length into the driver's seat and revved the engine; Audrey's heart beat like a pummeling drum.

"Leif, please, let me speak to her—"

The engine went dead as he whipped around to talk to her. He didn't touch her, but the quaking power held check in his body brought her instantly to silence.

"Audrey—don't interfere. You step into my affairs again, and I promise, I'll step into yours. This is between Tracy and me now."

"Leif—"

"Shut up, Audrey."

She did. When the Jag chortled and then purred into the driveway, she was desperate to escape it.

"I've a horrible headache," she told Leif sullenly. "I won't be down to dinner."

Then she fled toward the house.

Blake came running past her. She stared at him and gasped out something, then disappeared.

"Can we play ball now, Dad?" Blake asked Leif, pitching himself happily into his father's arms.

"Yeah, sure, son. Can you give me about half an hour, though. I have to change clothes and talk to—talk to Tracy for a minute."

Blake nodded happily. "Maybe Tracy will want to play, too!"

Leif shook his head slowly. "Not tonight, son. Maybe

another time." He smiled. "Wait for me. I won't be long."

He started up to the house, then changed his mind and walked around to come in the back; he was in no mood to run into any of his guests.

He was about to head silently for the stairs when he changed his mind and slipped into his office instead.

Leif picked up the phone receiver on his desk and noted that his hands were still shaking. He clenched them tightly; they still shook. Grinding his teeth together, he dialed Rob's number. When Rob answered, he was quick and to the point.

"Don't wait for me at Kennedy; meet me in Zurich, at the Zweikel Inn."

"Sure. You're going to take your private plane? That big jet for one person?"

"Yes. Except that there will be two of us."

The good thing about Rob was that he never asked unnecessary questions.

"Fine. I'll find you."

Rob hung up. Leif called the hangar and made sure that his pilot and crew were available and that his 727— used for years for group tours—wasn't out on a charity mission. He never paid much attention to the scheduling of its use since it had been customarily idle for a long time.

There was no difficulty; the plane was in and it could be overhauled and serviced by morning.

He hung up the receiver again and saw that his hands still trembled. He stared at them, willing them to be still.

Then he quietly closed the door to his office and walked around back to enter his room by the deck stairs. He didn't want to see anyone yet. No one but Tracy.

* * *

She was half asleep when she sensed him in the doorway, framed by the slightly billowing drapes. Shivers penetrated the fog-swept clouds of her subconscious, warning her of danger at first. She rolled, not quite awake, her lashes rising and falling.

Rising, falling. There was no danger; it was Leif in the doorway. But she hugged her pillow to her because the sensation did not go away. He stood there for endless seconds, tall, his shadow cast across the room.

And then he moved.

Coming casually through the archway, his eyes swept over her form, naked beneath the terry towel haphazardly wrapped around her. She wanted to speak; she wanted to demand to know where he had been with Audrey so long.

She couldn't form words. The sensation of danger still tripped along her spine—icy little rivulets that had her silent and still. He, too, was silent. She clutched her towel to her instinctively. She fought the grogginess of sleep and confusion. She should be accusing him—and demanding answers. He stared at her with searing charcoal eyes that convicted and condemned . . .

And still she couldn't speak. She could only stare at him. At the startling male image he created in the tailored suit, the broad appeal of his shoulders, the way the material encased powerful thighs and enhanced the trimness of his physique. The way he moved within it. Dark hair, dark eyes, a grim smile slashed against the uncompromising line of his jaw.

He sat on the edge of the bed, his eyes never leaving hers. He brought a hand to his collar, discarding his tie. Something in his look disturbed her further. Something in his eyes, in the ruthless cast of his jaw, in the way his

175

shoulders seemed even broader as he doffed his jacket and tossed it over the foot of the bed. Something about him spoke of a raw and powerful masculinity that excited her even as it frightened.

And something was wrong. All wrong.

Tracy gave herself a mental shake with confused desperation. He hadn't said anything; he hadn't really done anything. He had just come upon her and . . .

She should be asking questions—not feeling that a trap was settling around her. That she should run, because an overwhelming danger was hard set upon her.

He touched her cheek, as if fascinated. His fingers were cold; his voice was light.

"You really are so exquisite. In my life, I have never seen bluer eyes. Felt softer skin. Seen lips so red, so lush, so formed to riddle a man with the desire to touch."

He traced her mouth with a calloused thumb as he spoke, his touch, the sound of his voice, hypnotic—dangerously so, for she narrowed her eyes in wariness, yet realized she could not run. His weight was upon her towel.

"Leif—"

She breathed out his name in a question that he did not answer. He smiled, and tugged at her towel. She held it closer, but to little avail, for he lowered his head over hers and took her lips with his own, gently. The tip of his tongue tracing her mouth then, sliding over her teeth, subtly penetrating past them, exploding into passion. She whimpered slightly; the sensation was instantaneous, as if his kiss were a font, pouring into her, instilling her body with a fevered heat that cast it into a liquid pool of arousal. She thought that she should fight him; logic so warned her. But logic was all too easily swept away. She brought her hands against his chest; she felt the roughness of his vest, and the heat and power of his flesh beneath. He didn't note her futile attempt to push him away; he swept the towel from her, settling his weight over her naked body as he held her head between his palms and drew his lips from hers to stare down into her eyes.

"So damned lovely," he told her.

"Leif," she found the will to whisper, "what is the matter with you?"

"What could possibly be the matter?" he returned, his stare so intent upon her, his body so hard that she quivered, longing to break the spell cast between them, to shake him into some kind of truth.

She tried to twist from beneath him; it was futile. He smiled as if she'd made no motion at all and shifted just slightly to avail himself of her form.

"Life—and love. So fascinating, Tracy," he murmured. His fingers traveled her cheek, stroked her throat and over her breast. "I remember it so well. That first time. The way you moved, the way you walked. The way you shed your clothing before me. I trembled, watching you; I felt like steel, I felt like silver. I thought, 'My God, I've never seen more beautiful breasts.' "

His strokes, soft, gentle, highly erotic, moved with his words. His eyes followed his touch. His fingers moved her, then his palm. He cupped the weight of her breast, then paused to dampen the nipple with his tongue and watched with fascination as he grazed it next with his thumb, over and over, fascinated as the bud tautened and peaked. A sound escaped Tracy, a strangling sound. Her body burned, and she could not bear it. She was painfully aware that her flesh betrayed her at every step. And she didn't understand him at all. She didn't understand his silky words, the hardness of his eyes, or the unwavering way he touched her—gently, but with fingers that trembled like a tide held back—a volatile dam that quivered, ready to burst. He spoke of love, but something there was savage. Something wasn't right.

"Leif!" She gasped out his name that time, slamming a fist against his chest, near sobbing in bewilderment. She wanted him; she was afraid of him. She didn't want him touching her anymore because she would give in to him —and somehow, it was wrong.

She might not have used the slightest force against him. He caught her hand and studied it. "So tiny a woman, such elegantly long fingers. Long fingers, long legs. Beautiful long legs. I will never, never forget the way you came to me. Liquid grace, and I longed for you to pour all of yourself over me, into me. Just from that, from the way you moved, I knew. I knew that you would be an extraordinary lover, sexual and sensual. I never trembled so over any other woman. I could not wait to touch you, to feel you, bask in your scent, taste the silk of your flesh . . ."

He kissed her fingertips, taking them into his mouth, sucking them, releasing them one by one. Tracy stared at him, caught in the sensuality of his touch, feeling again the fire that spread from her hand to her womb, that permeated through her.

She drew a ragged breath. "Leif—wait—"

He lowered his head to her. He touched her lips briefly, her throat. He caressed her breast with his hand and brought his mouth to it, and she gasped again with the chemistry, with the savage streak of desire that soared through her.

No . . .

But she was in love with him. She wanted to believe the tenderness, the silk and fever of his voice. And the heat inside of her could not be quelled. Her fingers curled into his hair; her body arched against his. He used his mouth evocatively against her breast while his hand stoked downward, over her hips, along the length of her thigh. Again and again, so light, she craved for more. Hungered.

"Tracy . . ."

He whispered her name against her flesh, nuzzling her belly, taunting her naval with the tip of his tongue. Softly breathing, barely touching, lower and lower.

"I never suspected, never remotely imagined, that you could be a virgin. That it was maiden territory I transversed, I adored, revered, worshiped. You were so good—such a damned good actress, so beautiful."

His lips hot and passionate, seared her flesh. She cried out softly, oblivious to his words—only aware that she loved his touch, his dark head, the feel of his hair beneath her fingertips . . .

The pulsing hardness of him as he held her, still clad, still blatantly male.

"You smell good, you taste good, you are beautiful," he said, harshly, and rose up again, bracing his hands on either side of her, staring down at her again.

And she was. Hair feathered about her beautiful features, her eyes so incredibly blue and wide and sensually glazed upon his. How could you remember a woman so thoroughly! he raged to himself in an agonized silence. Remember a beauty that drove him mad, a movement, a whisper; eyes—endless azure seas of innocence and desire.

Innocence . . .

She had lied to him. She was still lying, still lying . . .

It didn't matter. Her lips were curled into the softest smile, parted slightly, the breath coming so quickly from her. Her fingers were anxiously on the buttons of his vest, and he took the task from her, ripping the garment from his body. She parted his shirt and tiny kisses fell on his chest—tender little bites that aroused him to fury. He crushed her against him, not bothering with the cuff links at his wrist or any other hindrance. She fumbled with his belt buckle. That, too, he dismissed for her, planting his length firmly between her thighs and melding into her with a swift and sudden plunge that stole both their breaths away, rocking with the vehemence and wonder, one at last.

He buried his head against her shoulder, feeling that he filled her with every inch of him—body, mind and soul— that he had never wanted a woman so badly, that no other woman had ever held him as this one. Her body a velvet blanket, her arms bars of silk that wound around him.

She'd used him once; God alone knew what she was doing now.

Still lying . . .

He raised himself and stared down and smiled slowly, bitterly. He saw the hurt in her eyes, the sudden mistrust, and knew that she was about to clamp her hands on his shoulders to escape him.

He caught her shoulder, and held her to him, and began to move. And he saw the fire catch hold in her eyes again, heard the soft gasp that assured him sensation moved her. He moved—with urgency, with love. He could never escape her. If he filled her enough with himself, perhaps he could hold her. Perhaps she could never escape him.

He closed his eyes. His palms closed around her buttocks and he lifted her and whispered to her and brought her ever closer to him. Tremors shook her body, damp-

180

ness sleeked it; he heard the gasp and cry that escaped her, and he thrust into her one last time, seeking his own release, pouring into her.

They lay silent, gasping. He rolled from her then, pulling a pillow behind his head, leaning against it and lighting a cigarette. Staring at the ceiling, then into space—waiting for her questions to start.

They did come. More slowly than he would have expected. She didn't look at him; she wrenched the top sheet from the bed and wandered to the window, staring out with her back to him.

"Leif! Damn it! What is it?" she raged suddenly, swinging back around.

She was beautiful. So beautiful. Soft, silken strands of hair falling about her in a fan, her eyes so deep and blue with passion. Quivery, tousled, she had just left his bed, just left his touch; her flesh still glowed.

He'd been duped before. Badly. Lies had fallen off her tongue like rain off the eaves.

Tracy was lost; totally lost. He just sat on the bed, comfortably relaxed, watching her. His shirt remained opened, the tails falling low, but with the deep tan breadth of his chest still visable. He'd adjusted his zipper and belt, and idly inhaled and exhaled, without once breaking contact with her eyes. He looked wonderful there, hair tousled and shirt open, rugged and virile and striking as ever, and she thought that she should be feeling a comfort that they had come together so easily after so much time. That he had cared, still cared. That maybe the time was right now, and maybe they had a future.

But she didn't feel comfortable at all. She felt acutely uneasy at the fact that he had not disrobed and she was in nothing but a towel, making her vulnerable.

She stiffened suddenly. Once, she had set out to seduce

him for seduction's sake. But now, if that was all that she was to him—a quick, easy sexual encounter—she didn't think that she could bear it. Or the fact that she did come to him so very, very easily. There was just something there with Leif. And seeing him again had fed all the flames. Of the men she had met in life, he was the one whose smile alone could arouse her desires, whose kiss could render her so totally vulnerable. Of all the men in the world, why Leif?

"Why were you with my mother?" She almost screamed the words.

He frowned, then he smiled, shaking his head with bemusement.

"Tracy, I think I know what you're thinking, and you're crazy. Rest assured—it was not a romantic interlude. I thought you would know that."

She swallowed, believing him—or desperate to believe him. If she were honestly to think that he had run from her mother to her, she would hate him for the rest of her life.

"Then what—"

A gray shield fell over his eyes; she broke off, knowing that no matter what she asked, he would not answer.

"Tracy, we went to lunch, for God's sake. We're friends, nothing more."

She shook her head, approaching the bed with new determination.

"What was the matter with you then!"

He crushed out the cigarette and in a sudden movement caught her arm, pulling her back down beneath him.

"What was the matter with what? Did I hurt you?"

"No."

He kept staring at her so intently. She closed her eyes

182

and leaned her face against his chest. Suddenly, she didn't want to know anything.

Slowly he rolled away from her. He went to his drawer and she heard him pulling out new clothing. "I promised Blake I'd play ball with him for a while."

A second later, he was staring down at her again.

She met his gaze. "You're trying to accuse my mother of my father's murder, aren't you?"

He smiled again, then shook his head. The smile faded, and those deadly gray eyes seemed to sear through her again. "No, Tracy. I'm not after your mother—not any more than I'm after anyone else."

He turned away. He disappeared into the bathroom, then returned a few moments later, showered and changed into a denim shirt and jeans.

"I've a surprise for you in the morning."

"Oh?"

He smiled. She still didn't trust his eyes.

"What is it?"

"You'll see in the morning."

He came over and brushed her lips with a kiss. An easy smile returned to his features. His eyes remained conversely cold and probing.

"Come out if you want to. Blake asked me if you'd come out and play with him."

She nodded, wondering what he looked for deep inside of her.

"I'll, uh, probably be out in a minute."

He straightened and walked to the door. Once he was there, he paused, his hand on the knob, his back to her.

"Tracy?"

"What?"

He turned around and faced her again, his words giving no hint of emotion other than mild interest.

"Are you taking precautions—this time?"

"What?"

It wasn't the question; it was rather an intelligent concern between consenting adults. It was the last two words. It was the sudden and total shock of it. It was the memories.

She knew that she went pale. She knew that her eyes widened and that her lashes then fell in a flash. Her fingers curled into the sheet, and she felt that she was sinking deeper and deeper into some kind of quicksand, and she didn't understand it all.

"Yes!" she snapped out. "You haven't anything to worry about."

"I never did, did I?" he inquired, and there was a grate to it.

"My Lord! What is your problem? Don't—don't worry about it!"

He was silent for a second. "That's just the point, Tracy. I like the right to worry about things. I can't just pass my responsibilities over to others."

"What are you talking about now?" she cried, staring at him.

He shook his head.

"Oh, leave me alone, will you! We can solve it all easily. I'll just stay away from you."

He chuckled softly. "Oh. You'll refuse to sleep with me?"

She gazed at him sharply and the simmering arrogance in his eyes sent hostility racing through her. "I mean it, Leif!"

He lifted his hands innocently. "Tracy, as long as it is yourself that you are suiting, do what you wish."

She threw the pillow across the room in a convulsive

rush of fury. "You're such an egotist! You think that I can't stay away from you!"

He was silent for several seconds, then the slow smile that touched his sensual lips had a rueful and tender touch to it.

"I don't know. I do know that I can't stay away from you—though God knows I should."

She sighed, her fingers still quivering and clenched into the sheets, a rampant little drumbeat controlling her heart. She probably couldn't stay away from him. But what kind of a fool was she? He was definitely on the prowl for something, and he was definitely dangerous when he chose to be. When he chose to be . . .

He came back to the bed one last time. He lifted her chin and looked into her eyes, his own a dark enigma. "Are you coming out?"

"I—probably."

He kissed her lips with a strange, aching tenderness.

When he looked at her again, though he smiled, she had the awful feeling that he was just waiting to slip a rope around her neck.

"See you downstairs—with Blake."

He opened the door and left, closing it quietly behind him.

Tracy threw the second pillow across the room. She needed to be wary of him—so wary!

It was so hard to be wary when you were falling in love. When you were in love. When his smile, when his touch, were fire.

"Oh, damn you! What are you after?" she cried out loud.

And then she fell silent, shivering again. *Are you taking precautions—this time.* As if he knew that she hadn't the last!

She shook her head, swallowing painfully. What difference did it make now? Her infant was dead and buried years and years ago and there was no sense in telling him now.

No sense whatever.

CHAPTER TEN

Just as she was exiting Leif's room, Audrey came hurrying past her, heading for the stairs like a runaway train.

"Mother!" Tracy grasped Audrey's arm; Audrey nearly brought Tracy crashing down in her headlong flight. They righted one another, then Audrey stared at Tracy with the greatest dismay.

"Tracy!"

"Mother, I want to talk to you," Tracy said firmly. "What is going on between you and Leif?"

Audrey gasped and stared at her as if she were a great grizzly who had crawled in out of the woods. She wrenched her arm furiously away from her daughter's grasp. "It's you and Leif that the things are going on between, isn't it?"

"Mother, you went to lunch—"

"I don't want to talk about it! Talk to Leif!"

"I want to talk to you—"

"Well, I've wanted to talk to you many times! You never wanted me. You left—you hid! Now it's my turn, Tracy—I don't want to talk to you!"

Audrey was very close to tears, Tracy saw. She didn't want to upset her mother—she just wanted to know what was going on.

"Mother—" She hesitated. Audrey looked much,

much younger than Tracy felt at the moment. So pretty, so tiny, so soft—and so vulnerable. What had Leif done to her?

"Mother, there was never a time that I didn't want to talk to you! I just had to leave home. I had to have my own space—can't you see that? Oh, Mom! Grandpa has told you and Ted what to do and who to do it with every day of your lives! I couldn't do that. He ruled me as long as he could, and that was it. He made a nightmare out of my life—"

"No! No!" Audrey protested vehemently. Her eyes fell, then they met Tracy's again filled with tears and that frightened look. "You ran away—you were underage! You got pregnant!"

Tracy felt as if she'd received a blow. She gasped for breath and couldn't help her retort. "You did, too! But I'm alive and—"

"You were lucky, you idiot! It all came out that you didn't have to pay for any of your mistakes. I did!"

Tracy released her mother's arm, stepping back. "I'm sorry that I was such a terrible mistake."

"Tracy—" With a pained expression, Audrey reached out to her. Then her hand fluttered like a butterfly's wing back to her side. A little sob escaped her, and she turned, running back down the hallway.

Tracy leaned against the wall, then sank slowly to the floor, shaking. She felt tears well in her own eyes, tears for Audrey—and for herself. For the child who had lived; for the child who had died.

Liz came upon her as she sat there, sunk into a frightened and miserable oblivion.

"Tracy?"

She gazed up, quickly realizing the absurdity of her position on the floor. And Liz looked so concerned.

188

She stood hastily, blinking away the tears and giving Liz a weak smile.

"What's wrong?" Liz asked anyway. "Leif? He's my brother, and I love him dearly, but what a stubborn stickler he can be when his mind is on something! Oh, Tracy! Are you really okay? I'll just go out and talk to him and tell him—"

"No, no!" Tracy said quickly. "Really, I'm fine. I had a few words with my mother. I'm worried about her."

"Oh," Liz murmured. "She'll be fine, I'm certain."

"She usually is," Tracy agreed. But she wasn't so sure this time; Audrey hadn't looked well at all.

"You're in jeans," Liz commented. "I'm already dressed for drinks. With this household, I felt I needed it. Lauren and Carol have been at it all day." She paused, then looked squarely at Tracy. "And your grandfather is wandering about like an outraged vulture."

Tracy burst into laughter at that discription.

"I was going to go down and play ball with Blake and Leif for a while," she told Liz. "If you'd rather, I'll change quickly and come down and have drinks with you instead."

"Oh, no! No! Blake will love it if you come out and play with him." She grinned ruefully. "I'm not much good outside, I'm afraid. And Celia used to go out with him all the time. He's taken to you, Tracy. Of course, he adored Jesse, and Jamie is like a brother to him."

"I'll go out then," Tracy murmured. But when she would have started for the stairway, she paused and turned back. "How did Blake—how did he handle it when his mother died?"

Liz shrugged. "He's a child," she said softly. "He was only four the night her heart finally gave out. He missed her, of course. Now I believe he really only remembers her through her pictures. He—he needs a stepmother. A mom. Aunts don't quite cut it."

"Oh, Liz, I'm sure—"

"I hope that you stay with Leif, Tracy."

Tracy smiled. "Thank you, Liz. That's nice."

"It's sincere. The three of you could use a nice stable life."

Tracy lowered her eyes for a minute, then met Liz's again ruefully. "Nothing is stable right now. Leif doesn't trust me and—I'm sorry—I don't trust him. But whatever, Blake is fine, I'm certain. He adores his father. And he has you."

Liz smiled.

"You're smiling just like that nephew of yours right now!" Tracy charged her. "Like your nephew—and your brother."

Liz stiffened with a frown. She shook her head. "Tracy, Blake can't look like me. I told you it was quite impossible."

"Why?" Tracy said blankly.

"I'm surprised that Leif didn't tell you."

"Tell me what?"

"Really, Leif should—" Liz began, then she shrugged, and smiled once again. "I'm sure he intends to tell you somewhere along the line. Blake was adopted."

"What? He can't be! His expressions, his—he can't be! He's so much like Leif!"

Liz shrugged. "Well, you know the agencies these days. And Leif was ahead of a lot of other people—he could afford to make an expectant mother very wealthy. The adoption agency probably tried very hard to match up characteristics. In fact," she laughed, "it's very nice to hear that you think he does look so much like Leif."

Tracy nodded. "He—uh—does."

"Go play, please! And hurry back! Tiger and Sam will probably hide out until the last minute and I'll be down there with the fur flying. Oh—and please don't mention what I said about Blake. It isn't common knowledge."

"I—I won't say anything," Tracy murmured, then she stopped Liz before she could start down the stairs.

"Liz—how was Leif?"

"When Celia died?"

A little shamefully, Tracy nodded.

"Everyone loved Celia," she said softly. "She was simply someone very rare and special—a totally giving woman. I know that Leif grieved her deeply. I also know that he cares for you, Tracy. I don't understand everything that happened, but I do know that you are very important to him."

Tracy thought that she was going to start crying again —for different reasons. Was it true? If it was true, it was something to fight for. But why then was Leif acting so strangely? And how could she forgive a man who had rendered her own mother to such a state?

She was still thinking about Audrey when she wandered outside. Neither Blake nor Leif saw her at first; they were busy running around passing a little football back and forth, rolling and laughing in the island grass off the driveway when they tripped and fell together after one of Blake's "passes."

Then Blake's eyes turned to her, and he smiled slowly, a little shyly.

"Daddy! Tracy did come!"

Leif's eyes were instantly upon her. One of his dark brows slowly arched and he offered her a questioning smile.

Full of mockery.

Tracy ignored him, certain she would tear into him

191

right in front of his son if they came too close at the moment.

The two of them stood up. Leif eyed her with heavy lids and his strange smile, then tossed the football her way.

"Tackle, Tracy!" Blake yelled—and he rushed at her like a little bullet. She wasn't quick enough or ready enough to sidestep him. He pitched into her legs and they both fell together, and she discovered herself laughing breathlessly as he very triumphantly stared down at her.

The picture of his father . . .

But he couldn't be, she remembered then. And she didn't know if she felt any better—or worse. It had always hurt to think that not a month after he had fathered her own child, he had sired another. But now she knew he hadn't. His own son had lain dying while he and Celia had feverishly sought an agency who would give her a child quickly, a child she could give to Leif and love herself in the time that she had left.

"Get Dad!" Blake said suddenly, full of grins.

"Oh, you bet your little—uh—rump that I'd like to get your dad!" Tracy replied.

But she didn't go near Leif. She let Blake tackle him. She stayed with the two a little longer, then said she was going to change, trying to make sure she could shower and dress before Leif returned to the room.

She almost made it. But just when she was exiting, he appeared, that sardonic expression still on his face.

"What's your hurry?" he asked her.

"Oh, I'm not in a hurry," she told him, planting her hands on her hips. His eyes swept over her, then met hers again, and she discovered that she was blushing. Her cocktail outfit was a mandarin dress in black silk. But the thin stream of embroidery on it was in an elegant gold stitch—a stitch that belied the modest collar along the leg where it provided two daring slits. It was a striking, sophisticated outfit. Tracy had chosen it because she would be in the company of her father's assorted women.

"That's striking."

"Thank you."

"I'm not sure I want you walking around in it."

"I'm not sure that it's any of your business what I wear."

"Oh?" He planted his hands on his hips to match her stance. "What is this now?"

"My mother is in tears. What did you do to her?"

"I bought her lunch."

"You're a liar!"

He gave her a smile that chilled her to the bone. It was somehow sensual, somehow completely sardonic, cold and contemptuous.

"I'm the liar?" he inquired softly.

"What did you do to her?" Tracy repeated.

"Tracy—go downstairs," he said, suddenly weary. He stepped aside to open the door for her.

She stepped out and turned back to him. "Please be so kind as to have someone transfer my things from this room."

"I've already asked for that to be done," he told her, and the door closed in her face.

She even heard him bolt it.

Stunned, she thought that she would cry out. She couldn't go down to have drinks now! She wouldn't be able to handle it.

She brought a knuckle to her mouth, biting down as tears stung her eyes. That wasn't the way it was supposed to happen! He should have said no; she should have told him that was the way it had to be until he explained what was going on, and then he should have succumbed. They should have solved whatever it was and fallen into one another's arms, too necessary to one another to ever give up again.

That wasn't the way that life went; she should know that by now. He hadn't fought for her; he had stared at her as if he hated her.

She was going to cry; she had to see someone. Leif and she had come together only to part. She and her mother had spoken, and the words between them had been terribly cruel. She hadn't felt this wretched since she had learned via the evening news that her father had been slain.

Blindly, she tore down the stairs. But she realized then that there was no one to go to. She raced into the maze, into the rose garden, until she came to the fountain. There she sank down to the bench at last—and burst into tears.

"Tracy?" It was a shy, hesitant little voice that accosted her. Quickly she looked up, wiping away her tears.

"Blake. Hi."

"You're crying."

"No. I'm not." How silly.

"Can I do something for you?" he asked her earnestly, his eyes very troubled, his little body still sweaty from their football game.

She shook her head. "No, thanks, Blake. There's nothing you can do."

He walked closer to her and sat down on the bench beside her. "I come here when I'm going to cry, too," he confided to her, and she smiled, because it seemed so sweet that he was willing to stay beside a zany adult who was crying like a child.

"It's a nice place."

"Please don't cry."

"I won't. I won't cry anymore, Blake."

He stared at her a long moment, then suddenly flung his arms around her shoulder and gave her a little kiss on the cheek. He sat back swiftly. "When Aunt Liz is unhappy, she always says a hug and a kiss can make it all better. I don't know if it works for everything, but maybe it will help you a little."

"Thank you, Blake. Very much. It has already helped a whole lot."

He stared at her quite pointedly—reminding her again of his father's blatant stare. But then, he couldn't really look like Leif. Maybe the years together had given them the same expressions.

"Are you going to marry my father?"

She gasped at the question from a six-year-old, but then shook her head. "No, I don't think so, Blake." He kept staring at her, and she found herself questioning him in return.

"What would you feel if I did marry him?"

"I don't know. I guess you're a lot better than some of the other girls he's dated."

Well, it was qualified, but the honesty made her smile.

"Thanks. Actually, though, Blake, your dad and I don't get along very well." She glanced at her watch. "I guess we'd better get in. I'm sure you have to take a bath, huh."

"Yeah, I guess so," Blake said with a grimace. He stood up; Tracy did the same. He placed his little hand in hers. "Just till I get you out of the maze," he told her.

"Oh. Thank you."

But when they came out, he gave her hand a little squeeze before releasing it and tearing off for the house.

Tracy followed more sedately, staring down at the ground, still trying to compose herself.

At the pool, she literally ran into Ted. He righted her with a gentle smile, then frowned, noting the distress in her eyes.

"Hey! Tracy. What is it?"

She shook her head. "Nothing. Nothing. I was just thinking about, about—"

"Jesse?" he asked her, concerned.

"Yes," she lied with a little qualm of guilt. But she had no intention of dragging Ted into another of her personal traumas. None of this was his concern.

"Ah, sweetheart!" He gave her a hug. "Jesse had a good life. Remember that. Remember the good. Come on in, kid, and I'll buy you a drink!" he teased.

She nodded, then glanced at his face, at the concern in his dark brown eyes. She tried to smile, but still sounded a little nervous. "Where's mother?"

"She's not coming down. She has a horrible headache." He sighed. "If you ask me, she's still jealous of Carol and Lauren."

Tracy gasped. "Why should she be! She has you."

Ted didn't answer her. He opened the back door and led her into the parlor, where Katie was supervising the young man at the bar. Ted ordered wine for them both, then wound up in conversation with the bartender. Lauren came in with Tiger, then Sam showed up. Tracy talked idly to them both.

But then Leif came down, and Lauren instantly became a clinging vine on his arm, and Tracy just didn't want to be there. She slipped out of the house, thinking that she desperately needed more sleep or something, because she felt like there was a running cascade of tears dammed up behind her eyes—ready to flow like Niagara Falls at the slightest word or motion.

Or the simple condemning brush of Leif's eyes.

Someone moved over by the umbrella. She started to back away, then realized that it was Jamie.

"Oh, Jamie!" She cried, and impulsively she rushed over to him, hugging him fiercely.

"Hey, hey! Don't spill that wine on me! It will clash horribly with my after-shave."

But he rescued the wine from her hand, set it down on the cast-iron pool table, and hugged her in return.

"What's the matter, Tracy?" he asked her, sounding wonderfully and fiercely protective.

"Oh, everything. I shouldn't be here, Jamie. None of this is working. We've still no idea who wanted Dad murdered. I've had words with my mother and—"

She broke off, biting her lower lip.

"And with Leif?"

"Yes."

He inhaled, looking out over the pool. He tried to cheer her up with a little chuckle. "If it helps any, I had words with my mother, too. Everyone is so tense."

"So why did they all come?"

"Who knows? The guilty person probably came to keep an eye on things."

"Great. Who *is* guilty—and what are the others doing here?"

"The ladies are all trying to see which one is aging the best," Jamie informed her.

"Lauren, obviously. She isn't even thirty."

"Ah—but she's never been, nor will she ever be, as beautiful as Audrey."

Despite herself, Tracy smiled. "That was nice," she told him softly.

He shrugged. "Tracy, things will work out. You and Leif will make it all up."

She shook her head. "I have this horrible feeling that if we ever do discover the truth, it won't matter anyway. The truth is going to be horrible and ugly—and it will split us all apart forever."

Jamie shook his head vehemently. "We won't let it. Tracy, if nothing else comes out of all this, we have each other."

"Oh, Jamie. That's sweet. I barely know you yet, but I do love you. I love you very much."

He kissed her cheek and gave her a broad grin. "Let's go show 'em who's boss, eh?"

She nodded, and they walked back into the house, arm and arm.

Tracy made it through dinner with a certain amount of hard, cold armor in place. Leif was at the head of the table—seated between the two Mrs. Kugers. Lauren talked about her house and her business affairs all night —and how wretchedly hard it all was without a man, batting her lashes at Leif all the while. He was remote, but unerringly polite. Tremendously courteous. And every once in a while his dark head would bend intimately toward her, and the shock of jealousy that touched Tracy was overwhelming.

She had asked that her things be moved from his room. She had handed him right over to anyone else who saw fit to pursue him. What else could she have done? Nothing.

She was next to Tiger and Jamie, with Blake and Liz— and her grandfather—just beyond them. Arthur Kingsley was remote all night, but Tracy noted that he watched Leif throughout the night. Her grandfather was next to Blake, though, and surprisingly attentive to the little boy.

Coffee and brandy were served outside by the pool. By

that time, Tracy had a horrendous headache. Leif approached her, bearing a mug of coffee, passing it toward her.

"Black." He said simply.

"I don't think I care for coffee—"

"Take it," he said, scowling. "I can't hold it any longer."

She took the cup he handed her. He stared at her a second; she returned the scowl. He walked back to answer something Carol was saying.

They were talking about Jesse. Naturally. They were all here for the coming memorial service. She couldn't take any more of it. No one was watching her; she decided to fade into the background.

The coffee was still in her hand. She sipped it quickly to get rid of it, then set the mug down on the tile step of the pool. Slipping back into the house, she hurried up the stairs, then paused, realizing that she hadn't asked where her things had been moved. She didn't want to go back down. With a sigh she decided she would try to discretely open doors and hope that she didn't walk in on anyone.

But she did; the first door she opened, the one that was right down the hall from Leif's. Someone was there; someone tall and lean.

Leif.

But she frowned, because she saw that her luggage was neatly stacked by the closet door. Her purse was on the bed—and Leif was busily examining it.

"What the hell are you doing?" she gasped out in outrage. How had he gotten here before her? she wondered, but then realized he had come to his room via the deck and simply slipped next door.

He swung around. His face was hard.

"Good. You're here."

"Why— And get your hands off of my purse! What in God's name are you looking for now?"

He didn't reply, but glanced quickly over her cocktail gown, then shrugged.

Then he strode toward her, gripping her arm before she could back away. "You want to know what ticks in my mind, Tracy? Well, let's go. You'll find out."

"Go where?"

"To the car."

"No! I'm not going anywhere with you!"

He ignored that completely. Before she could protest again, they were halfway down the stairs. "Leif, I will not go with you! If you don't leave me alone, I'm going to scream."

He stopped so abruptly that she slammed into his back. "Tracy—tell me the truth!" he stormed to her.

"What truth?" she raged back.

He sighed. "Are you coming with me peacefully. Let me start over. Please, Tracy, come with me."

She didn't like the tension in his grip, nor that which radiated through his body, rippling the muscles of his shoulders beneath his light jacket.

She didn't like the way he was staring at her. A challenge, a dare. A ruthless demand.

"I'm not going—"

"Yes, you are."

Before she could draw in another breath, he swept her up and deposited her neatly over his shoulder. Even as she struggled from her position, they were down the stairs and at the front door.

"Leif! Put me down! I'll scream! My grandfather—"

"Your grandfather will get what's coming to him, too, Tracy," Leif vowed savagely.

"You can't do this!"

"Sorry. I'm doing it."

It was nearly impossible to carry on a rational conversation from her position. She swung her fists in sudden panic against his back. She lifted herself against his shoulders and desperately tried to bite him. Her effort failed because he swung open the door to the Jaguar, threw her in, and locked the door. Then he got in the other side and started the engine.

Tracy sat back incredulously, wondering how it was possible to love someone and hate him, too. And then she felt sick, because she didn't want a life like her parents'. Audrey had loved Jesse. And she had hated him, too.

Leif didn't look her way. He drove; his hands white-knuckled against the wheel, his face as hard as granite.

"Where do you think you're taking me?" Tracy demanded coolly.

"We'll be there soon."

"Leif, damn you! What were you doing in my things? Why were you rummaging through my purse?"

He glanced her way at last, with a strange indifference. "I was trying to see if you had your passport on you or not. I assumed you had. You came into New York from Austria, didn't you?"

She didn't answer him, but looked at her hands, suddenly more afraid than she had been, trembling. Yes, she'd come in from Austria. She rented a little townhouse there in a small town where the largest populations were those of the cows and the geese and where the residents were friendly and quiet. No one knew her there—or anything about her. She loved Austria—she even loved Switzerland. Despite the past.

It was simply the last place in the world that she wanted to go with Leif.

"Leif, you have to stop this car somewhere, and when

you do, I'm going to scream and scream until someone gets a cop, and then I'm going to have you arrested."

A small, small curl touched his lip. She saw it as the light from a passing car streamed into the Jag. It was a bitter smile.

"We're almost there," he said.

"Where?"

"The airport."

"Airport!" Tracy screeched.

"That's right," he said calmly.

She started to shake her head. It was fuzzy. Of all the things to happen in the middle of this crisis situation, she felt as if she were going to keel over in a ridiculously sound sleep.

"We're taking my plane. The old group plane," he further clarified for her.

"Taking it where?"

He glanced her way again, then looked ahead to make a smooth right. "Switzerland."

"No! Oh, no! I'm not going to Switzerland—ever again! And you're really an arrogant fool, Leif Johnston, but it won't work this time. You have to get me through customs—and I won't go. I'll scream and have a fit and there is no way at all—"

"My plane is private, Tracy, you know that. And I've traveled enough to make a few friends. We'll be cleared at the plane."

She stared at him, fighting for cognizance. The urge to lay her head back and sleep was overwhelming.

"You're still crazy," she said thickly. "I'll pull a tantrum. It won't work."

"But it will, Tracy." He stared at her, interested in her appearance. "Lay your head back, Tracy. Relax. There isn't a damned thing you can do about it. I have your

202

passport. And by the time we get to customs clearance, you're going to be sound asleep."

"You drugged me!" she charged him in a sudden realization. "Oh, you bastard! The coffee—"

"Nothing serious. Just a little pill. Liz takes one now and again when she's desperate for sleep."

She knew that the battle was lost; she couldn't keep her eyes open, and a sweet, lulling lethargy was stealing away all her will. Her eyes were simply closing, and she hadn't the strength left to do a thing about it.

"You are despicable. 'Please come with me, Tracy!'" She repeated scathingly. "You liar! You'd already planned this!"

"If you weren't a liar, it wouldn't have been necessary."

"You are brutal and cruel!"

The car suddenly went off the road. His arms were around her and suddenly he was trying to keep her awake.

"Why, Tracy, why?"

"Why what?" she mouthed.

"Why am I being cruel?" he was shouting. She didn't care.

"I don't ever want to go back—"

"Why not?"

"I hate you!"

"Tell me the truth, Tracy!"

"I hate you! I despise you!"

"The truth! We can end it all now!"

"No—"

"Then I have to prove the truth to you, Tracy. Cruel and brutal as you seem to think it is."

"What—"

"Tell me!"

She couldn't tell him anything else. The sweet, pleasant, overwhelmingly urge to drift from the present overwhelmed her.

CHAPTER ELEVEN

They were somewhere far over the Atlantic when she awoke.

Curiously, her first sensation was one of mild interest —or perhaps it was merely that she awoke still feeling exhausted and too lethargic to give way to her growing sense of resentment and fury.

And so, awakening slowly, it was with interest that she looked around herself. She knew where she was—she'd heard about the groups' various jaunts and tours on the plane. She'd never been on it, though, and despite everything else, she was intrigued.

She was on one of two very plush recliners that lay against either side of the renovated plane. A table sat between them. There was a bar just beyond the sofas, and beyond that was a large round table surrounded by captain's chairs. It was fantastic, Tracy thought, that an airplane could so resemble a living room.

And then she remembered why she was on the plane.

Abruptly, she sat up, pausing to grip her temples as it seemed that bells went off in her head. A moment's panic seized her as she realized that she was alone, and the fantasy living room high in the air seemed like a corridor in the Twilight Zone. With a swift movement she turned to the windows, sliding open the slim plastic cover with a vengeance.

They were in the clouds. High, high above the earth, moving with a quiet hum through some strange eternity.

Switzerland . . .

Switzerland was their destination. *He knew.*

She shivered suddenly, then forced herself to swallow back an irrational fear. He knew.

So what!

He knew that she'd had a child; that the child was long dead and buried. What was his point? He was taking her back to prove it, but to what end, she wondered in anguish.

It just all seemed to be the height of cruelty; to prove that she had been nothing short of a fool to stay anywhere near Leif Johnston. Once burned . . . but she had come back anyway. She'd come back in memory of her father, but she'd been compelled to relive another memory, and she'd even begun to believe that memory could become truth—that he loved her.

She should have known. She should have been forewarned. She knew him well enough to be certain that his tenderness could be hypnotic—but that his temper was ruthless, and little ever stood in his way once he was determined.

The door to the cockpit suddenly opened. Leif stood there, quietly closing it in his wake, looking at her pensively, but saying nothing. Tracy returned his stare with cold reproach. There was nowhere that she could go—no way to avoid him. He walked down the length of the plane to the bar. The distance seemed very long, yet he filled that distance with his strides, with his silent presence. He slipped behind the bar and spoke to her.

"Can I get you something?"

"No."

"We've still got several hours in the air."

She gave him no reply. He poured himself a drink of something amber and came back around, sitting on the sofa opposite her. Idly he crossed an ankle over his knee and sipped his drink, but his eyes didn't waver from hers.

"You still don't feel talkative?" he inquired softly.

"No."

He lit a cigarette, inhaled and exhaled. "Tracy—"

"I haven't anything to say to you. You are cruel and obnoxious and totally without principle."

"*I* am cruel?" he inquired with a sardonic smile curling his lip.

Tracy clenched her teeth tightly together. How could he possibly switch the tables at a time like this? And yet that bitterness in his voice proclaimed him the one wronged, and it cast her into a pool of confusion, where she felt near tears again.

"How do you intend to manage the rest of this, Leif?" she asked him smoothly. She would not cry, she would not break, she would not give him the least satisfaction. If she closed within herself, if she could talk, walk, and feel with cold disdain, she would make it.

"Have you got more pills up your sleeve, Mr. Johnston? Unless you're planning on murdering me, I'll exit the plane sooner or later. And when I do, I plan to charge you with abduction."

"Do you really?" he replied as coolly.

"Of course."

"You're not afraid of what I might decide to do?"

"What can you do?" she demanded heatedly, then warned herself that she was not maintaining calm. But it was difficult; it was nearly impossible. The plane, which

207

had seemed so huge for two people, seemed ridiculously small. He was so close.

The same man who had taught her from the very beginning what love could be. Who had come to her in her dreams. Who had spoken so recently in a haunting voice that tore at her heart about the caring he had felt . . . the caring that had lingered.

Lies. It did not seem that he cared about anything.

The same man who had held her yesterday. Made love to her; filled her and touched her—and left her lost and confused. He'd been planning this. All along. But for the love of God—*why?*

Tracy lowered her eyes. She couldn't look into the smoldering gray eyes that could hold love and passion and then hide away all emotion. She couldn't look at his strong body, handsomely encased in his suit, somehow more distant because of the formal attire. His hands, long and powerful, capable of gentleness, capable of force.

Capable of touching her . . . and God help her, she still wanted this all to be only a nightmare. She wanted to be able to fly across the distance between them and curl into his arms. She wanted to smoothe the lines of severity away from his lean cheeks, run her fingers over the grim line of his mouth and watch it ease into a lazy, crooked half-smile, full of sensuality and laughter.

The distance grew between them. She couldn't touch him. She could never go near him again. Not after this.

He was frowning at her, slowly arching a brow. "What can I do?" It seemed that it was a whispered query, full of outrage and incredulity. He stood, and she braced herself, because she wasn't going to back away, but neither was she going to let him come near her.

He didn't. He walked around the bar, restless, filled with tension and a chilling energy barely held in check.

Then he laughed dryly and she couldn't tell which of them he mocked.

"What can I do? Maybe nothing—since apparently you didn't care to begin with. And the last few days didn't make any difference."

What was he talking about? she wondered. She shook her head, easing somewhat, but lacing her fingers together tightly as she looked down at them.

"How could I care when you behave like this?"

"What the hell does my behavior have to do with it?" he exploded suddenly.

And then she tensed all over, because he moved again, a swift stride that brought him instantly to her, on one knee, wrenching her hands into his, bringing her startled eyes to meet his glare, silver now with a burning intensity.

"Why did you come back?" he demanded fiercely.

She tried to wrench her hands away. She could not. With a little cry she fought him wildly, wrenching and pulling, succeeding only in finding herself on her back— with his legs straddled over her and he showing no apology at all for his crude behavior.

"I did not come back!" she spat out, furious. "I came to find my brother! Because of my father! You had nothing to do with it! You should have never had anything to do with it!"

"Is that the truth?" he whispered so softly that she barely heard him, but the skepticism in his voice was like a shout. "You didn't come back to take something from me?"

"No!" she screamed. "There is nothing that you've got that I want, Leif Johnston! Nothing! Get off of me!"

To her surprise, he inhaled deeply—then abruptly released her. "Well," he murmured, pouring himself another drink at the bar and lifting his glass to her, "that is a relief. Or it should be. Actually, I'm even more disappointed."

Tracy leapt to her feet, not about to be cornered again. "I don't know what you're talking about. I think you're mad!"

He studied her over the rim of his glass, then lowered it back to the bar. "Oh, yeah, Tracy. Sure."

He left the bar and she moved out of his way. He paused, watching that movement of hers with high amusement. "Don't worry, Tracy. I promise—no more violence. My apologies for that last disgraceful episode. I just keep thinking that I can get the truth out of you one way or another."

She closed her eyes, exhaling raggedly, clenching her fingers into tight fists at her sides.

"What truth! What do you want me to say? What are you getting at? Yes, I had a child! It lived for eight hours! That's where we're going, isn't it?" she inquired coldly. "Zurich. A cemetery. Who are we proving this to—you or me?"

He stared at her, a shocked look on his face. They stood so rigid; both of them, she realized. Rigid and apart, burning with heat and fever. Longing to tear into one another, longing to . . .

Let the fire burn, and see what remained in the ashes.

No. There would be nothing but those ashes. Loss and bitterness and all the things that had come between them. All the things that they had been; a child, learning that love was a greater thing than vengeance, learning it too late.

And a man—betrayed. In so many ways.

She felt the horrible urge to cry again. Tears that loomed in anguish and bitterness, pressing like a flow of lava against her eyes. For her mother and her father, for herself and Leif. For the infant who lay beneath a little stone in a cold cemetery where perhaps even the little headstone would be under a layer of snow.

For the young girl she had been; seeing that child buried after holding it only once—then turning her back on all that her life had been in the hopes of finding a life of her own.

She should have never returned. Nothing could bring her father back. Jesse was as cold and dead as that long-dead child, and there would probably never be any way to prove that his murder had been conspiracy. Judgment would have to lie in some greater court than any on earth.

She lowered her head, moistening her lips slightly. "I can't believe you're doing this to me, Leif. I really thought that if what you felt wasn't eternal love and devotion, you at least—you at least cared."

He was very, very still for a moment. He moved toward her then, and though she stiffened, she didn't resist. He raised her chin, and when she looked at him then her heart leapt, for oddly, in the silver-and-gray depths of his eyes, she could have sworn that he was as torn as she, that he felt an anguish greater than her own.

"I couldn't believe what you did to me, Tracy," he said quietly. "I—"

He broke off and shook his head. Then he released her abruptly and his long strides took him away, toward the cockpit once again. He paused there with his back to her.

"Tracy, we're going through with this. I can't tell you exactly why right now, but I'll do whatever it takes to see that it happens."

"I don't know what—"

"We have to refuel in London, then we'll be in Zurich. You are coming with me. One way or the other."

"Bast—"

"One way or the other," he repeated. Then he returned to the cockpit.

Tracy fell back to the couch, shivering, exhausted, horribly spent. She closed her eyes tightly, wondering what she would do. If she screamed and fought, they'd have to help her in London. And she should charge him with kidnapping and assault.

She found the brandy and poured herself a large snifter. It burned its way through her and she shuddered again. Her stomach felt like an empty pit. The brandy didn't help—it made her feel more wretched.

She slowly walked back to the couch and sat, and then even more slowly stretched out again, resting her head against the throw pillow, delighting in the coolness against her hot cheeks.

Suddenly she closed her eyes again because the pain that streaked through was like the tearing blow of a red-hot poker. How cruel in the scheme of things that memory could be so clear and vivid! But it was abruptly there, with her, as it hadn't been in years. A picture painted across her mind in bright and crystal colors. The little house in the mountains, her room, all in white and softest mauves. The snow beyond the windowsills; the flowers her mother had flown in every day from Italy . . .

The doctor who came. The hours in which she struggled, and he assured her in his guttural German that she was doing fine. And then being in that beautiful white room with the cool snow outside, but drenched in sweat and laughing, and excitedly holding the tiny, tiny newborn life that had been her son, her very own son. It hadn't mattered that Leif was married to Celia; it hadn't

212

mattered at all. She had been in love with the baby, and so triumphant and pleased and cocooned in the wonder of that love.

But not even that was to be hers. She'd fallen asleep in blissful dreams and awakened to a nightmare. Her grandfather, sitting beside her, holding her hand. Telling her in the kindest fashion that it was just one of those things, and that maybe it was for the best—she could start her life over.

She could remember standing on the hill as the cold swept around her. And the cold hadn't mattered, because nothing could have touched the ice within her. She'd been eighteen, and she had felt as if she had lived forever.

And when she'd walked away from that hill with the light drift of snowflakes falling on the little coffin, she'd walked away from it all.

Memories . . .

He meant to take her back. By threats, by force, by coercion. She should fight him every step of the way. Maybe not. Maybe she could find that cold again, the cold that had brought her the past. Let that ice settle over her heart.

Go with him. And end it, once and for all.

Leif stayed away from her the remainder of the flight. She knew that he watched her carefully the entire time they sat on the ground at Heathrow—but he didn't speak, and neither did she, except to the pilot and co-pilot, who took a stroll back. To them she was charming. Both of them had been in private hire for over ten years, she discovered, and they spoke kindly of her father and she was grateful to them. But when she asked them if it didn't get quite boring these days with so little to do, they both talked about the many uses for the plane, such as jaunts with underprivileged children to special events and transportation for the elderly for medical care in tenuous situations.

Leif had bought out the other group members' interest in the plane, she knew, and she wasn't particularly pleased to hear that he kept it for his own occasional use —and such charitable endeavors. Tax write-offs! she decided. But she didn't want to hate him any more than she wanted to love him; both were passionate emotions, and she wanted to feel cold.

In Zurich they were met by a driver in a handsome little beige Mercedes. Tracy went through customs without blinking an eye; when Leif went to take her arm to escort her to the car, she stared at him without tensing and asked him with admirable aplomb not to touch her; she would endure his awful charade without protest—as long as he wouldn't touch her.

He shrugged, and let her be.

They were taken to a lovely little European hotel outside of the city. It was a chalet that had sat on a small precipice for centuries, the hunting cottage of some long-ago knight now modernized with beautiful, fresh new paint and tiled baths in quaint rooms with marble mantels, working grates, and huge curtained windows that looked over the forest beyond, just lightly dusted in spring snow.

Tracy knew that Leif was amazed when she didn't protest the fact that he procured connecting rooms. She accepted it all without a word, without the flick of an eyelash. She didn't do anything but walk to the window when she came into her own room, although she realized that Leif had had someone pack her a small bag. When she realized that he had opened the connecting door and stood watching her, she didn't move. Still staring out at the beautiful countryside, she asked him, "Well, what now, Mr. Johnston?"

"Freshen up, take a nap, do whatever you like. We'll meet down in the lobby in an hour. You should be hungry. Order something to eat."

She turned around at last, smiling with no emotion, leaning easily against the window seat.

"I imagine it's about ten A.M. by now in Connecticut. Won't we be missed? You have a houseful of guests—or did you forget? We were all assembled to catch a murderer. And instead we're sitting in Switzerland for you to prove some—some point that has absolutely nothing to do with it."

"We won't be missed. I asked Liz to take care of things."

She nodded, crossing her arms over her chest. "You're quite lucky you have her. Blind loyalty and obedience."

He shrugged. "You've got Jamie."

She shook her head. "No, not really. Jamie really belongs to you, too, doesn't he?"

Leif tilted his head, staring toward her with mild interest. But his eyes wore a silver gleam of tension once again.

"If I have Jamie, Tracy, it's simply because I was there. I cared for him. I loved him. He spent more time with me than he did with his mother or father. You could have been there—you've been of age for a long time. You could have done a lot of things, Tracy."

She turned back to the window.

"What, Leif? What could I have done? Walked into the center of your marital bliss? I think not."

"You could have told me."

"It's over Leif. Why can't you just let it lie."

215

He was silent; suddenly he was explosive. "It's not over! And it won't ever be over—not in our lifetimes!"

Tracy spun back around, but he was gone. She went to the door and slammed it shut, locking it.

In the end, she did take a shower. The water was wonderfully hot, the jet spray stringent and good against her. She thought that she was exhausted—she really wasn't sure. She seemed to be living on tension.

She wondered when she unpacked the little bag if Leif hadn't been through her things himself—there were only two outfits in the bag and two sets of underclothing. Obviously, they weren't staying long. But both sweaters and skirts that he had chosen were right for the weather; fashionable, but comfortable. She dressed, feeling more tension steam through her. She began to doubt her wisdom about going along with him—she should have screamed her head off at Heathrow.

But just as that thought faded, she gave herself a helpless little shake. She had to go through with this. Just as it seemed that it was a compulsion with Leif, she felt that she had to go through with it herself.

Just like that day when she had walked away—when she had buried her son and walked away. Maybe she would feel the same now. Her mother had screamed when she'd learned Tracy's intentions; her grandfather had yelled. Only Ted had remained silent, maybe respecting her decision.

And she hadn't felt anything. Just cold. She hadn't hated them; she had loved them, but nothing they had said or done had touched her. Her only salvation had been in getting away. In creating her own life, far, far from the influences that had been.

She found boots in the overnight bag—and stockings. Thinking that Leif could certainly be deliberate and thorough, she slipped them on and called the lobby to adjust her watch to the proper time.

Then she lifted her chin and met her own eyes in the mirror. She was dismayed to see that they were very wide and very blue. Frightened.

"No," she whispered aloud, and she turned then, quickly, ready to go down and meet Leif.

He was there, in the lobby, somehow absurdly appealing in a trenchcoat, his hair damp with a tendril over his forehead—his eyes as cold and hard as she had wanted her own to be. He glanced at her, sweeping his eyes over her with no emotion.

"What are we doing?" she asked him curtly.

He glanced at his watch. "Waiting. Let's get some hot chocolate or something."

He set his hand on her elbow to lead her from the lobby to the dining room beyond it. She spun on him.

"I'm here, Leif, and that's it. I don't ever, ever want you touching me again. You are a cold and brutal man, and I don't ever want anything to do with you again."

"Tracy—move."

She did so, irate that he was so tall and hard, that his voice could be so low and controlled. That she walked as he had told her—with his elbow still on her arm. And all around her there were people. Most of them in ski clothing, all of them chatting and laughing warmly and carrying on conversations in German and French. They talked about the slopes, about the shopping, about the beautiful way the weather was holding out. They seemed so happy.

Leif led her to a small table with a single rose in a vase upon it. The rose reminded her of her mother's penchant for flowers. No matter where Audrey went, she had to have flowers.

Sitting, Tracy was at last freed from his touch. But not his presence.

"What are we waiting for?" she demanded with what she hoped was bored impatience.

"A man," he said simply.

A pretty waitress with beautifully colored cheeks came by. Tracy ordered hot chocolate and a croissant. Leif ordered coffee.

They didn't speak again until they were served. Tracy picked at her pastry. Leif lit a cigarette and stared at her. She tried to ignore him and not care that everyone else was laughing and chatting. Not to care that they were all happy and enjoying vacations while she and Leif . . .

He leaned toward her suddenly. She pretended not to notice.

"Tracy, look at me."

She did, hostility stark in her features.

"I know what you look like, Leif. Inside and out."

"You think I should just forget it."

"What can we prove?" She almost shouted the words. She swallowed, determined to lower her voice.

He shook his head at her, disgusted. "Well, for one, Tracy, we're going to prove that your family is capable of anything."

She stared at him, startled and confused by his words. Maybe she should have told him that she was pregnant. No! She hadn't owed him anything. He had been a married man by then. And if anything, she thought that her family's love and loyalty had been proven by their tender support of her.

"There he is," Leif said, rising suddenly.

Tracy looked up. A pleasant-looking young man was coming toward them. As soon as he greeted Leif with a

218

handshake and a few quiet words, she knew that he was American, too.

Leif introduced them briefly. "Are we all set?"

"Yes, the coroner should be there by now, with the cemetery people," Rob said.

The room seemed to swim. "What?" Tracy gasped out.

Leif grasped for her elbow, propelling her out of her chair. She'd barely touched her chocolate or her croissant.

In the lobby she desperately tried to free herself from his grasp. Too soon, she was out the steps and approaching a car.

"Leif—"

"Get in."

She had no choice; he pushed her into the back. Rob got into the driver's seat. They were all like little peas in a pod in the small vehicle, and she knew that anything she said was going to be overheard.

"You're going to open that grave?" she demanded, near hysteria.

"That's right," Leif said impassively.

"No! How could you! How dare you! It's illegal— they'll stop you. You're an animal! You're worse! You're—"

The tears she'd held back at last came to her and she twisted in the small space to pummel her fists against him, blinded. He caught her wrists with no mercy and no patience. Rob cleared his throat uncomfortably.

Leif didn't say a word. He held Tracy in an implacable grasp and stared straight ahead.

Tracy didn't know what she said then; she knew that she kept talking, that she railed, that she pleaded—that she labeled him a monster and more. And none of it made any difference.

They kept driving until they came to the wrought-iron gates and passed through them, driving uphill. Some of the graves were new, some of them were weathered and aged. It was stark here, and cold, and it seemed that even the beautiful blue that had colored the sky faded and paled and turned to a dismal gray that echoed all that was dead and lost.

Tracy remained in a state of shock.

Rob parked the car. Leif reached to help her out—she turned truly hysterical then, trying to refuse his hand, trying to pummel against him again. She tried to enlist the mysterious Rob's aid, swearing that she would have them both arrested.

Rob glanced at Leif in accute discomfort, but remained silent. Leif didn't twitch or blink or falter. He set his arm firmly about Tracy's waist and dragged her along while she balked.

They came to it—to the tiny gravesite in the soft, light snow. To the gravestone. There were other men there. Three of them. Two men in sweaters and jeans with crowbars, and a graying, dignified man who could only be an official.

"Please, please!" Tracy screamed, begging for help. She pleaded in German, and she pleaded in French. She was barely coherent, and she knew it, but she couldn't believe it. She couldn't believe that they were going to dig up the dead and decaying flesh of her infant son.

Rob gave the official a paper. They all looked at Tracy a bit sadly, but ignored her.

She looked at Leif at last, face tearstained, eyes brilliantly blue as she beseeched him. "You can't do this! Please, I beg you! Why? How can you do this to me?"

Something—perhaps a hint of confusion, remorse, or maybe even tenderness—touched his eyes.

220

"Please, Leif!"

He shook off her arm then. "I have to!" he grated. The gray-haired official nodded to the workmen.

"No!" She slammed both fists against his chest. He caught her arms, crushing her against him.

"Tracy! Don't you understand—or are you still fighting the truth? Damn you, Tracy! It's empty! The grave is empty!"

"What?"

She stared at him in disbelief, and his eyes met hers. What was in them, she wondered desperately against the awful confusion. A question, an accusation? Pity? His own uncertainty?

And again, just a touch of silver tenderness?

The workmen kept digging; the coffin came up. One of the men stepped forward with a crowbar. Tracy pressed her face hard against Leif's chest. She hated him with all her heart, but his tense, heated body provided her with the only way she knew to hide.

The coffin was opened. She could not look.

"Tracy—it *is* empty!"

She looked then and saw that it was.

She sagged against Leif's form. She was unaware that he caught her and lifted her into his arms, unaware that he held her against him with grudging tenderness and a torn heart.

She was unaware of anything. The world had spun far beyond her grasp. All she knew was darkness.

CHAPTER TWELVE

Unfortunately for Tracy, the blackness lifted nearly as quickly as it had come. She didn't think or rationalize; none of it meant anything to her at that moment.

None of it—except for the fact that everything was terribly, terribly wrong.

She opened her eyes and stared into his. They were as dark as night; charcoal gray, probing, condemning. Ever watchful and ever wary—and if there were the least caring in the granite lines of his facial structure, she didn't see it. He'd brought her here for a reaction, and she was giving him that!

Nevertheless, she stared at him for what seemed like a long time. Snowflakes were falling—light, light, like the wings of butterflies . . . beautiful, crystal, so soft. Falling from the gray sky. People were talking; the workmen and the officials and Rob. The words were in English, though they might have been in an entirely alien tongue. Tracy didn't hear them. She felt the caress of the snowflakes against her cheeks and the steel of Leif's arms. She shivered, and felt that his eyes were a threatening fire that simmered and darkened and tore into her.

She cried out suddenly, hurt beyond feeling and logic, hating him with all the raw emotion that swept through her. She struck out at him so suddenly and with such ardent force that he released her. Her feet touched the ground and she was gone.

Running, running blindly.

Angels surrounded her, angels and saints. The dark sky, the white snow. The air was cold, her body hot. She heard her own heartbeat and she heard the rush of her breath. She rushed past mausoleums, small and beautifully wrought homages to the honor of great family names. She ran uphill, not knowing where she tried to go, only that instinct told her to run, desperately.

As if she could escape it all. As if she would not think, and understand what it meant.

"Tracy!"

She veered around a tree, then grasped its trunk, inhaling. She stared at the spidery limbs, still naked from winter's death.

"Tracy!"

Against the new-fallen snow, she heard the crunch of his footsteps, and she started running again. But this time something caught her. Some broken stone, cast into the earth centuries ago. It caught her hard, sent her flying down face first into the snow, slamming into the ground. Feverishly, she gasped to regain her breath and roll and scramble back to her feet.

Too late . . .

He made a flying leap upon her, tackling her back to the snow. Holding her there even as she sobbed raggedly and pitched and rolled to escape him until exhaustion overcame her again.

Panting she stared at him. So coldly. All the ice she might have desired lay in her heart.

"Why are you running!" he demanded harshly. "You knew! Dammit, Tracy, you knew!"

"I didn't know."

"Audrey said you knew all about it!"

"I will never forgive you, Leif, as long as I live," she said softly. Renewed energy came to her and she tried once again to dislodge his muscled legs from his grip about her. His lip tightened, but he gave no other sign that he recognized her struggle, and he waited until she lay still again.

"Should I forgive you?" he whispered. "If your grandfather hadn't felt a slight twinge of guilt and gone through the channels to get him to me, God knows where he would be."

"What are you talking about?" Tracy screeched. "You're condemning *me* but you're the one who knows everything!"

For the first time, a true flicker of doubt passed through his eyes. Gray clouds masked it quickly, and he sat straighter.

"Tracy, I have firsthand experience. You're a wonderful liar."

"Oh, God!" Miserably she closed her eyes and cast her head back, heedless of the snow in her hair or that which fell so lightly against her face.

"You knew that there was no corpse in that grave. *I didn't!* For God's sake, before you hang me, tell me the crime! Why? Where is my—my child?"

He released her hands and balanced his weight still atop her, but not against her. He studied her for what seemed like eons before he spoke at last.

"Tracy, you've just spent several days with the 'child' who was supposedly buried in that grave."

"What?"

"I'll refresh your memory. You had a child. Not just illegitimate in the eyes of Arthur Kingsley—but damningly illegitimate, since he was the son of a musician. Just

224

like Jesse. The man who ruined your mother's life, in his opinion. There's an easy solution—get rid of the child. Easier still when you hear that the natural father and his wife are desperate to adopt an infant."

She stared at him, and she didn't believe it. Couldn't believe the harsh words that bit out at her in clipped tones. How could she believe it? Believe that they had lied to her. That her own mother had taken her child away. She shook her head at him, slowly, watching him as she would the most dangerous snake in the world.

"You're a liar, you're a liar! It can't be! Get off of me, get away from me—"

He did the opposite. He leaned down to her, sluicing his fingers through hers, knotting them together in the snow. All around them the wind played; it seemed to moan out a death knell that touched the naked branches and the quiet hill and made it a place far apart from the world—far, far apart. As if she and Leif were alone, cast into some mocking play, and she couldn't get off of the stage.

"Tracy, swear to me that you knew nothing about this!"

"I'll never swear anything to you! I hate you. My God, I never want to see you again—"

"Or Blake, Tracy? You see, that was what I couldn't figure out. If you hadn't wanted the child—or anything to do with him. Or if you had come back into Jamie's life just to step into mine—because you had decided that you did want him back, after you had given him up."

"Damn you, I didn't know!" She shouted those words, then they both fell silent.

And then it struck her full force.

Blake. Blake was the child she had held only once. It was true, her mother and grandfather had told her that

225

her child was dead—and they had given him away. It hurt. It hurt so deeply that the pain was staggering—and then completely numbing.

Blake was her child.

The numbness settled over her. She didn't know what she felt. She didn't know if she hated her mother and her grandfather. A sick rage settled within her that they could do such a thing to her, and then even that ebbed.

"Leif, let me alone. I don't want you near me. Before God, you've made your point! Get away from me!"

"Tracy—"

"Damn you, get away! I hate you for this! You might have spoken to me, you might have warned me, you might have trusted in me, you might have given me half a chance! Oh, my God, that child is mine—"

"I have a history of bad luck with trusting you. And no, Tracy. He is mine."

She let out a strangled cry, her heart suddenly torn apart by all the wasted years. She hadn't seen his first smile, and she hadn't seen him take his first steps. He was alive, and she was glad, but suddenly, fiercely, she wanted him, and she couldn't bear that Leif could have done this to her—and have her baby, too.

"How could you be so cruel? And how can I ask that? You are the coldest human being I've ever met!"

"Leif—?" They were interrupted by Rob. If she weren't so wretched, Tracy might have felt sorry for the man, cast into this.

Somehow Leif managed to crawl from Tracy and help her to her feet with a semblance of dignity.

"They want to know if charges will be pressed."

Leif looked to Tracy. "I doubt it."

"The Swiss government might have a few," Rob said,

226

looking at Tracy apologetically. He felt sorry for her, she could tell. But he still gave Leif his total respect.

Leif shook his head. "It doesn't matter. Arthur Kingsley can buy himself out of anything. I'll tell them thank you, and we'll get out of here."

Tracy went straight to the car. Seconds later, Rob and Leif joined her. She didn't look at either of them, but stared ahead of herself, blindly, for the drive back to the hotel.

Once there, she let herself out and hurried up to her room, casting herself on the bed. She didn't cry; there were simply no more tears. Nor did she feel hysterical. Just cold, and numb. And when that numbness started to warm, she fought the feelings. She had to, because the rage and ragged pain would come again, and she would want to scream. How could they have done it to her?

And Leif . . .

She didn't want to think about any of it; she couldn't help herself. She got off the bed at last and picked up the phone. She had no conception of the time in Switzerland or in the States. She didn't care.

Katie answered the phone at Leif's, asked after her welfare, and then went to find Audrey.

And as soon as Audrey came to the phone, Tracy knew that it was all true.

"Mother, how could—how could you—have done it? I have to know. Or I'll go mad."

Tracy pressed her palm to her temple then, because she could hear Audrey crying, all those many, many miles away. She started saying incoherent things, pleading, begging that Tracy understand. That her own life had been a travesty. If it hadn't been for Tracy, for the link that remained, she might have stayed away from Jesse.

"Grandfather kept the two of you apart," Tracy said

with surprising calm. "And he did it to me. The two of you— But a child, mother—my child! You had no right!"

She started crying again, and Tracy felt terribly weary. Audrey said then that Tracy hated her, and for all of it, Tracy couldn't add another blow to her mother's life.

"I don't hate you, Mother." She didn't even really hate her grandfather. She wasn't terribly sure that she could forgive and forget, and so she determined to hang up the phone.

"I don't hate you, Mother. I'll see you soon."

She bit her lip, because Audrey was still talking through a torrent of tears, telling her that Blake was really so beautiful, and she'd been so afraid to touch him.

"Good night, Mother," Tracy said, and hung up the phone at last.

She'd wanted to ask to speak to Blake; she'd wanted to hear his voice. But like Audrey, she'd been afraid.

Tracy walked back to the bed, wretched. She started then, when she heard a sound at the connecting door.

She thought she had locked it from her side. Apparently she hadn't—or else Leif had the key. He stood there in jeans that snugly encased his lean hips and a sweater that emphasized his height and the breadth of his shoulders.

She stared at him, fighting back the rush of emotion. She wanted to strike out at him so badly. She inhaled and prayed for poise.

"Leif, I think you should understand that I do not want to see you."

"And I think that you should understand that you have to."

He strode across the room, not touching her, and picked up the phone. To her astonishment, he calmly ordered that a bottle of wine and food be sent up.

She rushed over to the phone, ready to grasp the receiver from his hands. He warded her away with his free one until he was ready to hang up.

"Leif—I do not want to be with you!"

"Sit down, Tracy."

"I won't—"

"You will!"

He proved his point by walking her backward to the bed, where the edge caught her knees, forcing her to sit. She was ready to lash out when he moved away from her, facing her at the window seat.

Then, somewhat to her surprise, he inhaled, hesitated, then gave her an apology.

"I'm sorry, Tracy."

"Sorry?" she repeated softly. "For what, Leif?"

He shrugged. "For—today."

She started to laugh, and the sound frightened her, so she sobered quickly. "You abducted me, and dragged me into a cemetery and forced me to look into a coffin that I believed held my child. And you're sorry. That's just great."

With an explicit oath he was on his feet, hands locked behind his back, pacing before the window, as if he were afraid to come too near her and—

Touch her.

She was just so exhausted and torn that it didn't matter.

"Tracy, your mother told me that you knew. You lied to me once—and you kept lying to me. I'd thought at first that Arthur and Audrey might have done something without your knowledge. But I gave you every opportunity in the world to tell me about your pregnancy—about our child—and you kept lying."

"I didn't lie, damn you! I couldn't see any reason to

tell you that you had a child who had been dead over six years!"

He stopped his pacing and looked at her. "I believe you, Tracy."

"That's really big of you, Leif," she stated flatly, meeting his eyes. She just felt so tired. And so confused. Afraid—and unwilling to face her fear.

She felt shaky when it came to Blake. He was hers. Her son, her flesh and blood. Her baby. And she wanted to get back and pick him up and hug him and inspect him and kiss and cry with the wonder of it all.

And she couldn't do that, of course. What could she do? Without harming him. Without his father's consent.

Her hands began to shake and she clenched them tightly in her lap, looking down at them. He couldn't be so cruel as to prove his point and then deny her! But look at what he had done today.

She lifted her chin. "You might have warned me. You had every opportunity, too, Leif. You could have confronted me with what you knew. Why—why did you have to drag me over here—confront me at the grave?"

"Tracy—" He paused, rubbing his temple. "I asked you. I asked you and asked you and asked you if there wasn't something that you wanted to tell me. You wouldn't talk to me. I knew that if I brought you here, you couldn't deny it anymore. And that you'd be forced to realize that Arthur and Audrey might be capable of anything."

She leapt to her feet, all her fury exploding.

"Oh! Oh! This is all part of it, I see! They did this—just an inch away from murder, no doubt."

He shook his head in disgust. "Tracy—they took your child and gave it away, and by some mercy I have my son. And you still refuse to remove your blinders."

230

"I have removed my blinders!"

"I did not intend to be brutal or cruel, Tracy. You had to see the truth!"

She flew across the room at him, slamming her fists in a rain of fury. And the tears that had gone cold started to fall again. He held her, and stood rigid to her attack, not stopping her, but letting her play her energy out.

"Leif—leave me alone."

"Tracy—I'm sorry—"

"Once, Leif, you didn't seem able to forgive me. Well, I'm damned sorry, but I can't forgive you this time."

"Tracy—"

She felt him coming toward her and she swallowed, stiffening further and placing her hands to her cheeks, wiping away all remnants of her tears and swearing that she would be strong, she would not cry again. Nor would she touch him, in anger or in love.

Before he could reach her, there was a light tapping on the door. Leif stepped on past her, opened it, and greeted the man from room service cordially, displaying an easy shift of personality that irritated Tracy thoroughly.

He and the young Swiss kept up an idle conversation as the table was set, the wine uncorked and approved, and everything arranged.

"Madame?"

Tracy was not so glib. She did manage a tight smile as she was seated, and a forced, "Thank you."

Leif tipped the man. He locked the door in his wake, then hesitated only briefly before sitting down across from Tracy.

He lifted his glass to her, watching her sardonically. "To life, Miss Kuger."

She didn't lift her glass. She just sat there.

"The food is delicious here," he said, studying her impassive features as he idly continued to sip his wine. "The steak is excellent, and I've never had potatoes like this anywhere else in the world."

"That's fascinating."

He emitted an impatient sound and leaned toward her.

"God, Tracy, I gave you back a living child! What—did you prefer a dead one?"

Tracy lifted a brow to him. "Oh? Are you planning on giving me back my son?"

He smiled slowly, sardonically. "Ah, so that's the gnawing question at the moment."

"Well."

"Drink your wine, Tracy. Eat."

"I asked you a question."

"Hmm. Do I mean that to infer that we're going to have a rational conversation?"

"I'm trying very hard."

He lifted her glass and handed it to her. Tracy's fingers curled around it, and she knew he wasn't going to have any kind of a conversation at all unless she ate.

She sipped her wine and sat down and picked up her utensils. She ate a bite of the steak and it was truly delicious, but her stomach felt as if it were leaded and heavy with rocks.

She felt his eyes on her; she didn't know his feelings or what he was thinking. "What?" she demanded, setting her fork down and swallowing a sip of wine to alleviate the sudden parched feeling that came to her throat.

He shook his head. "I really don't know. You tell me, Tracy, what you would like to have happen. How do you think that this should be handled."

She wanted to meet his eyes. They were hard upon hers, blunt and unwavering. She couldn't.

"I—I realize that he has lived with you for over six

years. That I mean nothing to him at all. That—that Blake is the one who matters here, and that he must be dealt with very gently. He's not really old enough to understand. Perhaps we could arrange something where I have him for a few days at first, then a few weeks, working up to an even situation where—"

"An even situation?" he inquired tightly, his eyes narrowing. "You mean like split custody."

"Well, yes—"

"You're insane, Tracy," he said coldly. "Forget it."

She shouldn't have lost her temper; she did.

"He's my son! I lost him through a cruel hoax—I never gave him up on purpose! Surely, I can get him back legally. His birth certificate must still exist somewhere, and since my grandfather began the hoax, he'll certainly be willing to get me out of it now! You're the one who always says it—Arthur Kingsley can buy anything!"

Leif pushed back from the table, not answering her at first, but studying his wine as he swirled it in his glass.

"Not my son, Tracy. You're forgetting—my financial situation may not put me in the billions, but I'm affluent myself. And if his birth certificate can be discovered, I'm willing to bet that you did name the father on it."

"So—" she said, her voice low, and to her horror, quivering. "So we'd be back where we are now. Split custody."

He shook his head at her, displaying no anger except for a telltale tick in that long vein in his tightly corded neck.

"No way, Tracy," he said softly. And then he smiled. "Legal battles can also take forever and forever. You've lost six years. At this rate, you might make it for his high school graduation."

She exploded with some oath, throwing her napkin on the table and stalking away.

The soft sound of his laughter followed her, with only a slightly hard edge to it. Her back was to him; it was all she could do to keep from throwing herself at him again in a futile expulsion of her fury. And pain. Her heart ached as if dagger after dagger had been slammed within it. Why had he done this?

Given her back her son . . . only to keep him away.

He'd wanted to prove how callous the Kingsley side of her family could be. That they were capable of taking a newborn infant, that they were capable of murder.

She winced; she didn't dare think about her father now. That was a quest that would have to wait. She knew she couldn't bear knowing that her child lived. That he was six and healthy and sweet and adorable . . .

And she didn't have him.

"Blake is my son, Tracy. Biologically, I'm his father. In his eyes, I am his father. I have raised him. I held him through the night when he cried; I changed diapers, I caught measles from him. I'm not saying that to be cruel —only to point out the undeniable truth. I will never give him up. He will never leave my house."

Tracy spun back around. "You have to give him up! I —I'm his real mother!" She didn't want to plead with him; after today, she had never, never wanted to ask anything of him again. But she had no choice. Because she was desperate to have a part of Blake. Of her own son.

He shrugged, and stared straight at her. Evenly, implacably. He actually appeared relaxed and comfortable and totally at ease with his own position.

"I will have a place in his life!" she flared with sudden passion, willing herself to remain still.

"Then you will come to him," Leif said softly. He

stood too, coming nearer her, but not close enough to touch.

A distance gaped between them then. A great, vast distance.

"I can't come back to your house! Ever!"

"You said that once before."

"I didn't hate you with all my heart before!"

It was a lie; she knew it was a lie. And yet the burning pain and rage she felt toward him made it very nearly the truth.

It seemed that his jaw tightened; he blinked, but still betrayed no emotion toward her. Not anger, not tenderness.

"I suggest that you learn something about forgiveness, Tracy," he warned her softly. "I told you that I was sorry; I tried to explain—"

"Leif, you are merciless and ruthless!"

"Tracy, if you want to be his mother, be his mother. Don't disrupt a decent home, all the stability and love that the child has already. I swear to you—I'll fight you into the ground if you try anything. If you want to learn how to become his mother, you are welcome to do so. In his home."

"I will not live in your house!"

He arched a brow, as if mildly interested—and amused.

"You've lived quite nicely in my house—in my room and in my bed—twice now. I'm sure you'll manage to do so again."

"What? You think after what you've done that I'll just come back as a permanent—mistress?" she demanded incredulously.

"Not at all. I'm his father. You want to be his mother—"

235

"I am his mother!"

"I repeat, you want to be his mother. That's a damn nice and normal situation. Good for a child. A father and a mother. It's a very good way to grow up."

She couldn't breathe suddenly. She felt very weak, both frightened and anticipatory, on fire—and shaking with chills.

"What—what are you saying, Leif?"

"I'm saying that if you want your son, Tracy, at this very late date, that you'll play by my—'house'—rules. You'll marry me," Leif stated simply, "and it will be that old anachronism—a family."

"I—I—"

She was actually speechless, so stunned by his words that she couldn't begin to combat him. Inwardly she struggled, and then her words rushed out.

"You can't be serious!" Tracy cried. "I told you—I despise you and I'll never forgive you for today!"

"Have it your way, Tracy," he said with a shrug.

He turned away, and there was an awful finality about the way he so determinedly walked from her. Could he do it? Could he keep her away from her son? A child she had barely seen. A child also biologically his—and legally adopted as well. She could fight him, but it might take years and years, and before the law, too, it might appear that she had willingly given up her own infant, having been a teenaged and unwed mother . . .

"Leif, wait!" she cried, rushing to him, catching his arm to spin him back to her, then dropping it hurriedly. It burned to touch him.

Again, she wanted to face him. She couldn't at first. She fought to raise her chin and meet his eyes. They were gray; as hard as stone.

"You—you can't be serious."

"I am."

"Leif—a marriage like that would be a disaster! Legal, but meaning nothing. In name only and all that!"

"In name only?" With mild interest he folded his arms over his chest and waited expectantly.

"It couldn't be anything else."

"It would have to be something else."

"I will not go to bed with you again!"

"You never had any problems before."

She glared at him. "I've had problems every time I've ever seen you!"

"Tracy, if you marry me, you sleep with me. I can't imagine it being that terrible a hardship. But that's your dilemma to solve. I can't make you talk to me or jump up and down with joy over the situation. I'm just warning you—no lies, no surprises. If you're my wife, you'll be just that." He added, with a hard glint in his eyes: "In the bedroom as well as outside of it."

Fire swept through her. She knew that she quivered from head to toe, and she certainly didn't intend to capitulate to his crude proposal.

"You'd be miserable," she said coolly.

"Why is that?"

Color rose to her cheeks. "I could marry you, I could follow your rules. Sleep in your bed. And never protest your touch. But—" Her voice lowered, she could barely breathe. She sought for the right words. "I wouldn't, I couldn't—"

"Do go on, Tracy. This is fascinating."

"I'd be a log!" she shouted. "You'd have an empty shell every time you touched me."

She was suddenly afraid that he'd be violently angry with the tension that coursed between them. She tensed,

237

willing herself to keep her chin high, little help against his towering size.

He wasn't angry.

He started to laugh and eye her with a silver ridicule that made her long for violence.

"Tracy," he said smoothly, "I've known you rather—well. You might hate me from now to eternity, but—well, let me put it this way. I've no qualms about enjoying a certain amount of marital bliss in the least."

"You—"

He stilled her urge to slap him before her hand could come anywhere near his face. She was held tightly to him; he stroked her cheek, then stared down at her, still smiling with high amusement.

"Egotist!" she snapped.

"No," he said softly. "I just know you very, very well. Every—delectable inch. And you are made of fire, my love, not ice."

He released her and reached for the connecting door. "We've an hour before the courthouses and license bureaus close. If your hatred for me is deeper than your belated love for your son, by all means go your own way. And if not, well, meet me downstairs in fifteen minutes. Prepared to marry me—and give me each night that sweet empty shell!"

He smiled, opened and closed the door. Tracy slammed a fist against it, shouting her rejoinder. She doubted if he heard or cared.

CHAPTER THIRTEEN

Tracy had had her fantasies about marrying Leif. His house would have been the place—out in the back with the sun reflecting off the water, the roses in full bloom, the lawn alive with friends and family. She would have worn white, albeit it slightly tarnished in truth—traditional to the end. A gown with tiny seed pearls sewn in by hand, a veil that rippled and cascaded down her back. And she would walk, of course, with a brilliant smile, ready to take his hand.

And Leif . . .

His eyes would glimmer with smoke and silver; he'd wear white, too, for it would be an afternoon wedding. He would be resplendent, for the cut would be perfect and fit to the lean contours of his body with an unmatched elegance. His lips would curl into a wonderful crooked smile, and she would feel the wonderful warmth and radiance of love sweep over her.

Once she had harbored such a fantasy. When she had dreamt those many years ago. Dreamt—so near here, right outside of Zurich!—that it had all been a nightmare. She hadn't been taken away; Leif hadn't married Celia. He had combed heaven and earth to find her and swept her away to be married in a field of roses. Her mother had been reconciled; Jesse had given the bride away, and clasped his best friend's hands with tears in his eyes as he bid him care for his daughter . . .

The real wedding wasn't her fantasy—and yet, perhaps, in a way it was. For despite it all, at the crucial moments, she felt a blazing sizzle of happiness. Illusion, perhaps, but there. His awkward smile for her right before the ceremony began. The warmth of his hand on hers. The little squeeze of his fingers that seemed an unspoken promise. A touch that might have hinted at the things that could not be spoken, not when so much lay between them.

Perhaps, even, fact was greater than fantasy. The light in his eyes when they touched hers as he placed the gold band around her finger, that slight trembling in his hands. Greater, perhaps, than fantasy, because she had never imagined the emotion, the warmth—the way she would feel when the words were spoken out loud that in fact, not fantasy, she was Leif's wife.

It should have taken days; Leif seemed to have some influential friends who managed to secure a license immediately. Two strangers served as witnesses; she barely understood a word of the ceremony.

But she was his wife.

She wasn't in white; she wore a soft red scooped-neck sweater and a navy shirt. Leif was in a sweater and beige jacket—nice, but very casual. They were already married and it seemed his hair was still damp from the shower.

It *was* fantasy, Tracy decided. It didn't matter what was said, what was worn. It mattered that she had those moments to believe, with all her heart, that *he loved her* as deeply as she loved him. Precious, precious moments, because the past was doomed to come between them again.

It was dark outside. Only the very slim sliver of a

moon gleamed down upon them as they left the church, with Leif anxious to reach the corner—and Rob and the car.

But he paused suddenly, looking up at the sky.

Then, looking at Tracy with a crooked smile: "Liar's moon, Tracy. So it would seem that not all truths have been told."

They'd procured the papers they had needed last night and this morning; he hadn't come near her since until it was time to leave for the little church. He'd suggested that she sleep—she didn't think that she'd actually slept more than an hour since they'd gotten here.

And to make matters worse, they'd passed her grandfather's house on the way. The house where she'd lived all those months. The house where Blake had been born.

"Oh, but you're convinced you know all about truth, aren't you, Leif?" Tracy asked him wearily. "Either my mother or my grandfather had my father killed—you just have to decide which."

He was silent, not replying to her sarcasm.

"Let's get back to the hotel," he said simply. He caught her hand and hurried to the car. The ever quiet and uneasy Rob greeted them both with a hello and drove them back to the hotel.

Tracy was suddenly loathe to go up the stairs to their room. She hadn't had a decent word for Leif in nearly two days, but she suddenly hung on his arm.

"I'd like a drink."

He gazed down at her and slowly, slowly smiled. "Whatever you wish."

They didn't sit down in the restaurant, but in the lobby near the fire, where a pretty blond waitress served cocktails in elegant attire. Again, the flow of easy conversation seemed to be all around them. Skiers and partiers

241

vacationed here, lovers and friends, and they were all so comfortable, so at ease.

Tracy ordered a double Tom Collins and she felt again Leif's wicked amusement. She didn't look at him, but stared into the fire. He sipped a Scotch without comment, too, and eventually the silence dragged out so long that she leapt to her feet and hurried up the stairs—without him.

Then she wondered if that action wasn't even more tearing upon her nerves—because he didn't follow. She paced so long that her feet began to hurt. She cast off her boots and trod in her stockings to the door between the two rooms and entered her own, longing for a shower—without Leif around.

She kept the water running for a long, long time. It was far better than speculation. Far better than stepping out.

But at last she emerged, surprised that someone from the hotel hadn't beaten on the door to demand that she leave the water be. She toweled herself hurriedly dry and donned the one night garment she had—thankfully a red flannel gown that had a wonderfully chaste neckline and fell all the way to her toes.

But before she could leave the bath, she gripped the sink. Dizzy, expectant. She stared at herself and saw her eyes again—blue and wide and dialated. She slammed a fist against the counter with a choking little cry.

She was warm, flushed, tremulous. Because she wanted to be with him. It had become as natural again as breathing, as feeling the sun against her face. She had to hate him for what he had done; for his manipulation.

But hadn't her grandfather and mother manipulated her life with a greater cruelty. And she didn't hate them.

242

She was hurt and wounded and horrified; she despised what they did. But not them.

She loved Leif. A part of her was secretly thrilled that she had become his wife—but to what cost?

Still shivering, she closed her eyes and sank to the floor, hugging her knees to her. It was frightening. She didn't want to love with the type of obsession that had sent her mother back to her father time and time again. Yet, hadn't they created their own hell? She and Ted might have gotten a divorce—sad, but better than the life they had led. Jesse might have given up something. Had they both been cowards—or had life simply played against them at every turn?

Tracy bit her lower lip and felt around the sink to find her watch. It was nearly midnight, and still Leif hadn't come for her. She trembled all the more thoroughly. Where were his demands now—now that she admitted she was more than willing to fulfill them, even if she was still too wounded to offer the truth to him? She stood and rinsed her face with cool water. She straightened her shoulders and came out.

Leif wasn't in her room. She crossed to the connecting door and silently opened it. He wasn't there either. Where had he gone? To celebrate the bitterness of her surrender. And then she heard it—a soft, clacking sound. Like pebbles against a glass pane.

Frowning, she walked to the window seat and cast the curtains aside. A second clattering of pebbles fell against the window. More perplexed, she hefted up the glass and stuck her head outside.

Leif was far below her in the snow, still dressed in his wedding attire, but now adorned with an acoustic guitar about his neck. He smiled at her and waved.

And began to play a love song.

Oh, it was one that she knew. Not written for her, she knew, for it was nearly twenty years old. But it was one that she loved. Jesse's work, Leif's work. A tune that haunted the mind and the senses, where the music and the lyrics combined to create magic.

It had, she knew, topped the charts for weeks on end. It was different now. There were no drums; no keyboard hummed in the background, no base sounded, there was no sax, and no flute. Just the simple sound of the guitar and his voice. A sound uniquely his—a tenor with a husky rasp that defined it, that should have been a flaw—that was instead an evocative asset, a signature of the man, known instantly by generations.

Known to the core, to the bone, by Leif Johnston's new wife.

She closed her eyes; she felt it. She opened her eyes, and she couldn't still the slow smile that came poignantly to her lips. She met his eyes and knew a harmony and a sadness, thinking of all the suspicions and lies and bitterness that lay between them and could not be erased overnight.

But she thought then that, yes, she loved him. And yes, she'd been given back the son that she thought she had lost.

And listening to the love song, she began to believe in magic. The song ended. The last chords of the guitar faded away. He looked up to her, and she could not see his expression, but she thought that there might be tenderness in his eyes.

The night was still—and then there was a sudden round of applause—and a burst of noise.

Tracy hadn't thought that anyone would be on the street that late; Leif was suddenly surrounded by people —recognized now that he held the guitar. Now that the

244

unique sound of his voice had been for her. To her surprise, Tracy thrilled with a sense of pride. Even in Switzerland the Limelights were remembered.

She watched as he signed autographs, and she heard him laugh as he thanked a young man for the use of the guitar, returning it to him. Then he gazed up at the window quizzically and extricated himself from the situation, telling them he had been serenading his new bride.

There was more applause.

Blushing, Tracy swiftly brought her head back through the window and hastily closed the glass and the curtains.

She was more nervous than ever. Keyed and tense. Trying for a facade of calm, she sat before the dressing table and picked up her brush, threading it through her hair mechanically.

He came at last. He paused in the doorway, watching her. She should have told him that his song had been beautiful, that the action had been whimsical and romantic, and a wonderful thing to have done—for her. But she couldn't speak. Her throat was tight.

He came up behind her. She saw his reflection in the mirror. He came so close that she paused with her brush in midair, for the back of her head was flush with his stomach and his hands were on her hair while his eyes held hers in the mirror.

He didn't speak to her, nor could she yet find the words to say to him. His fingers just played through her hair in a gentle massage, then moved over her throat. To the button at the neck of her very chaste gown. He slipped it, and lowered his head, placing the lightest kiss upon her collarbone, then upon the arch of her throat, then upon her shoulder as the material gaped and opened.

He straightened again, behind her, wrenching his

sweater over his head, moving closer again to rub the silky tendrils of her hair against his stomach in subtle motion.

And still he held her eyes, the soft stroke of his touch brushing her nape, her neck, her throat once again. Watching the blue pools of her eyes in that mirrored image all along. At last slipping his hands beneath the shoulders of her virginal flannel gown and causing it to fall from her shoulders. His gaze fell at last as the bronzed length of his hands cupped and curled over her breasts, thumbs rubbing over the nipples until a little sound escaped from her. Her lashes fluttered over her cheeks, hiding her eyes from erotic contact.

Tracy turned in a sudden motion, her own quivering, small white hands upon his hips, her face buried against the taut flesh of his stomach. She nuzzled against him, feeling the short coarse hairs tease her lips and cheeks and nose. She began to scatter kisses there, tenderly nipping at his flesh, taunting it with the soft flick of her tongue. Her finger delved beneath the belt line, stroking absently as she kissed him. He caught a mass of her hair with his palms, inhaling sharply as he brought them trailing through his fingers, against his flesh.

Tracy paused suddenly, hiding against him, caught in a turmoil of longing and truth. The night was cool; his touch was fever. Evocative fever rippled and danced all through her, and her greatest desire was to cast herself into his arms.

Not exactly an empty shell . . .

She was his wife, at long last. And if the fantasy of a white and traditional wedding had faded, the magic of his touch had not. She had fallen in love with him years ago and lost him. And now he was hers—only pride stood in her way.

246

"Tracy," he whispered suddenly, raggedly, "Don't stop now!"

He didn't really give her much choice in the matter; his grip, tender, gentle—urgent—fell upon her naked shoulders, bringing her from the chair and into his arms. His fingers thread through the hair at her nape, tilting her head. And again his eyes met hers. No mirror image now —just naked in glistening silver and boldly intent with thirst. His eyes closed, a shudder raked through him, and he brought his lips to her.

She'd never known a kiss so totally consuming. The delving of his tongue, the movement, the erotic sensations of its very tip, coming to her, withdrawing.

And she, in hunger, catching him, drawing him back, seeking each elusive thrust. Pressing against him with greater urgency. Barely aware that her very chaste gown was no longer on her at all, but had fallen to her feet in total disregard. She was consumed with the need to touch. Feel the exhalting sexual tension in the corded muscles of his shoulders and chest, warm, rippling, and moving to the softest caress of her fingertips. Feel his hips, hard and urgent against hers. Feel that kiss that promised everything else to come.

She found his belt again. She slid her hands around to his spine, forcing material away, exploring the fine lines of his back and the hard power of his buttocks.

He made a hoarse sound, kicked off his shoes, shed trousers, socks, and boots, and swept her in his arms. The breath escaped her in heady excitement, and when she lay beneath him, she could not lie still.

Empty shell . . .

She mocked herself, and it meant nothing. A fever was upon her, potent, demanding, and she could not deny it. She made love to him, allowing herself to refuse no temp-

247

tation. She kissed him, she trailed her hair over him again —brought all of her body in contact with all of his. Heard his whispers, flowery compliments, graphic truths —all spoken as only a lover could speak them, and all beautiful in the arousal they brought forth in her blood, in her limbs, in the spiraling crest of her desire.

She felt deliciously powerful; more powerful still when his eyes and face first betrayed his intention, when his arms enwrapped her again, when the tide swept and ebbed, and brought him to be aggressor again. Did one take and then give, give and take, or was it all one? Lips meshing, fingers touching, bodies burning—all in one.

All in one.

Making love had never been like this. And yet she felt that each time he touched her again. He'd been her lover; he'd become her lover. And tonight, beneath another liar's moon, she knew again that wonderful fascination, that spell. He coming into her, she being filled with him. Each stroke, each thrust a bonding, a beauty. Rising in earthbound passion, somehow more. Shimmering magic. This was unique. No one had ever loved like this before.

Minutes passed, bodies cooled. He continued to stroke her and she was ready to talk, ready to say the things that might make life right between them. But then, right then, was when he chose to open his mouth, chuckling softly.

"An empty shell, huh?"

Something rushed through her like brushfire; not passion now, but burning anger. She twitched with the near irresistible urge to move her hand just a bit and twist some wrenching damage upon that piece of his anatomy that just brought her such sweet pleasure.

He might have sensed her deadly intention; the next thing she knew his arms were about her, pulling her on top of him, laughter in his eyes.

"Tracy—"

"Let me go! I'm getting out of this bed—"

"No, you're not," he said serenely, still amused. "You promised to sleep with me."

"Oh! I should keep my promises when you don't?"

"What promises have I ever made and not kept?"

"You were supposed to find my father's murderer, remember?"

The laughter faded from his eyes. He rolled, leaving her beside him. He reached to the nightstand, found his cigarettes, and lit one. His back was to her and despite it all, she wanted to take back her words. She wanted to stroke her fingers down the length of his spine.

She didn't touch him. A moment passed, and then he spoke.

"Tracy, Rob is a detective. He discovered the grave, he slipped some money to a retired official to give him a garbled account regarding Blake's birth and the preadoption circumstances. He's also been working for me where your father's death was concerned."

Tracy tensed, wondering what the quiet Rob had discovered. The man she had hired had discovered the money situation, then reported to her that there was nothing else he could do.

"Go on," she said.

Leif turned back to her. "The cop who shot your father's killer rather conveniently fell off a roof and died very recently."

Tracy swallowed. "Police work is dangerous—"

He made a ticking sound of annoyance.

"Tracy—face it. He was paid to kill Smith after Smith killed Jesse—just to make sure that Smith didn't talk. And now the cop is dead, too. No connections."

She grasped the covers, pulling them nervously to her breasts. "When—when did this man fall off the roof?"

"Right after my invitations to get together for the memorial service went out. When everyone that we might suspect could easily have been in the city."

Tracy lowered her eyes. "What does that matter? You're convinced that it was either my mother or my grandfather," she said bitterly.

"Tracy." His voice was surprisingly gentle. "I have reason to suspect that Jesse thought Blake might be ours —your child and mine. You never told him about Blake, did you?"

She couldn't answer him.

"Tracy, did you?"

She shook her head at last. "No. When I—when I thought that the baby was dead, it didn't seem to make any sense to tell Dad. I hadn't seen him—not after Mother determined to take me to Europe, where I could be completely beneath her wing. And then, of course, when I discovered that I was pregnant, you were already married to Celia. It seemed to make the best sense to stay here and have my baby. I didn't leave until—until after the funeral for the baby. I didn't see Jesse until a month or two after that—and then it just seemed that it would cause needless pain to tell him."

Leif took in a deep breath and exhaled slowly, then murmured. "I don't think that it was an accident. I think that your grandfather made sure that Blake came to me, once he knew that we were hoping to adopt a child."

"You're granting him that concession?" Tracy asked bitterly.

Leif eyed her coolly. "Blake is his great-grandchild. Arthur probably did want him raised by one of his natural parents and cared for in a sound home, lacking nothing. Before our month together, Tracy, I'd gotten on rather well with your grandfather. But Arthur came to see Jesse about a week before he was killed. They fought. I think that Jesse told him that he was pretty damn sure that Blake was his grandson and that Arthur had been playing God again."

Tracy moistened her lips. "That's an assumption!"

"Yes, but your father called me the day before he was killed. He seemed upset. I think that Jesse knew, Tracy."

"So," she murmured distantly, smoothing the sheet down. "My grandfather had Jesse killed rather than let him tell you that he thought that you had adopted your own natural son." She stared at him with hot eyes and a wretched effort at contempt. But for a moment, she just didn't know anymore. "Tell me, if grandfather didn't conspire to kill him—just what was my mother's motive?"

"She couldn't stay away from him," Leif said softly. "Or perhaps she didn't want Jesse coming out with the truth, either. You would have believed your father," Leif added bitterly. "You would have told him the truth. He would never have had to drag you to a cemetery to find out what really happened."

Tracy rolled away from him, grinding her teeth together as a cacophony of emotions seemed to scream within her.

Blake . . . It was still incredible that people who supposedly loved her could have stolen her child away.

Jesse . . . It was still incredible that he was dead. Gone from her forever.

Leif . . . Determined to nail the people she still loved despite it all.

Audrey . . . Never, never able to break her ties with Jesse.

251

Herself . . . She would do anything to be with Blake now. She did love Leif, and marriage had once been a dream. But tonight . . . tonight she had fallen to his seduction without feeling love, and she was faced again with a moral horror. I am his wife. But is it enough? It is an empty marriage—a demand, not a proposal.

"Tracy?"

He placed a hand on her shoulder; she shook it off. "I'm in your bed, Leif. Or rather, you're in mine. Promise fulfilled. May I go to sleep, now, please?"

She felt him stiffen. "Certainly, Tracy. Go to sleep," he muttered with disgust.

But she didn't sleep. She lay there as far away from him as she could get. She didn't know how much time passed, but he knew she wasn't sleeping. He spoke again.

"By the way, Tracy. Rob was able to tell me that your mother, Ted, and Arthur Kingsley flew into New York on Friday, a day before the cop was killed. And by some odd, odd coincidence, they all happened to be there the week before Jesse died. Jesse and Arthur fought at the office, Jesse had dinner and I'm not sure what else with your mother, and Jesse even met Ted for lunch."

"And you live in Connecticut and the two of you saw each other constantly. So tell me—what does that prove?" Tracy asked.

"Not a thing," Leif said. "Maybe the lovely Lauren did it after all. Or Carol. Or Sam or Tiger—or the damned butler. Go ahead. Go to sleep, Tracy. You're living with blinders on."

"Go to hell!" she snapped.

"Yeah, yeah. Sweet dreams to you, too, Mrs. Johnston," he said with a very weary sigh.

They kept their distance then. It was near dawn when

she slept, just in time for him to wake her and tell her in a very foul temper that it was time to start for home.

It was daylight when they left, daylight when they returned to Leif's home in Connecticut.

Leif must have called Liz, and Liz must have told Blake that they were returning, because he was standing on the porch, waiting.

Tracy stared at Blake as Leif parked the car. She and Leif had barely spoken on the long flight home; they hadn't exchanged two words in the car. Now he gazed her way before exiting the car, and she knew that it was with speculation. He hadn't given her any guidelines in dealing with Blake and she knew that he was curious to see what role she would take.

He was too young; they both knew that. Way too young to deal with the intricacy of the situation.

And at this particular moment, Tracy just wanted to be his friend. Well, that wasn't really true. She wanted to run to him and sweep him into her arms and break into tears and tell him that now that she had found him, no one would ever, ever take him away from her again. She wanted to hold him and marvel at him and absorb the fact that he was her son. Hers.

"Daddy!"

He didn't give her a glance, but raced forward to fly into Leif's arms. Tracy stood in the background, inhaling, exhaling, trying to still the sharpness of the pain.

Leif hugged him tightly, the massive length of his hands and fingers cupping the dark little head close to him. Tracy's throat tightened; there was so much love there. Love earned in constant days and nights of caring. Days and nights that she had lost.

"Hey!" Leif said at last, settling Blake on his hip and

smiling. "Say 'hi' to Tracy. I've got a big surprise for you."

Blake glanced over his father's shoulder at Tracy and gave her a little smile. Leif's smile.

Leif's smile. Leif's eyes. Jesse's beautiful blond hair—all these things. His—hers.

"Hi, Tracy." He gave his attention back to his father. "What's the surprise?"

"You're the first to know. I hope you like the idea. Tracy and I ran away and got married. What do you think?"

Tracy wasn't at all sure that Blake was thrilled with the idea. He gazed at her with his father's own wariness apparent in his charcoal eyes.

"Will you be leaving a lot again?" he asked his father.

"No," Leif said, shaking his head.

"Tracy plays the piano, too, you know. She might want to go on the stage like Jamie," Blake continued, not sure.

Leif hesitated, Tracy stepped forward. "I like to write music, Blake. I don't like crowds, and I really don't like traveling a lot."

He lowered his head and shrugged, then grinned at his father. "She's a lot better than some other girls you might have married."

"Blake!"

"Can I tell everybody?" he asked his father.

He shrugged and glanced at Tracy. Her fingers were still itching to wrench *her* son from Leif, and she knew she couldn't do it. She shrugged in return.

Leif set Blake on the ground, and he went running up to the house, screaming out the information.

By the time they reached the door, it seemed that the household was there, waiting for them, asking if it was true or not. Jamie was thrilled, kissing Tracy and telling

254

her he had known it would happen all along. Liz was much more quietly pleased. Carol congratulated them nicely, Lauren with more of a barb to her words. Tiger and Sam gave her a kiss. Ted was there, mildly pleased.

Only her mother and grandfather were missing.

While Leif went to the bar to produce champagne, Tracy learned in a soft aside from Liz that her mother had barely appeared since Tracy had spoken to her on the phone. She was out back by the pool with her father right now.

Tracy slipped out back, finding her mother and grandfather beneath the sun umbrella. Arthur remained sitting at the sight of her, Audrey jumped to her feet. Tracy could see that she had been crying. She was still beautiful, but she didn't look her customary ten years younger than her true age—she looked ten years older.

"Oh, Tracy!"

Audrey looked as if she wanted to reach out and hug her. She didn't. Tracy stepped forward and took the initiative, wondering if she shouldn't tear into her mother. She sighed, holding Audrey close. She couldn't help it; she couldn't bear the pain.

"Mother, please, it's all right."

"It's not—"

"Audrey, hush!" Arthur said wearily. Seated, dignified, he touched Tracy as deeply as her mother had—Arthur looked close to a hundred today. He stared at her with a strange honor in his weathered face, like a man condemned to hang, but certain that he acted on principle and couldn't have changed a thing.

"Tracy, I hope, girl, that you will forgive us. If you can't, I can only offer this—what I did, I did out of love. You were so young." He glanced at his daughter; Audrey's head was still bowed. "Audrey didn't breathe a

255

happy breath from the time you were born because every time she looked at you, she thought of Jesse Kuger. She wrote him, she called him—she saw him—to tell him about you." He lifted his hands. "Tracy, a child is a tie. And Leif was married. I couldn't bear to see your life go the same way. I—I did see to it that Blake reached Leif."

Tracy sat down. "I just married Leif, grandfather."

He digested that information in silence, then spoke to her softly. "I wish you every happiness. I mean that, granddaughter."

"Grandfather, what you did was wrong. To mother's life, to my own."

"Tracy, we all have to do what we think is right at that time. Only hindsight can prove us right or wrong. Your father—" He paused, glancing at his daughter's bowed head again. "I don't think that your father had it in him to be a one-woman man. But he needed Audrey in his way. If Audrey could have forgotten him, she might have been a great deal happier."

He paused and leaned toward her. "Forgive me, Tracy?"

"Oh, Tracy!" Audrey sobbed again.

"Mother!" Tracy murmured awkwardly. "For God's sake! Please quit crying. I forgive you!"

Audrey looked at her—then past her—and tears started to well in her red-rimmed eyes again. And this time, Arthur Kingsley came to his feet. Tracy turned around to see that Leif had come out and was walking toward them. She jumped up, gazing at Leif herself, mutely beseeching him to go gently with these two.

He stopped behind her, locking her to him with his arms encircling her waist. "Has Tracy told you?" he inquired softly.

256

Her mother didn't answer; Arthur nodded. He sighed. "I assume, Leif, that you'd like me out of your house."

Tracy curled her fingers over Leif's hands. She felt all the tension in their steel hold, and again, in her touch, she tried very hard to beg in silence. She tilted her head, gazing up into his features. He shook his head ruefully.

"No, Arthur. This is Tracy's home, too, now. You're her family—always welcome here. Audrey—we're opening champagne. Will you come in and toast us, please?"

Audrey broke into another spasm of tears. Leif released Tracy in order to go to her, leading her to sit, kneeling before her, and taking her hands. "Look at me, Audrey. It's all right. It's—all—right. Really. Now, please, come and have some champagne."

Audrey nodded, her eyes very, very wide on Leif. He helped her back up, and they all returned to the house.

Tracy was exhausted—that was half of her problem with the evening. She felt as if she had been digging ditches all day, but then she had heard that mental trauma was far more draining than physical exertion.

There was so much activity that night. They barbecued at the pool, and since it was the last night before they were to drive into the city for Jesse's memorial service, everyone was nostalgic, and all the conversation centered on her father. Tracy drank too much champagne to soothe her jangled nerves, then she kept looking at everyone and wondering once more which of these smiling people had decided that her father should be murdered.

And then there was Leif . . .

She had wanted to kiss his hands for the way he had dealt with her mother, yet she didn't feel close to him at all. To her, unless he was holding her or touching her for someone else's benefit, he remained as cool and distant as he had been since they had exchanged the bitter words in bed.

Lauren was the last straw. She sauntered over to Tracy with her charcoaled chicken plate and a frozen daiquiri in her hand and offered congratulations again.

"I do hope it lasts," she said with wide, innocent eyes. "For a few years, at least."

Tracy smiled. "Lauren, marriage is for a lifetime."

"Ah, Tracy! More than fifty percent of all marriages end in divorce! And you two have the age difference and all."

"Lauren, Leif would be two years younger than Dad. You're about two years older than I am? Did you marry him with that attitude?"

"I—" Lauren stared at her with her mouth agape for a second and then snapped it shut. "I—was more mature, Tracy. You've led a sheltered life. Fifteen years is a big difference. I mean, your husband is one of your mother's friends!"

"Yes—nice, isn't it?" Tracy said smoothly. "Oh, do excuse me, Lauren. I think I hear my mother calling me!"

"Just one minute, Tracy! I was your stepmother; I'm trying to give you a friendly warning. You are young. At some time your eyes might start straying and you might be tempted—"

"Oh? Did you cheat on my father, Lauren?"

"No!" the blond snapped out. "He cheated on me, and Leif is exactly the same. Do you really think that you can hold him?"

Tracy laughed. "Lauren, make up your mind! Who is going to cheat on who?"

She left quickly; she simply wasn't up to Lauren anymore that night. She wasn't up to the truth.

I am afraid, Lauren! Damned afraid! He married me because he wouldn't give his son up in any way, shape, or form, and I have no idea what he really feels. Bitter, for one. But maybe we will manage, because we are capable of sleeping together very nicely, thank you.

And if he left me for another woman now, I think that I might curl up and die.

She managed to escape to the maze; she so desperately wanted to be alone. But when she had reached the rose garden, she realized that someone was there before her.

To her astonishment, she realized that the silhouettes against the silver moon were Sam and Liz.

Sam and Liz—in a passionate embrace.

Quietly, quietly, she slipped away.

For lack of anywhere better to go, she hurried into the house, listening to the laughter and conversation that followed her. She started up the stairs, wondering what would happen when Leif came up at last. Would he miss her downstairs? Would he hunt for her?

Would he come to bed in silence, still so distant? Or would he touch her? Was it all a travesty? Would they lay together, yet eons apart, for night after night after night . . .

She reached the door, then closed her eyes, leaning against it. Leif had been good to Audrey and Arthur. Had that been only to lure them into a trap?

"Tracy!"

At the sound of the urgent whisper, she started. At first she saw nothing, then down the darkened hallway she saw a little head peering out from a softly lit doorway.

Blake. Her heart began to pound, her hands to tremble.

She walked down to him and kneeled before him. He was in the cutest little teddy-bear pajamas.

He touched her cheek. "Were you crying again?"

She shook her head. "No, Blake."

"Your skin is wet."

"Is it?"

He nodded gravely.

She wanted to touch him so badly. She did, just stroking her palm over his cheek, then letting her hand fall. She couldn't smother him; he wouldn't want her at all then.

"You need to go to sleep, big boy," she told him. "We're going to drive into the city tomorrow."

"I know. To pray for Uncle Jesse."

"Right."

"You *were* crying. Was it because tomorrow is when we remember him?"

"Maybe."

He cracked his door open wider. "You can come in with me if you'd like. It might make you feel better. I'll let you hold my Wuzzle."

"Thanks, Blake," she murmured, and her heart leapt again. He took her hand and led her into his domain. It was a big wonderful boy's room with bookshelves and train tracks and toys.

"That's my bed. It's big. Want to lie down with me?"

"Oh, yes, Blake, thank you. I'd like that very much."

She lay down beside him, holding the Wuzzle. Trying not to cry, trying not to grasp him to her.

He stared at her, and smiled. "I really didn't want to be alone tonight," he admitted.

"Neither did I," she said.

In time, his eyes closed.

She couldn't make herself leave him. In time, her eyes closed.

Thirty minutes later, Leif gave up searching the house for his disappearing and wayward bride—it had been hard to keep up a celebration dinner without her. Grimly he wondered if she hadn't decided to back out of the whole thing anyway. And if she had . . .

He inhaled, knowing that if he found her, he would drag her back, back to his arms, back to his room. Back to his bed.

On sudden intuition, he went to his son's room. He saw the two of them sleeping there. He saw the tears on her cheeks. He saw their fingers, entwined between them. He pulled off her shoes, drew the blanket over them both, and silently closed the door as he left.

CHAPTER FOURTEEN

Tracy tried to pray but she couldn't. All that she could see or feel was the sun, reflecting through the beautiful stained-glass windows.

Bessie Tibbs, a popular soul singer and old friend of Jesse's, was singing "Ave Maria." It was beautiful. Her tones reached throughout the church like crystal magic. Everything was beautiful. The candles, the flowers. The church was full, and outside people lined the street. Some in tribute to Jesse; some to see the personalities who would eventually come from the church.

Tracy closed her eyes. She felt the fabric of Leif's jacket brush her arm, and though nothing was right between them, she was glad. He'd made no comment at all about her falling asleep in Blake's room; he'd been beside her all the way today. They'd driven together with Liz and Blake in the backseat, and, thankfully, the two of them had kept conversation going. And once they'd reached the church, Leif hadn't left her side. He still hadn't really spoken to her, but he'd been there for her, and she felt the strength of his presence—a bastion today, when she needed it.

She closed her eyes more tightly. She wanted to pray for her father. All she could keep thinking was that it had all been such an awful waste. Jesse lost to them. Young,

262

full of laughter, full of talent. He hadn't been just a pop star, but a musician and a poet. Not a personality, but a man, with all his human frailties. She missed him today with all her heart.

She opened her eyes again. She heard the words of eulogy, the prayers for his soul.

God grant that he have peace . . .

Once she caught Jamie's eyes. He gave her a rather sad smile of encouragement, and she returned it, thinking, We are here, we are together—and we loved him. That is in itself the greatest testament!

Leif prodded her. She gazed into his eyes and realized that the service had come to an end. Stumbling slightly, caught by his strength, she started to walk from the pew.

Outside on the steps, the sun nearly blinded her. There were a number of policemen and security officials around, holding back the crowd. But suddenly a man approached Leif, motioning him aside.

Leif didn't seem to be surprised. He excused himself huskily to Tracy and stepped aside. She gripped Blake's hand.

"What a circus," Liz murmured.

It was indeed.

"Hey!" someone shouted. "Mrs. Johnston! Is it true?"

Liz nudged her. "Tracy—you are Mrs. Johnston."

"Mrs. Johnston! Is the story true?"

What story? She felt very disoriented. Jamie and Tiger were suddenly in front of her. Like a wall of protection. A group of teenaged girls started shouting at the sight of Jamie.

What story? She'd seen the morning paper. There had been an article on the service today—and on Jesse. It had been a nice article, commemorating his accomplishments in music.

"Ah, come on, Mrs. Johnston! There's a great story out in the tabloid! All about you and Leif Johnston being lovers a long time ago! That you actually had a child together, and that all these years later you're finally together! What a romance!"

Tracy was stunned. Who could know? Who could know but her intimate family—and who of them would have called in such a story? She couldn't believe it. She couldn't react—she couldn't function.

She realized then that her mother was behind her on the steps, and that Arthur was with her, and Ted.

A flashbulb went off in her face. When she could see again, she instantly noted Blake—staring at her in a horrible way.

"Leave her alone!" Jamie shouted in her defense.

Numb, Tracy stared across the steps. Leif was still talking to the man, nodding and frowning with his dark brows drawn taut across his face. He saw Tracy's pale face and inclined his head in a worried question. He pointed toward them. The strange man looked their way —and nodded. Leif started walking toward her. But he seemed so distant. There were so many people between them.

"Mrs. Johnston! Is Leif's little boy your own son?"

Who? Tracy raged silently. Maybe one of the others had known; maybe Jesse had told Lauren or Carol what he had suspected. Lauren, surely! She couldn't be trusted.

A woman's voice came at her next, giggling, excited.

"Tell us! Please, what is the truth? Is he your little boy? He's adorable!"

Blake wrenched his hand from hers and stared at her in a horrible combination of reproach, fury—and hatred.

"My mother is dead!" Blake cried out, wrenching from her. "I hate you!" he screamed to Tracy. "I hate you, I

264

hate you!" He burst into tears and disappeared into the web of humanity coming from the church.

Chaos broke out. People were forging everywhere. The police began to lose control.

"Blake!" she screamed. She was shaking. Tears started to burn behind her eyes. How could anyone be so cruel?

Liz gripped her shoulders. "Tracy—I'll find Blake. I promise. I—I don't think he'll come to you right now. Do yourself a favor—get out of here, quickly."

Liz disappeared. There were too many people. She could no longer see Leif, nor could she even find Jamie.

"Is Leif Johnston's son really yours?"

"When was the affair?"

What in God's name possessed people? Tracy wondered desperately. There were strangers all around her, crushing her, smothering her. Grabbing at her. At her hair, at her clothing.

She was about to panic, about to scream, when she saw a familiar, kind, gentle face at last. Ted Blare reached out a hand to her and wrenched her from the frenzied crowd.

"Come on," he whispered. "Let's get out of here!"

She followed him with the greatest relief, running down the steps in his wake. There was a taxi at the curb. Ted ushered her into the back, hopped in beside her, and told the cabbie just to drive, to get them going.

Then he turned to Tracy, his dark eyes full of concern.

"Are you okay, sweetheart?"

She nodded, gripping his hand. "Oh, Ted!"

She was shaking; she had sworn she was done with crying, but tears streamed silently from beneath her lids. "How could they? How could somebody print a story like that? How could that horrible man have shouted that way? Oh, my God! Blake will never speak to me again.

What is the matter with people? It was supposed to be a memorial service for my father—"

"Hush, hush, Tracy, it's going to be all right," Ted assured her. He wiped the tears from her cheeks, smiling. "Look around you now. We've left it all behind. It's just a quiet Sunday afternoon and everything is going to be all right."

"I don't know if it will ever be all right. Blake—"

"Tracy, his aunt will find him. They'll control that mess back there, and Leif will reassure him. He is only six, Tracy. He didn't really understand any of it—only that they were nastily attacking you. And somehow threatening what he remembers of Celia. He's young— he'll be okay. He'll spring back, and he won't hate you."

Oh, God, he hates me now! she thought wretchedly.

"It's all, all, all such a mess," she murmured.

She gazed up at him—at the kind, steady face she had always known. Ted, always there in the background. She laughed suddenly. A bitter sound, a sad one. She gripped his hand and held it tight.

"Oh, Ted! How did you ever wind up stuck in this absurd family!"

He smiled back. "I was what your grandfather had in mind for your mother. A good, steady, boring businessman. And once I saw your mother, I was hooked. I still think she's the most beautiful woman I've ever seen."

Tracy discovered herself looking quickly away from him. She couldn't bear to look into his eyes with the thought that her mother had cheated on him for years and years and years. With her father.

He sighed softly. "You don't have to look away, Tracy. I know that your mother saw Jesse until the day that he died."

"Oh, Ted. I'm so sorry."

"Don't be. I have your baby brother now. Anthony makes everything all right."

She swallowed and nodded. Anthony was only two now, but when he was older, she wanted him to spend time with her and Leif and Blake.

If there was anything left. If Blake could forgive her, if Leif could love her. If they could create a family in the wake of all of this.

She shook her head, suddenly, violently, misery rising high within her once again. She looked out the window at the city, wishing desperately that she could just run, feel the breeze—feel free from the burdens of the heart that seemed to hang about her neck like heavy bricks.

"Stop!" she cried suddenly, leaning over to tap the cabby on the shoulder.

The taxi veered off the road. Ted, confused, gripped her arm. "Tracy! What are you doing? Let me get you back to the hotel. We'll go to your mother's and my suite. No one will be back for a bit. We'll be all alone—"

Tracy smiled at him. "I know you think I'm crazy. I just have to get out. I have to walk for a while. You go on back."

"Not on your life, young lady."

"Ted, see the bridge? I'm going to take a walk over it."

He inhaled impatiently. He was annoyed with her— she knew it. He'd wanted her to go to the hotel with him.

"Tracy, come on, now, just come back to the hotel with me!"

"Ted, really—go on. I'll be all right. I just feel like walking. Ted, you're a dear, but—"

"Do something!" the cabby interrupted them irritably.

"Maybe the bridge will do just as well," Ted muttered. Tracy frowned. He smiled and urged her out of the taxi, following quickly behind her.

Ted paid the cabbie; they stepped out on the pavement. The bridge loomed before them in silent majesty.

"Come on!"

Ted took her arm. He seemed quite content now to walk over the bridge with her. They walked in silence then for the next fifteen minutes. The air was cool, the sun was out—New York was enjoying a fabulous blue sky that day. The breeze cooled Tracy's cheeks. She noted moments later that she wasn't shaking anymore, that her footsteps, hurried to keep up with Ted, were both exhausting and calming. She did feel better.

"Look at the old scow down there!" Ted told her, pausing. Tracy came beside him to stare down to the river—far, far below them now.

The sky was blue, but the water was greenish gray. Sunlight caught on it, and now and again it sparkled. Behind them, a group of cars whizzed by, creating a greater wind.

"It's magnificent, isn't it?" Ted said.

He took her elbow and they started walking again. "A sailboat—and that one looks like a merchant marine!"

They paused again. Tracy realized that they were high up and the boats below them were very, very small now. Not real at all.

"Toys!" she laughed again.

"It's a long, long way down," Ted murmured.

Tracy stepped back suddenly, wanting a distance from the rail. She was suddenly frightened, and she didn't know why. Heights didn't bother her. It was broad daylight, and though the Sunday traffic was slower than usual, the bridge was still busy with spurts of cars whizzing by them every few seconds.

"Very few people have survived a fall from this height, Tracy," Ted told her gravely. "And I believe that those

268

who have came out of it were terribly mangled. Death would be the better option."

She smiled at him, weakly, feeling the shivery sensation of an unknown fear once again.

"Ted—" she murmured uneasily, backing further away to start walking again.

He reached for her hand, holding it tightly with his own, leaning comfortably against that railing that suddenly seemed so small a barrier between life and death.

"I know that you know, Tracy."

"What?" she gasped. "Ted, I don't know anything—"

"Surely, you do." He smiled. "That cop's partner is telling Leif right now that your mother, Arthur, and I are the ones that he saw his partner talking to the week before dear Jesse departed. We just met him in the street, you know, and your mother can't resist flirting with anyone. But I saw something about him. I saw his lust for money, the way he seemed awed when he realized that he was talking to Arthur Kingsley. So I went back. I saw him alone—and I paid him to see that a criminal was killed. Easy. My benefit for years of being the neglected husband—Arthur Kingsley's money. Two hundred thousand dollars a year in personal allowance. I wanted it—but I discovered no amount of money was enough to watch your mother yearn for your father—year after year after year."

"Ted, no. I don't know anything of this! Don't tell me anything. I don't want to—"

"Tracy, Tracy, tsk, tsk. You and Leif decided that someone had paid Martin Smith to kill Jesse. I knew it as soon as Leif called about his get-together for a memorial service. Flush them all out. That was his plan. But you see, he's still going to think that Arthur did it. After all, Arthur did everything else. Arthur and your mother."

His fingers tightened around her wrist. Tracy was still so stunned that nothing escaped her but a faint protest.

"Tracy, you were a sweet child. But you were his child. God, the years I spent hating him! You should have hated him, too. He didn't bother much with you—he was too busy sleeping with your mother."

"Ted!" she protested suddenly, vehemently. Was he mad—he was so calm! And never, never in her wildest imagination had she thought that it was Ted!

Ted—telling her flatly that he had conspired to kill her father. He would only tell her such a thing if . . .

"Look down, Tracy. A long, long fall. I was so upset with you, I planted that story in the paper just to create havoc, my dear. Just to get you alone. I meant to get you up to the suite—forty stories above the ground—and watch you jump from the window. I thought the whole thing would be blown. But this is really much, much better. You casting yourself over the bridge. And, of course, I'll tell them you did it because you finally cracked. You came from such a messed-up situation, Tracy!" His smile deepened. "Jesse's bastard bears a bastard! I loved the story idea—such poetic justice, you know? Of course, I don't know the whole story, Tracy, or I could have told that smutty reporter more. Is Johnston really in love with you? Or does he hate you? Did he think that you gave your baby away? Jesse did know, by the way. I think that he planned on telling Leif—and you. Which makes it look all the worse for your grandfather. So few people knew! But then maybe it wasn't so odd that after a certain amount of time Jesse was able to recognize his own grandchild. And he knew Arthur. He knew that Arthur would stoop to almost anything."

Ted started to laugh. Tracy looked anxiously over her

shoulder. Where were the cars? It was a sunny day. Ted couldn't possibly be planning . . .

"It's so easy, Tracy. Leif will believe forever that Arthur killed Jesse. And anyone in the world would believe that you went insane and suicidal! Look at the pressure, Tracy!"

The pressure—the only pressure she knew was that of his grip about her wrist. She didn't know whether to scream in pure panic or to still the rampaging beat of her heart and try to rationalize with him. She still couldn't believe it. Ted! Of all people! Of all people, sweet, harmless Ted.

He wasn't harmless now. She realized that as she looked at him. At the grim, implacable smile in place on his lips.

She tried very hard to wrench her arm away. His grip tightened. She screamed, with all her heart, with all her breath, as long and loud as she could.

The cars just kept whizzing by, and there wasn't another soul on the walkway.

Ted's smile deepened.

"Tracy, it's perfect. Bless you for that stubborn streak of yours. The bridge is really far superior to a window! It's—perfect!"

She gasped for more breath. "As perfect as giving a petty crook a fortune to kill my father. Then having that petty crook killed. Then killing the policeman who had killed him! Who did you pay to do that for you, Ted?"

"Not a soul, Tracy. I did that one myself. It was easy— he had been blackmailing me. I picked a time for him to meet me on the roof, and the poor fellow went right over. I heard him tell his partner that there was a mugger up there. Some things do fall right in place. And you know

271

what, Tracy? He was a pretty hefty fellow. And you're just a little, little girl. You'll go over easily."

"Why?" she gasped out. "Why—"

"Why did I kill Jesse? Tracy, what a question! The bastard kept sleeping with my wife!"

She moistened her lips. Her head was spinning. He meant to cast her over. Over the rail. And she would fall. Fall and fall and fall into the grayish green depths so very far below her.

"Why me, Ted! What did I ever do to you?"

He shook his head. If she could keep him talking, maybe he would ease his hold. She could run. Pray God she could outrun him!

"Tracy," he said very softly. "I thought that you already knew. And then again, well—"

"Well?"

"You're Jesse's girl." He chuckled softly. "I can't tell you how much I hated Jesse. How much—or how long. Tracy, it was like worms eating away at my stomach, at my heart, day after endless damn day. Eating, festering. My God! How I hated that man."

Staring at him, Tracy realized with horror that there would be no reasoning with Ted—none at all. His hate had been so deep that he had come to an awful madness because of it.

With a violent wrench, Tracy tore her hand from his grasp. She shoved against him with all her strength and started to run, screaming for help. Someone had to have their windows down. Someone had to hear her . . .

She knew that she could be faster than Ted. But somehow he caught her. His fingers twined into her hair, jerking her backward and sending her flying down to the pavement hard, the breath knocked from her. She gasped; he was trying to pick her up. Wildly, she thrashed against him, tearing long grooves into his face with her nails. Oh, good God! Someone had to see the struggle!

"Ted!"

He jerked, releasing her. Tracy recognized the voice just as he did, and she spun around to see her mother standing twenty yards in back of them, with Arthur Kingsley beyond her, stepping from the driver's seat of a sedan pulled haphazardly against the curve.

"Ted!" Audrey cried again. "Stop! I see you, my father sees you. There are witnesses!"

He stared at her, then shook his head slowly. "No. No, I can't! Don't you see—she is Jesse's seed. And—yours."

"My daughter, Ted! Jesse is dead. I love Tracy! If you touch her—"

Ted let out the most horrible cry that Tracy had ever heard. Like a bellow, like a bull's roar of rage. Then he was up and running again, running toward her mother.

"No!" Tracy was on her feet, screaming.

"Audrey!" Ted shouted. "We'll do something together! We'll go out of this world as one!"

Tracy started running, too, but something whizzed by her. A man.

Leif.

And just seconds before Ted reached Audrey, Leif reached Ted, pitting himself against the man's back like a tackle, smacking them both flat against the cement.

"Audrey, damn you, run!" Leif shouted. Tracy heard the sickening sound of fists flying against flesh and bone. Arthur Kingsley reached his daughter and wrenched her wooden body back toward the car.

273

Arms sweeped around Tracy's shoulder. She turned. It was Jamie, grim and tense, holding her.

She stared ahead of herself. The two men were up. Ted swiped at Leif; Leif ducked.

Ted didn't strike out again. He very simply caught hold of the rail—and catapulted over it.

Tracy heard a long scream. She didn't even know that it was she that was making the sound until Leif, tattered and mussed, and gasping, staggered back over to them and took her from Jamie, gently sliding a hand over her mouth.

"Shh, Tracy. Shush!" He held her as she broke into a spasm of tears. He tried to ease the shaking in her body.

"Look at me, Tracy!" he commanded her. "Look at me!" And he raised her chin so that her eyes met his. Gray and level and tender and caring.

"It's over, Tracy. It's going to be all right. It's really going to be all right."

He kissed her forehead and hugged her to him again. "I love you, Tracy. I love you. It will be all right."

And suddenly she stopped shaking. She believed him. She pulled away from him and stared searchingly into the handsome lines of his face, and she felt again the silver caress of his eyes.

"Leif?"

"I love you, Tracy. I love you," he whispered again. He caught her hand and brought their fingers between them, entwining them. "We can make it all right," he told her, firmly.

And by then, the police were there. Someone called his name, and he handed her back to Jamie's care.

Jamie hugged her tightly. "We've made it, Tracy. We've made it, and we can go on from here."

It wasn't to be quite that simple. Tracy had to give a statement to the police, and although Leif tried to handle most of it, she did have to speak with them.

Audrey was so hysterical that she had to be taken to the hospital, sedated, and kept overnight. But before she was parted from Tracy, she begged to talk to her. Tracy had to know, she said, that her baby brother, Anthony, was—was Jesse's child, too.

Audrey was so remorseful, so hysterical. Tracy tried to tell her that it didn't matter; Audrey said that it did. She hadn't wanted Tracy to believe that her little brother could be mad—like Ted. Tracy had kissed and hugged her mother again, and tried to assure her that everything would be okay.

And Arthur Kingsley was so shaky, pensive and morose that Tracy began to fear that her grandfather wouldn't make it either. She knew that he couldn't help but think that he had caused it all by his interference all those years ago. And he had been wrong; so terribly wrong. But Tracy believed with all her heart that he had never meant to hurt any of them, and she tried to tell him that she loved him, wondering if it would do any good. Arthur went to stay at Audrey's side in the hospital, and Tracy knew, too, that for all his interference, he loved his daughter very, very much, and that he was praying, too, that he might make several things up to her.

Through it all, Jamie was there. Pale but steady and totally supportive. He told Tracy that, just when she had left with Ted, Leif had learned from the deceased officer's partner that the two of them had met Arthur, Audrey, and Ted over a year ago. And that, once Leif knew Tracy was off with her stepfather, instinct had warned him that Ted had ordered Jesse's murder. For several seconds he had soared into an explosive panic, but he had sobered quickly, aware that he must find her.

Someone had noted the cab company and Leif had reached the dispatcher and contacted the cabbie who had remembered letting the two of them out by the river.

"I've never seen Leif like that, Tracy," Jamie told her with his wonderful, easy smile that was so like their father's. "He must love you very, very much."

"I hope so," she whispered. And she'd leaned against him, waiting for Leif to finish with the police, too worn to cry.

When Leif finished at last, he took her hand and suggested that they go to the hotel. Tiger and Sam would be there—and Lauren and Carol deserved explanations.

And most importantly, Liz would be there, waiting with Blake.

"What am I going to tell him?" Tracy whispered hopelessly to Leif.

He hesitated, and she had never been so glad of his arm around her, or the unwavering strength he offered her.

"Tracy, it might take time. But we've got time now. Years ahead of us." He paused again, heedless of Jamie, staring deeply into her eyes.

"That is, if you love me. I—I only forced you to marry me because—"

"Because you're both stubborn idiots!" Jamie chimed in. "Tracy, face it, you married him because you love him. Let the poor guy off the hook."

She discovered that she could still smile after all. She gazed up into eyes that were silver and charcoal and tense and fascinating and demanding and tender and smiled.

"I married you because I love you. I do love you, Leif, so much."

"Then together," he whispered softly, "I know that we'll do fine with our son."

She was afraid. So very afraid to talk to her own son.

"He's in the second room," Liz told her after hearing the complete story of what happened. "Go see him."

"Liz—I can't!" Tracy protested in panic. "He hates me! You heard him."

"Go talk to him, Tracy. He's your son! Your little boy! You go in there and tell him what's what!"

Liz gave her a shove. Tracy walked hesitantly to the door. She knocked on it.

"Go away!"

She almost did just that; then she asked herself just what kind of a coward she was. So she twisted the knob and went in. Blake was lying on his bed. He turned around to look at her, then swung his back to her face once again.

"Blake, I need to talk to you."

"I hate you. I don't want to talk to you."

She took a deep breath and walked over to the bed and sat at its edge. His little body stiffened.

"Blake—"

"You're not my mother! I don't care what they said! I remember her! She loved me! She was beautiful!"

"Celia was beautiful, Blake. Kind and gentle and very wonderful. No one wants to take her away from you. She did love you. So much."

He spun around, staring at her with his cheeks tear-stained, his blond hair a tousle—and his eyes as dark and stormy as his father's.

"They called you a 'bastard.' And they said that I was

277

your 'bastard,' and that's bad—I know it! And it isn't true! Tell me that it isn't true!"

She lowered her head for a minute, then looked up at him, shaking her head. "Blake, if I start at the beginning, will you listen to me?"

"You're too big for me to throw out of my room!" he told her grudgingly.

Tracy inhaled and sought for words.

"Blake, in the eyes of the world, I suppose, I am Jesse's bastard. But please don't use that word—people really shouldn't. Blake, Jesse and my mother fell in love. But they were kept apart. I believe that they cared very, very deeply when they—when they made me. I loved Jesse, Jesse loved me."

He didn't say anything. She didn't know if he was still crying or not. She inhaled another deep, deep breath.

"Blake, I met your father many years ago. And after I came to know him, I thought that the sun rose in his face. In my life, Blake, I never cared for anyone more. But I—I was too young. And my parents took me away."

How, how did she explain this to a six-year-old? Her heart cried out.

"Blake—you are my son."

"No!" he screamed, then he spun around with a gasp and a worse accusation on his lips.

"You didn't want me! You didn't love me! You gave me away! That's why I used to be 'adopted.' "

She shook her head vehemently. "No, Blake, no! Oh, Blake, listen to me! Sometimes people who aren't really bad do some things that are! You were taken away from me." She tried to smile. "I—I didn't even know when I met you that you were my son. Oh, Blake, this is so much to understand. I'm an adult and I'm having trouble with it all! Please . . ."

He stared at her, but he didn't take the hand that she had outstretched to him.

"So you are a bastard—and I'm one, too," he said distantly.

"Blake, I asked you not to use that word, please!" Tracy murmured.

"It's true. You just said so."

"No—it's not. Not at all."

Tracy and Blake both started at the interruption. It was Leif, standing silently in the doorway. He walked over to the bed, looked at Tracy and saw the lost appeal in her eyes, and sat. He squeezed her hand, then took the protesting Blake into his arms.

"Blake, listen to me, son. Listen to me, well. I loved Celia, and she was your mother. No one will ever take that away. She wanted you very badly. But before I married Celia, I knew Tracy and I loved her, too, son. You were born out of that. Two people who loved one another deeply and who both love you now more than anything else in the world."

Blake looked at his father. He didn't protest. He just sobbed softly and buried his little head against Leif's broad chest.

Leif bent his head down to whisper. "Please, Blake. Please tell Tracy that you don't hate her."

Tracy waited, her heart aching. Waited and waited . . .

And at last Blake turned to her. He stared at her with his massive gray eyes for several wrenching moments.

"I—I don't really hate you. It's just that they are suddenly saying that you're my mother and—"

"Blake, please!" She reached for his hand a little feverishly; this time, he accepted it. "Blake, you knew that I was going to be your stepmother, and that was going to be okay. If we can start out by trying to be friends, maybe the rest will—will work out."

He didn't say anything for the longest time. Leif prompted him.

"Blake?"

He nodded slowly. Leif smiled at him. "Son, I promise you, we're going to have a wonderful life together. Tracy loves you, too, you know that."

"Do I have to call you 'mother'?" He asked.

She shook her head. "Not until you want to."

"I might never," he warned her.

"Well, we'll wait and see, okay."

"Maybe I will," he conceded.

"Give me a big hug," Leif said to him. "It's getting late. You need some sleep."

Obediently—and with a love that Tracy envied—Blake hugged his father and kissed his cheek. Then he looked at Tracy again. "Does that mean that I'm kind of related to Jamie, too?"

"He's your uncle," Tracy said.

"I like that," Blake mused, and Tracy smiled, lowering her eyes. The little things might win him in the end. It would be difficult; she had to move slowly. But Leif was right; she loved him. And sometimes love did win out.

"Want to give Tracy a little kiss on the cheek?" Leif suggested. "Just so that she really doesn't think you hate her anymore."

He hesitated. Then he gave her a bird's peck on the cheek. She smiled, then she and Leif rose together to leave him. They got as far as the door. Then a flurry of movement followed them; Tracy discovered herself almost knocked over by a force at her knees.

"I really don't hate you," Blake told her. "I wanted to hurt you at first, but I—I don't really want to anymore."

She knelt down beside him, near tears of joy when he wrapped his arms around her and gave her a fierce hug.

"Thank you, Blake," she murmured.

He nodded, quickly released her, and raced back to his bed.

"Good night, son," Leif said, and he led Tracy from the room.

Another door closed somewhere in the suite. Tracy realized that her sister-in-law had gone to bed, discreetly leaving her and Leif alone in the salon.

Leif led her over to the window. A breeze was blowing the drapes about, far below them horns still honked on a busy street.

He stood behind her, holding her close to his body, lightly brushing her nape with a kiss and then holding her closer once again. Far above them, the moon was high in the sky.

"No more 'liar's' moon," Leif commented softly. "The new is coming."

"Yes," she murmured.

"Tracy, I'm sorry."

She winced. "I am, too. All those years Ted raised me. I can't believe that he wanted to kill me."

He didn't reply. He stroked her shoulders soothingly.

"Your mother is stronger than you think, Tracy. She will pull out of this. But I was thinking—maybe you'd like to send for the baby to come and live with us."

She spun around, her eyes bright. "Oh, Leif, could we? I mean, when mother is well, of course, she should have Anthony back. Maybe they should both be with us for a while. That is, if—"

He smiled at her, kissing her fingers. "Tracy, I'm not the one who can't forgive and forget. When we can, we'll bring Audrey home. And Anthony."

She turned into his arms. "Oh, Leif, I do love you!"

"Tracy Johnston, I do love you with all my heart."

She sighed softly and buried her head against his chest.

"It's so easy now. So very easy. I love you. I love you. To feel, to say—"

He lifted her chin, smiling crookedly, lazily—rakishly.

"To show, Tracy? I didn't mind you in your son's bed, but I did spend a rather lonely night."

"To show," she whispered in return, and lacing her fingers with his, she kissed him with all her love and need and passion.

And the breeze blew gently around them while the fading moon beamed down a gentle blessing.

EPILOGUE

She came to him in darkness, in the coolness of the night, beneath the glowing cast of the moon.

He could almost reach out and touch her. Smell the sweet aroma of her perfume, feel the curve of her breast, the whisper of her caress.

He saw her smile. Standing in the doorway, framed by the glow of the moon. A full moon tonight. Huge and silver and shimmering. Casting its benign eye upon love and lovers, come full season at last. A love that had endured and conquered endless sins.

That moon, that ancient moon. It played so beautifully against her—against her silhouette. She paused there in the doorway and slowly bent to cast her heels away. He saw the grace of her feline stretch, the supple shape of her legs, and heard the soft thud of her shoes as they fell.

She came into the room then, slow again, elegant in her walk, easy, luxurious, unhurried. So confident, so sensual. She came that way to the center of the room, where that full moon could fall upon her from the bay window that opened to the garden, to the night breeze. She reached for the string of her gown at her nape, releasing it, shaking back the lustrous waves of her hair as she did so.

The gown fell to become a pool at her feet. Beneath it,

she was naked. No slip, no teddy, no frothing lace, no stockings. Just bare and elegant beneath the moon glow . . . a glow falling upon her breasts, the fullness of their shape, the firmness, the beauty against the slender curves of her body. Skin like satin, taut and sleek, so breathtaking. Everything . . . everything about her so perfect. The slope of her shoulders, the line of her back, the flare of her hip.

Her eyes were indigo. Sparkling, reflecting, catching the moonbeams, so deep and dark, so touched by brilliance. He knew, because he came to her, scarcely able to breathe. Touched her shoulders and felt her trembling.

Touched her, his love, his wife.

The very essence of him—his wife.

They smiled to one another beneath that moon, smiled with deep understanding, unspoken knowledge.

No love could be deeper.

He took her into his arms, kissed her—and it was, as always, just like that first kiss. Deep and shattering, evocative. Her hair brushed his chest in silk, her touch made him quake.

She raised her hand, spreading her fingers. He raised his own. They hesitated, touched, entwined together.

From the open window the breeze blew in, the fresh scent of roses. Clean and sweet and wonderful.

They walked to the bed, curled upon it, loved upon it. Touch for touch, kiss for kiss. Sweet remembrance, soaring new heights. The wonder, the awe, the beauty.

And all that came after. A time to hold, a time to cherish. To be blissfully aware of all that was theirs, for time had taught them loss and pain, and yet time had taught them, too, that love could well prevail.

Leif lay awake after she slept. Staring at the window, to the drapes fluttering there. To the moon, full and new and high in the sky. He stroked her hair, and kissed her forehead, and thought what a heaven they had here. In their rooms.

Oh, not in the house. The house was full. Jamie was back from his latest tour of Europe, occupying half of the west wing with all his equipment. Anthony had been with them for some time, and Katie had thrilled again to the patter of toddling footsteps and greasy handmarks all over the place again.

Audrey was here, too, now. Looking too slim, but smiling easily, and as beautiful as ever. Leif had invited Arthur down for the weekend.

In the darkness he smiled, for Audrey was not alone. After so, so many years, it seemed that she and Tiger were becoming very special friends. He hoped so. Tiger—the old bachelor—needed to settle down. And Audrey deserved some happiness.

Then, of course, there was Liz.

Leif frowned absently, hoping that he wasn't interfering with others' lives. But it had seemed that Liz and Sam spent more and more time talking together. That Liz smiled more like a girl when Sam was at the door.

Maybe it was nothing—but maybe . . .

He smiled to himself a little sheepishly in the darkness. He was just so damned happy. He wanted everyone else to be happy, too. To know what it was like to feel this wonderful emotion of loving—and being cherished in return.

He closed his eyes again. A full house. Jamie, Blake, Anthony—and Jessica.

In a few minutes, he knew, like clockwork, Tracy would stir. Leif still couldn't fathom it—she simply had some kind of inner mechanism that warned her when the baby would awake.

Jessica was nearly four months old. And she was stunning. Blue, blue—endlessly blue—eyes, and a mop of strawberry blond curls. And when Tracy wasn't out playing with the boys, she was with Jessica, and Leif never said a word because Tracy would look at him and he would know. She had never been able to share in Blake when he was a baby. This time was very precious to her.

And, of course, he was endlessly proud of her, too. She had that very special beauty that belonged to Audrey and Tracy. She charmed, she captivated, she would never grow old.

And she would never be hurt the way that Tracy had been hurt, Leif vowed. She and Blake would be chastised and loved, held under a strict thumb—sometimes given their way. There would be problems, there would be joys. But above it all was that very, very special quality.

They were a family. Committed, caring.

Blessed.

It had been a long hard road.

But they had come home.

Beside him, Tracy stirred. He smiled above her and kissed her. In silent agreement, they donned their robes and tiptoed down the hall.

First to Blake's room. He always got a kiss first, even though he was sleeping. Tracy was determined that he would never think that there was any favoritism going on.

Then they joined hands again to go for the baby in her canopied crib.

But just before Tracy plucked her from her snug nest of blankets, she turned to Leif with no words but a radiant smile. She kissed him quickly, and he knew that she was thinking the same thing.

We have come home, my love.